SWEET ESCAPE

A SUGAR RUSH ROMANCE

NINA LANE

SNOW QUEEN

PUBLISHING

Sweet Escape
A Sugar Rush Romance

Published by Snow Queen Publishing

Cover photography: Sara Eirew
Cover design: Perfect Pear Creative Covers

ISBN: 978-1-7360527-7-8

SWEET ESCAPE
NINA LANE

✿

Heartbreaker Evan Stone offers to teach world traveler Hannah
about love, but can they keep the lessons temporary?

Warning! Contains Sparkle Pops, knee-high socks, wanderlust,
road trips, and wicked acts involving a chocolate mousse cake
laced with Kahlua and ancho chilies.

The Sugar Rush books are sexy contemporary romances by New
York Times bestselling author Nina Lane. They can be read as
standalone novels or enjoyed as a series.

SWEET DREAMS
SWEET ESCAPE
SWEET SURRENDER
SWEET TIME
SWEET LIFE

www.ninalane.com

PROLOGUE

"*E*nd of messages."

The monotone voice of the answering machine ended with a click. Evan Stone rubbed his chest and stared out the kitchen window at the ocean—gunmetal-gray water beneath an overcast sky.

Something was wrong.

The realization poured through him like thick, black oil. His doctor wouldn't have asked him to come in to the office on Monday if his test results had come back normal.

He turned away from the window. The knowledge of his defective heart always simmered at the back of his mind, but most of the time he was able to forget about it. Dealing with his medical condition was part of his life, almost a routine. He didn't know life without it.

But he saw life without it. He'd spent many hours in the hospital with a tutor while other kids went to school on the bus. He saw his brothers playing football and baseball, heard about Adam's treks through the Himalayas and his climb to Machu Picchu, high altitude places Evan might never see.

And every time Evan took off his shirt, every time he showered, every time he swam and caught people glancing at the vertical scar on his chest, he was reminded that his heart, the most vital organ he possessed, was defective but still his.

It was the only heart he'd ever have, the one that had been damaged at birth but repaired, the heart that had pounded nervously when he had a crush on a girl, the heart that had stuttered over exams and competitions, the heart that had both broken in love and soared with happiness. His heart had gotten him to the age of thirty-three and was still beating.

But Evan would never stop wishing his heart was whole.

CHAPTER 1

*S*ix more months of evil whipped cream.

To Hannah Lockhart, it might as well have been six years.

Royal icing? Bring it. Sprinkles? No problem. Powdered sugar, marzipan, buttercream? She was on it. Even delicate, easily torn fondant didn't faze her. But one look at the stainless steel whipped cream charger with its secret nitrous oxide chamber and specific rules for temperature, shaking, and dispensing—and dread pooled in the pit of her stomach.

She wiped her forehead with the back of her hand. *Keep it together.* She had to rally. She *was* rallying. When you were asked —okay, *told*—to cater the extensive dessert table at a high-society bachelor auction called "Cream of the Crop," you had to bring your A-game. Even though Wild Child Bakery's new pastry chef was sick with the stomach flu, and the coordinator of the event was a massive pain in the ass.

Hannah set the serving utensils on the dessert table, which was draped in silky black cloth and spanned half the length of the wall in the great room of the historic, Spanish-style villa nestled in the foothills of the Santa Cruz Mountains.

Open doors led to the back terrace and majestic courtyard surrounded by wisteria and slender palms. Laughter and conversation flooded into the house as guests floated around the marble fountain in a sea of tuxedos, glitter, silk, and champagne glasses.

Hannah hurried back to the industrial-sized kitchen and opened the refrigerator. She could do this. Pastry Chef Sophie who had actual professional certification in cake decorating and therefore knew what she was doing, had explained everything. All Hannah had to do was pipe a few ribbons, stars, and swirls onto the desserts before bringing them to the display table.

She transferred the multitude of trays and platters from the refrigerator to the granite counter. She'd brought all of Wild Child's specialties—cream puffs, custard-filled éclairs, layered trifles, mango napoleons laced with caramel sauce, apricot rolls, chilled pineapple mousse dotted with pistachio slivers, hazelnut-praline torte, lemon charlotte encased in ladyfingers, and of course the famous Declairs, the hybrid éclair-doughnut confection her sister Polly had invented before she'd gone off to study with famous pastry chefs in Paris.

"Hope none of the guests are lactose intolerant," Hannah muttered to herself as she pulled a blackberry pavlova from the fridge and set it on the counter.

Time for a whipped cream throwdown.

She turned to the sink, where the charger parts were strewn like the detritus of a grenade with its chambers and valves.

Dispenser chilled.

Cream poured.

Sugar and vanilla added.

Hannah dropped the piston into the charger, screwed on the head, and inserted one of the gas cartridges into the chamber. She repeated the process three times.

She felt like she was readying for battle instead of piping a rosette onto a mille-feuille. This bakery business wasn't even her real job. She was just running Wild Child for a few months while Polly completed her pastry-making course and internship.

When Polly came back to Rainsville and took over Wild Child again, Hannah would be free to get back to her regular life of traveling and blog writing. The life she'd lived for the past decade of her twenty-eight years.

But until then, she had to get this done. After inserting the last cartridge, she shook the charger exactly four times, as Polly had instructed her, turned it upside down and squeezed the lever. The canister spat and hissed like the devil.

Shit shit shit.

Cream leaked out of the crack between the head and the base, spilling all over her fingers and the delicate puff pastry. She slammed the canister on the counter—right next to the rubber head gasket she'd forgotten to insert.

Hannah grabbed a towel and wiped her hands. She picked up the dispenser again and pressed the lever to discharge some of the gas. She fucking hated pressurized devices or anything with explosive potential. She didn't even like balloons.

She carefully twisted the lid. The canister emitted another seething hiss that sounded like air escaping a tractor tire.

"I wouldn't do that if I were you, Lockhart," said a male voice.

Hannah looked up irritably. She froze. Her heart bumped against her ribs. Evan Stone, one of the heirs to the Sugar Rush Candy Company, was coming toward her, his eyes narrowed.

And...*damn.*

Although Evan was the brother of her sister's fiancé and therefore almost family, Hannah didn't know him well. He'd come into Wild Child for coffee and a Declair a few times during the three months she'd been in Rainsville. They'd chatted briefly. Exchanged observations about the weather. She'd told him to have a nice day. He'd complimented her muffins.

But—clearly because she had lost crucial powers of perception—not once had Hannah imagined he could look like *this*. A beautifully fitted tuxedo sheathed his tall, muscular body, and his glossy, dark brown hair shone under the lights. With his strong features and thick-lashed, laser-blue eyes, he looked like a classic movie star come to living, breathing life.

She couldn't stop staring at him. Heat flickered through her, like the strike of a match. He looked more delicious than an endless bowl of savory ravioli laced with parmesan and accompanied by a robust Chianti.

She could dive into him headfirst, swirl her tongue around his fork, lick up his sauce and—

"Opening a pressurized container can be dangerous," he remarked.

With effort, Hannah returned her attention to the unwieldy charger. She was an independent world traveler, for heaven's sake. She had this situation under control.

"I know what I'm doing," she informed him crisply.

She twisted the lid again. Sweat trickled down her temple, though she didn't know if she was getting warm from whipped cream exertion or Evan's sudden and very sexy appearance.

Hormones, she told herself firmly. She'd experienced a whole new meaning of the word *abstinence* since returning to Rainsville four months ago. It was no wonder her body was reacting with all sorts of inappropriate hot cravings to the sight of Evan Stone in a tuxedo.

And she did not have time to deal with a hormonal surge right now. She had to wrestle the charger into submission, decorate the damned pastries, and get them to the dessert table before the bachelor auction started.

"I'm sure you know what you're doing." Evan extended a hand toward the charger. "But can I please help you with that?"

"No, thank you." Hannah wiped her wet hand on her chef's jacket and turned the lid again. "I read about how to do this on the internet. If you open it slowly, millimeter by millimeter, the nitrous oxide leaks out gradually and the whole thing won't—"

Boom!

The lid exploded off the canister. A volcanic spray of cream shot upward. Hannah shrieked and dropped the charger. Splatters of white flew in every direction.

Evan darted between her and the spluttering device from hell. He grabbed her shoulders and pulled her a distance away.

A dull roar filled Hannah's ears. She squeezed her eyes shut and dragged in a breath.

"Are you all right?" Evan asked.

"Yes. Just a little...uh, creamy." She wiped her sleeve across her face and slowly opened her eyes.

Evan was looking at her, runny whipped cream dripping off his hair and onto his immaculate tuxedo.

"Oh no." Hannah grabbed a dishtowel and scrubbed at the cream on his lapel, which only smeared it over the black wool. "I'm so sorry."

"It's just a tux." He released her shoulders.

"But you're one of the bachelors, right? You have to go onstage." Hannah hurried to wet the dishtowel under the faucet. "If we get it off now, it should dry by the time it's your turn."

She swabbed at the cream on his tux, and then reached up to wipe it off his face and hair. Though she tried to remain clinically detached, she couldn't ignore the brush of his breath against her wrist, the tickle of his hair on her palm.

She stepped away from him, her pulse racing. Evan took the damp towel and gave her a wry grin.

"Sparkle Pops are safer," he said.

"What?"

"Just came out last year in a new line of Sugar Rush candy." He stepped toward her. "A hard-shelled lollipop with a fizzy chocolate center that bursts in your mouth. The beauty of it is that you never know when the explosion will happen, so it's a surprise."

"Sounds awful," Hannah said. Oops, she'd just insulted his

family's candy company. "Er, but I'm sure plenty of people love it."

He studied her. "You don't like surprises."

"Depends on the surprise. Things that explode…no."

"Hold still."

He put his hand under her chin and lifted her face slightly, then wiped the cream off her forehead and cheeks with the wet towel. Her whole body reacted to his touch with a surge of pleasure. She focused on the crease of concentration between his eyebrows, the impossible length of his thick lashes. He had a straight nose like that of a Roman emperor, and a beautifully shaped mouth that had drawn her attention in the past as he'd licked a speck of chocolate from his lower lip…

Heat bloomed inside her. *Hormones*, she reminded herself. Plus, she was totally out of her element trying to deal with all these fancy desserts and a whipped cream explosion, so it was hardly a wonder that her defenses were weakened and she was noticing things about Evan Stone that she never had before. Or hadn't wanted to admit that she'd noticed.

His gaze met hers, the crack of energy jolting heat through her entire body. A flush burned her cheeks as she turned away from him. She forced her attention to the damage wrought by the explosion.

Watery cream dripped off the granite countertops, the stainless steel refrigerator, and spread in a pool across the tiled floor. Some of it had also splattered onto the trays of mille-feuille and Declairs, but thankfully most of the desserts had been spared.

"I hate whipped cream," she muttered.

"Interestingly, it was a popular dessert in the sixteenth century." Evan bent to pick up the parts of the charger and toss them into the sink. "There are recipes in the books of several Renaissance chefs about mixing cream with rosewater. It was called *neve di latte* or *neige de lait*. Milk snow."

Milk snow. That was rather charming. So was Evan's knowledge of the history of whipped cream, even if it was also a bit dorky. Who knew that kind of obscure fact anyway, and why?

Evan turned on the water and wet a couple of paper towels before crouching to clean the spilled cream off the floor.

"I'll do that," Hannah said quickly, grabbing the towels from him. "You shouldn't get any messier. I know you're expected to inspire some heavy bidding."

Though she suspected Evan would inspire heavy bidding even if he was wearing a stained T-shirt, parachute pants, and sandals with socks. The Cream of the Crop bachelor auction was exactly that—the most eligible bachelors from the coastal California town of Indigo Bay and neighboring cities were going on the auction block with expensive date packages to raise money for charity.

Hannah was unsurprised that Evan Stone was one of those bachelors. Even if his aunt Julia—the massive pain in the ass—hadn't been the coordinator of the event, Evan's *most eligible bachelorism* radiated from him like heat from a light bulb.

"Aren't you supposed to be chatting up the ladies at the VIP reception?" she asked.

"Yes." Evan straightened and wiped the front of the refrigerator. "But I had to escape because I'm being stalked by the lovely Lucy Clements."

"What's wrong with lovely Lucy Clements?"

"On the surface, nothing. She's attractive, educated, and is the daughter of a state representative. She's very *suitable*."

"So what's the problem?"

"She's my ex-girlfriend." His mouth twisted. "Who claims she wants me back, even though we broke up because she cheated on me."

"Ouch." Hannah grimaced. "Sorry."

Evan shrugged and tossed the paper towels into the trash. "We hadn't been dating long, but I have no interest in dating her again. Unfortunately she has a different idea."

Hannah couldn't imagine why any woman would want to cheat on Evan Stone. She could, however, understand why any woman would just *want* him—either back or for the first time. He was one of the six Stone brothers who owned The Sugar Rush Candy Company, the conglomerate that had transformed the economies of several coastal California towns, including Indigo Bay.

The company, once called Stone Confectioners, had been in the Stone family since the mid-nineteenth century, but within the last twelve years had transformed into the behemoth that threatened the biggest names in the business due in part to their focus on quality and expansion. The eldest brother Luke—Polly's fiancé—had been responsible for Sugar Rush's growth.

So aside from Evan's good looks, his family was both wealthy and, by all accounts, well-respected after having overcome both business and personal scandals. Hardly a wonder that Lucy Clements was still after him.

He nodded toward the splattered desserts that sat waiting for their creamy decorations. "What are you going to do about those?"

Hannah sighed. "I'll have to bring out my secret weapon."

She opened the refrigerator and took out one of several cans of Reddi-Wip she'd brought along *just in case*. If there was anything Hannah had learned from a decade of traveling around the world, it was the wisdom of preparing for a potential emergency. In her case, an industrial whipped cream dispenser definitely qualified.

"If you tell anyone I'm using this," she warned Evan, "the bakery will be scandalized. Polly is all about using fresh, real ingredients."

"That's about as real as it gets." Evan nodded toward the can. "Remind me to tell you about my childhood whipped cream battles with my brothers. Winner got to down a full can of the stuff."

"Ugh." Hannah rolled her eyes and handed him a second can of Reddi-Wip. "That also sounds awful."

"Explosions aside, you don't like to eat whipped cream either?" Evan eyed her with mild suspicion as they started piping rosettes and swirls onto the unadorned cakes.

"I don't like dessert," Hannah admitted a little warily. Her uncommon distaste of dessert was often met with surprise, if not outright shock.

"At all?" Evan asked.

"Not really. I'm not a fan of sweet things."

"*All* sweet things?" He put the can down and stared at her in astonishment. "What about ice cream? Cookies? Chocolate cake?"

"Not really. I could never see what all the hype was about."

"Dessert," Evan said emphatically, "is one of the great wonders of the world."

"I've seen the great wonders of the world. Cake isn't one of them."

"What about candy?" He lowered his head to peer at her, as if he were trying to determine if she was lying. "Tell me you like candy."

"When I was a kid, I liked candy." Hannah stepped back to scrutinize the symmetry of her whipped cream scroll. "Not so much anymore."

"Have you tried Sugar Rush candy?"

"Your brother gave me a bag of Sugar Rush Jelly Rolls before he and Polly went to Paris," Hannah said. "I mean, they were fine as far as candy goes. Just too sugary for me."

Evan frowned, his gaze tracking over her face. "I don't buy it."

"What?"

"You have a sweet tooth," he said. "Everyone has a sweet tooth. You've just misplaced yours."

"I assure you…" Hannah pressed her lips together to conceal a smile over the absurdity of this conversation. "I have not misplaced my sweet tooth."

"Yeah, you have." Evan narrowed his eyes. "But don't worry. I'll find it for you."

"You will, huh?"

"You're dealing with a man who has sugar in his DNA," he said. "I assure *you* I'm a veritable archaeologist when it comes to long-lost sweet teeth."

Hannah didn't look at him as she squeezed dots of whipped cream onto the pavlova. She was not getting soft and fuzzy inside. She was not on the verge of being charmed by a man who was cute, hot, handsome, and sexy all at the same time.

A man who was the brother of her sister's fiancé. A man whom she barely knew and didn't want to *get* to know because aside from Polly and Wild Child, Hannah couldn't have any other connection, no matter how tenuous, to Rainsville.

Not when she needed to *leave.*

"So you don't like surprises, dessert, or sugar." Evan squeezed florets onto the tops of the napoleons. "What do you like then, Hannah Lockhart?"

"Spanish tapas. Russian vodka. The flamingos in the Laguna Colorada in Bolivia. The Great Barrier Reef. Masala dosa from a street vendor in Mumbai. Spicy Moroccan coffee that's so good I learned how to make it myself. Watching the fog drift over the Paro Valley in Bhutan."

"That's it?" he asked dryly.

Hannah smiled. Evan winked at her. A warm, pleasurable current flowed between them.

"What do *you* like, Evan Stone?" she asked. "Besides dessert, I mean."

"Sex. Christmas Eve. Grilled steak and Hennessy. Kissing. Wild Child Declairs. Golden Retrievers. Navy blue. Running. Classic cars. A woman who calls me instead of texting so I can hear her voice. Sex."

Hannah's pulse sped up. Freaking *poetry*, that list spoken in his deep, hypnotic voice. She wished he'd keep going. She could have listened to him forever, his *likes* flowing into her like hot honey.

Sex. Navy blue. Declairs. Sex. Sex. *Sex.*

"The fact that you have whipped cream on your ear and don't know it," Evan continued.

She blinked. "I have…"

He drew his thumb across her cheek to her ear. He took her earlobe between his thumb and forefinger and rubbed. A flame flickered in Hannah's core. She struggled to pull in a breath. Had her ears always been such a heightened erogenous zone? Or was she simply reacting to the way he was caressing her earlobe with such gentle intent, as if he were enjoying the sensation as much as she was?

Her knees weakened. What would it feel like if he touched her in more intimate places with that same tender precision? Warmth collected between her thighs, and her nipples budded up against her bra at the thought of Evan gliding his hand over her breasts and down farther and farther until—

Hormones!

Oh, hormones, my ass.

It was *him.* He was the reason she was getting all hot and bothered. Evan Stone with his wine-and-ravioli deliciousness, his sweet tooth detection, and that ridiculously sensual way he had of fondling her earlobe…

"There you are." A sharply musical female voice chilled the air several degrees.

Evan stepped in front of Hannah so swiftly that he was blocking her from sight before she'd even had a chance to look up.

She drew in a breath and tried to calm her racing pulse. Behind his back, Evan held out the Reddi-Wip toward her. Hannah grabbed the can from him and quickly tossed both his and her cans into the cupboard beneath the sink.

She fixed a smile on her face and peered around his shoulder.

Tall, elegant Julia Bennett strode across the tiled kitchen floor, her silver metallic gown skimming her gorgeous figure like water.

In her late forties, her natural beauty enhanced to level ten with artfully applied cosmetics and sleek, honey-butter blond hair, the Stone family matriarch walked the earth like a medieval queen expecting the peasants to do her bidding.

"The auction has started," she informed Evan. "So I'd suggest you get backstage pronto."

"On my way."

Julia pursed her lips and studied the desserts. "They look lovely, Hannah. I'm glad to know you're running Polly's bakery with the same attention to detail and quality she employs."

Evan coughed. A laugh bubbled in Hannah's throat. She didn't dare look at him.

"Of course," she said.

Julia nodded and swept out of the room. Evan turned to Hannah. She swore the expression in his eyes was one of regret. Mirroring hers.

"Thanks for your help," she said. "I owe you one. Or a few thousand."

"It was my pleasure," he replied. "And now I have to go be auctioned off like a side of beef."

"Then you'd better get moo-ving."

He grinned, his eyes crinkling at the corners, as he walked backward toward the door. "We'll meet again, Lockhart."

"After you find my sweet tooth?"

"No," he said. "When I come looking for it."

He winked at her again and disappeared into the foyer.

CHAPTER 2

ocus.

Hannah attempted to smother her warm, Evan-inspired fuzzies as she finished decorating the pastries and brought them to the table in the great room of the villa. After the desserts were arranged with their Reddi-Wip rosettes glowing like snowballs in the lights, she hurried into the bathroom and shrugged out of her chef's jacket.

Underneath she was wearing a purple silk blouse that likely wasn't as fancy as what the other women were wearing, but her goal was to be invisible, not stand out. She pulled a pair of black pants and evening pumps out of her bag, changed, and did a quick check of her reflection in the mirror.

She pulled the band out of her ponytail and brushed out her long brown hair, leaving it loose around her shoulders. An application of lipstick and powder, and she could safely watch the auction from the edges of the crowd without anyone thinking she was slacking off on the job.

She grabbed her camera case and hurried through the foyer. The beat of "It's Raining Men" thumped into the house from outside, along with ear-splitting feminine squeals and laughter.

Hannah walked out to the courtyard. Lanterns glowed from between the trees, heat lamps chased off the evening chill, and a bar was set up near the mosaic wall fountain. The guests sat at the tables around the stage and runway, on which a handsome young man with chiseled features and dark blond hair walked out from behind the curtain.

A female announcer spoke into a mic, her voice animated and eager. "Thirty-one-year-old Adam Stone—yes, you heard me right, Adam Stone of the Sugar Rush Candy Company family—is the very hunky owner of an adventure travel company."

As Adam started down the runway, a palpable excitement lit the air. Hannah didn't bother trying to find an empty chair; she stood in the shadow of a colonnade and took a small notebook and pen from her camera case.

"Adam's date package is *A Walk on The Wild Side!*" the announcer called. "Join him for a trip to the Harley-Davidson store, where you'll be fitted with your own personal riding gear before you and Adam take an epic coastal ride on his Harley! End your ride in San Francisco and a gourmet dinner at Fresca on Union Square. Then you and Adam will enjoy a night of dancing at the Saint Francis Hotel and two separate rooms for the night… unless you decide that bunking together is more your style!"

Hannah scribbled a few notes—*women between the ages of twenty-five and forty, very expensive date packages, bachelors showing off their best assets.*

"Let's start the bidding!" The auctioneer, a portly man whose bow-tie was askew, stepped to the podium. "We'll begin at five thousand dollars, ladies!"

A frenzy ensued as Adam walked down the runway, casting meaningful glances into the crowd before pausing to unbutton his tuxedo jacket. The women screamed their approval, several standing to wave their paddles in the air. Hannah set her notebook aside and snapped several photos.

"We have five thousand…do I have six…six thousand five

hundred...seven from the lovely lady at table fourteen! Do I have seven thousand five hundred? Come now, ladies, all proceeds go to the Rebecca Stone Foundation, and you'll have Adam to yourself for a full day *and* night!"

Adam pulled off his bow-tie and tossed it into the crowd, then started slowly unfastening the top buttons of his shirt. Whoops and screams filled the air as the bids rose higher and higher.

After he'd unbuttoned to the waist, revealing rippling pectoral muscles and a strikingly impressive six-pack set of abs, the gavel finally came down at twenty thousand dollars. To thunderous applause, Adam descended the stage into the audience to plant a kiss on the winning bidder.

"Our next bachelor is twenty-five-year-old Brendan Deeds!" the announcer said. "An account executive in San Francisco, Brendan loves sports, traveling, and intimate moments with a special woman!"

The audience cheered. Hannah wrote down Brendan's date package—a two-night yacht trip to Catalina Island. Julia had told her that all the date packages had been donated by various companies, hotels, and restaurants, so one hundred percent of the auction proceeds would go directly to the Rebecca Stone Foundation.

Brendan and Catalina Island sold to a young woman with short dark hair who beamed with excitement when he swept down from the stage after the gavel fell. He grabbed her and bent her against his arm for a dramatic kiss. The crowd erupted into cat-calls.

As more bachelors paraded down the runway, the bidding frenzy increased, with most of the wins landing between fifteen and twenty thousand dollars. The whole thing was an elaborate mating ritual. The men strutted like peacocks showing off their feathers before descending on the ecstatic woman for the obligatory post-win hug and kiss.

Perfect. A lively post about a high-end bachelor auction would be excellent content to keep Hannah's *Lock Heart* blog readers engaged. She could make connections to similar traditions she'd seen around the world, like the Gerewol courtship competition of the Wodaabe people in Niger.

Hopefully the new content would also make the editor of Franklin Publishing happy. Elaine Miller had recently expressed interest in turning Hannah's love-themed travel blog into a book, which would be a dream come true—albeit one Hannah hadn't known she'd had until Elaine contacted her.

The new possibility of promotion and making money both for and from her travels now dangled before her like an airline rewards card with unlimited free miles.

There was no offer yet, though. At Elaine's request, Hannah had compiled a manuscript from her blog post archives, and Elaine had responded with an emailed *I'll get back to you soon*. In the meantime, Hannah had to prove she still had an active online presence, and at least the Cream of the Crop bachelor auction gave her something to write about.

She slipped her notebook and camera back into the case and started back to the kitchen.

"Our next bachelor is the delicious heir to the Sugar Rush Candy Company, thirty-three-year-old Evan *Heartbreaker* Stone!"

Hannah stopped, her whole body charging with sudden energy. She turned back to the stage. Before Evan stepped out from behind the curtain, the women were on their feet applauding and cheering. He appeared with a somewhat abashed smile, his hands in his pockets as he started down the runway.

Warmth bloomed in Hannah, swift and bubbling like hot springs. Unlike some of the other men, Evan appeared too self-conscious to engage in any gyrations or actual stripping—despite the calls of "Take it off, Evan!" "Work it, baby!" and "Show us your stuff!"

Couldn't these women see that was what he was doing? He didn't need to do anything but *walk* in order to work it and show his stuff. His stride was long and certain, his lean, muscular body moving with an unconscious male grace, his brilliant blue eyes skimming across the crowd with unerring perception. Even his shy grin didn't mask the touch of wariness surrounding him, as if he knew—

"Ten thousand dollars!" yelled a young blond woman seated at a table near the stage.

Evan blanched for half an instant. His smile remained fixed, but his eyes flickered with distaste.

Hannah craned her neck to get a look at the blonde. She looked like a porcelain doll in a green silk wraparound dress and glittery emerald jewelry, but this was clearly Lucy Clements, the Cheating Ex.

"Eleven thousand!" called another woman.

"Hold on, ladies!" The announcer laughed and held up her hands. "Let me tell you about Evan's incredible...er, *package* before we start fighting over him! Evan's three-date—yes, *three date*—package is *Wine and Dine*! It includes an incredible weekend in Napa Valley. The lucky winning lady will accompany Evan on a wine-tasting tour, a sunset hot-air balloon ride, a gourmet dinner aboard Napa's famous Wine Train, and...oh, yes, a two-night stay at Napa's exclusive Castillo Hotel. The second date is a gorgeous yacht trip on San Francisco Bay, and the third is a date of your choice. Now let the bidding war begin!"

The auctioneer came forward. "Let's start at nine thousand very generous dollars for this very eligible bachelor!"

"Eleven thousand five hundred!"

"Thirteen thousand!"

Paddles shot into the air as the auctioneer called for higher bids. Evan stood at the end of the runway, his hands still in his pockets and his gaze moving across the crowd with faint bafflement.

Lucy waved her paddle for every bid, so swiftly it might start smoking any second now.

"Fourteen thousand!"

"Fifteen."

The mood shifted. A subtle but unmistakable sharpness descended over the competition and diluted the sense of friendly fun. The claws were starting to show.

"Sixteen," snapped a woman in a red dress, standing from her seat and shooting Lucy a glare.

"Eighteen," Lucy replied coolly.

Hannah caught sight of Julia Bennett standing near the stage, her expression mask-like but her eyes gleaming with pleasure. She also appeared unsurprised, as if she'd known her nephew would incite this kind of feminine battle.

"Twenty-three." Lucy tipped her paddle toward the auctioneer.

A few gasps rose from the crowd. Evan's mouth tightened, the spotlights making his eyes glitter. Another woman stood from the back and lifted her paddle.

"Twenty-four," she called.

"Twenty-five," Lucy snarled.

Hannah's heart raced. She could practically feel Evan's rising anger.

She glanced at the program. Out of twelve bachelors, Evan was second to last just before his younger brother Tyler. Clearly Julia knew what she was doing, putting one of the Stone brothers near the beginning to get things going, and then saving two of them as the grand finale.

Hannah stepped away from the colonnade and toward the villa. She was hired help and shouldn't be lingering at the auction.

"Twenty-six five hundred!" called the woman in red.

Hannah stopped again. Tense silence, vibrating with expectation, descended over the event. The spotlights glared over the tables. Sweat shone on the auctioneer's forehead.

"Do I have a bid for twenty-seven thousand?" he asked.

"Twenty-eight!"

"Fifty thousand dollars!"

Everyone went still. People turned around in shock. A spotlight suddenly fell over Hannah, blinding her even as she felt the weight of dozens of stares. She lifted a hand to shield her eyes. Deep foreboding rose inside her, along with a flicker of panic.

But it wasn't until she met Evan's astonished gaze from clear across the room that she realized the voice had been hers.

CHAPTER 3

*H*annah struggled to pull in a breath. Her camera case slipped from her weak grip. She did not just bid fifty thousand dollars, not even a fraction of which she possessed, for a three-date package with Evan Stone.

No way. No freaking way.

The auctioneer shouted, "Sold to the lady standing in the back without a paddle!"

Or a clue.

The slam of the gavel sounded like thunder. Cheers erupted as people got to their feet and applauded.

Hannah couldn't move. Her panic intensified. She opened her mouth to try and say something, anything—*"So sorry, terrible mistake, I have an untreatable condition where I'm occasionally possessed by a crazy woman who can't control her impulses..."*

"Kiss her!" someone called.

Whoops and cat-calls rose as everyone took up the rallying cry. Chants of "Kiss her, kiss her, kiss her" surged like a wave across the crowd.

Oh my God.

A bead of sweat rolled down Hannah's temple. She stepped

away from the spotlight. The lack of glare brought the room into sharp focus—every eye now turned toward Evan, who was descending the stairs at the side of the runway. The women erupted into cheers.

Then Evan started directly toward her.

The crowd parted like the Red Sea to let him pass. His attention fixed on her. His stride was long and purposeful, as if each step he took was securing the earth in its place, as if everything else had fallen away and his sole intention was to reach the spot where Hannah Lockhart stood.

The spotlight followed him, a glowing halo making his dark hair shine. Hannah's heart kicked into gear. Surely he wouldn't... he couldn't...

He stopped in front of her. She stared with determined fascination at the perfect knot of his bow-tie nestled at the base of his throat. His gaze even *felt* blue—clear, strong, confident. And then his hand brushed against her wrist, his fingers wrapping around hers in a grip that was both gentle and unmistakably firm.

"Thanks for the save," he murmured.

"I...I did owe you for the whipped cream...er, *milk snow* incident."

Her whole body felt electrified by his touch—a collision of sparks with reverberations right to the pit of her belly. She took a breath.

Okay, so she'd done something stupid. Not the first time. All she had to do was apologize, send him back to the auction for another round of bidding, then escape into the kitchen to arm herself for the fallout of this disaster.

"I have no idea where that came from," she whispered. "I did *not* mean to bid on you."

"I'm glad you did," he replied, his eyes still holding hers in some sort of mystical blue steel trap that was somehow both unnerving and soothing at the same time. "Why did you come to the auction?"

"Your aunt told me I could write about it for my blog," Hannah explained, darting a glance past his shoulder at the expectant audience. "I wasn't supposed to *bid*, for heaven's sake. I mean, obviously I can't afford to pay for you. Not for anywhere near fifty thousand dollars. Not for anywhere near a *thousand* dollars."

"How much can you afford to pay for me?"

"If you include the change at the bottom of my purse," Hannah said, "maybe $8.56."

Amusement gleamed in his eyes. "Sold."

Sold?

"Come on, Evan!" shouted another woman.

A hush fell over the crowd, punctuated by occasional whoops or calls of encouragement.

Hannah steeled her spine. She'd gotten them both into this mess, and now she had to get them out of it.

"You don't have to do this." She gestured toward the villa. "If you'd let go of me, I'll just run away and everyone will have a fun story to tell about the dessert girl who made a scene over the eligible Evan Stone."

"They already have a fun story to tell," Evan replied. "Now they're just waiting for the end."

"Which is…?"

"A kiss." His eyes creased with a smile. "There's always a kiss at the end."

Not in my experience, there isn't.

He stepped closer. His scent—cedar and the fresh air of night —filled her blood. He caressed the inside of her wrist with his thumb, a gentle movement like the stroke of a paintbrush. The silver flecks in his blue eyes were like glitter sprinkled over the sky. Hannah swallowed hard, her heart beating faster.

Her gaze went unwillingly to his beautifully shaped mouth. There was a little notch beneath his lower lip, like a secret. The urge to press the tip of her finger there seized her with sudden force.

Evan slipped his hand beneath her chin and lifted her face. Her heart stopped.

He couldn't. He wouldn't...

He tangled his other hand in her hair and cupped the back of her neck. His grip was certain, gentle, as if he were securing her rather than holding her in place. Then he lowered his head and pressed his mouth to hers.

And inside Hannah, a light clicked on.

CHAPTER 4

*H*annah had seen the sun rise over the African savannah and dolphins leaping in Plettenberg Bay. She had been awed by the pyramids at Giza, the Great Wall of China, and the sight of Machu Picchu through the foggy reddish light of dawn. She had walked on Ireland's majestic Cliffs of Moher and felt as if she were standing on the edge of the world.

And yet for all the magnificence of those experiences, none of them had inspired a slow, billowing sensation like molten lava flowing through her veins. None of them had spun clouds in the middle of her soul.

But Evan's kiss did. The world with its ancient monuments and sweeping vistas faded beneath the sheer pleasure of his lips moving against hers. Hannah's body came alive, every nerve ending lighting up.

He brought his hands up to hold either side of her head, increasing the pressure of his mouth. Hannah's heart thumped with an emotion both painful and sweet, as some distant part of her mind wondered if any man had ever cradled her head while kissing her.

And Evan kissed her. Oh, did he kiss her. His mouth moved

with deliberate ease over hers, urging her lips apart so he could dip his tongue inside. He tasted like sweet, spicy peppermint, and his breath was cool against her lips. Hannah's pleasure blossomed outward, filling her veins with heat. He slid his tongue over hers, nibbled at her bottom lip, and licked the corners of her mouth.

It was a delicious, prolonged seduction, carrying the promise of so much more. Her whole body swayed toward him as she longed to press her breasts against his chest, to feel his hands slipping beneath her shirt and touching her bare skin.

He drove his fingers into her hair, threading his hands through the long strands. He tilted her head and deepened the kiss, gliding his tongue over the surface of her teeth before moving to press his lips to her cheek. His stubble scraped her skin exquisitely, igniting little fires in her veins. She trailed her fingers over his arms, feeling the muscles of his forearms beneath his tuxedo jacket.

She could drown in him, sinking into the heat of his body and never wanting to come out again.

A burst of light glared behind her closed eyelids, and dimly she heard the cheers and cat-calls of the crowd. A chill ran down her spine. She tore herself away from Evan, caught by the burn of his blue eyes.

"All right, folks!" Adam Stone stepped in front of them suddenly, lifting his hands to the crowd. "Our baby brother Tyler is next on the auction block, and you'd better believe he wants to beat both me and Evan in the bidding war."

Voices rose as people returned to their tables and servers started forward to refill wineglasses. The spotlight shifted back to the stage, casting Evan and Hannah in darkness again.

Their heavy breaths mingled between them. Hannah couldn't think past the haze of desire and shock. Evan tightened his grip on her wrist and led her away from the courtyard, back into the quiet of the kitchen. He closed the door and turned to face her.

"You...you should get back out there," Hannah stammered in a rush. "I mean, go up for auction again. I'll tell everyone it was a terrible mistake so someone else can bid on you, and you can go on the dates with a woman who can actually afford you."

He regarded her, his eyebrows drawing together.

"You owe me $8.56," he said.

Hannah swallowed. "I owe you fifty thousand dollars."

He shook his head. "You bought me for $8.56. I'll take care of the rest."

"The *rest*? You mean the fifty thousand dollar rest?"

Evan shrugged, as if the amount were negligible. "I mean the forty-nine thousand, nine hundred ninety-one dollars and forty-four cents rest."

"But that's a fortune!"

"It all goes to my mother's foundation anyway, so it's not that big a deal."

"Not a *big deal*?" Hannah stared at him. "This is an astronomically big deal!"

"Compared to other things, it's not." He skimmed his gaze over her, heat brewing in his eyes as if *she* rather than a stupidly impulsive bid were the "big deal" here.

"I can't let you do this." Hannah started to the door. "I'll find your aunt and figure out a way to make up for—"

He moved in front of her so swiftly that she almost bumped up against him. And *oh,* there was that delicious scent of him again, something aromatic and peppery like herbs, and that heat radiating from his body. There was that crackling attraction that pushed Hannah toward him rather than away.

She stared at the perfect knot of his tie, the mother-of-pearl buttons marching up the front of his shirt. She wanted to press her hand to his broad chest, to feel the beat of his heart.

Heartbreaker.

With his devastating combination of good looks and charm, Evan Stone was a natural seducer, but not in a smarmy gigolo kind of way. He was more like a rare combination of the boy next door, the hottie senior crush, and a singularly self-possessed male who knew exactly what he wanted.

And when he wanted a particular woman, he got her.

Hannah shivered a little at the thought of being *gotten* by Evan Stone.

"You saved me from the clutches of lovely Lucy Clements," he said. "That's more than enough payment for me. Thank you."

A smile tugged at her mouth. "Well, you saved me from an exploding whipped cream dispenser. So thank you too, though I'm still convinced that whipped cream is inherently evil and out to get me."

"Yet another misguided notion I'll need to correct." He brushed his thumb across her earlobe, as if a trace of cream still lingered there. "Sounds like we saved each other. That makes us even."

"I...I guess so." Her breath caught as he ran his finger behind her ear, eliciting that warm, melty feeling in her belly. If he started rubbing her earlobe again, she'd end up a puddle on the floor.

"So we're good?" Evan extended his pinkie finger, his eyes crinkling with a smile.

God, he was cute.

Hannah hooked her pinkie around his. "We're good."

He tightened his hold around hers and tugged. "Then we should kiss again."

A laugh bubbled in Hannah's throat. She ignored the flash of warning in her mind—*don't start anything with him*—as he slipped his hand beneath her chin and lifted her face to his. If Hannah believed the potency of their first kiss had been heightened by the crowd's excitement and the utter shock of the moment, she was proven wrong the instant Evan's lips touched hers.

Bliss flooded her. She sank into him, curling her hands around his lapels as all the heat and pleasure poured back into her like a waterfall. Except this time, they were alone without the glare of a spotlight, and that knowledge emboldened her. She parted her lips and darted her tongue out to touch his because —*oh my God*—it felt so good to feel so good.

A groan rumbled in his chest. He slipped one hand around to her lower back, tugging her firmly against him. Hannah shuddered as their bodies sealed together, his lean, hard length pressing fully against her curves. Her nipples stiffened from the contact, sending a bolt of pleasure to her core.

"Christ, you taste incredible." He drew his tongue across her lower lip. "Much sweeter than dessert."

He tangled his other hand in her hair, tilting her head to just the right angle before settling his mouth over hers again. Their lips touched, retreated, met again and clung.

So many types of kisses in the world. Hand kisses, cheek kisses, air kisses. Eskimo nose kisses. Kissing under the mistletoe, on New Year's Eve, the Blarney Stone. First kisses.

But was *this* what people meant when they talked about the perfect kiss? Was it this wild, riotous combination of tenderness and excitement, the sense that you were both simultaneously falling and floating? Was it when eternity folded in on itself, distilling time and space into the moment of one particular man and woman touching lips?

Was it a full harvest moon right on the edge of the earth? Was it the infinite colors of a rainforest, the churning rapids of a river, the silence and peace of a temple? Was it feeling as if you were being kissed right to your soul?

Yes, whispered a little voice at the back of Hannah's mind. *This is it.*

The light inside her burned hotter, brighter. She brought her hands up to cradle Evan's jaw, his faint stubble rubbing her palms deliciously. He gripped her hips and turned her so her back was against the door, and then he rested his hands on either side of her head, caging her in the secure circle of his arms.

Instead of kissing her again, he tracked his gaze over her face, her kiss-swollen lips and heated cheeks, down to the arch of her neck and lower to where her nipples tented her silk top. His eyes lingered on her breasts, which rose and fell with the force of her breath.

"Ah, hell," he whispered, smoothing one hand over her bare arm. "What is it about you, Lockhart? Aside from the fact that your body does crazy things to me, and I forget my own damn name every time I look into your eyes, and I've wanted to taste your mouth since the day I first saw you at Wild Child…"

Hannah's breath caught. "Really?"

"You couldn't tell?" Amusement flashed in his eyes. "Didn't you ever wonder why it takes me over an hour to eat a Declair? It's because I spend most of the time sneaking glances at you."

Hannah smiled, inexplicably warmed by the idea that he'd been coming into Wild Child as much for her as for the pastries. "Why didn't you say anything before now?"

"Not good to hit on the sister of my brother's fiancé," he said, rubbing his hand up and down her arm in a warm movement that melted her like butter. "Unless she nearly gives herself a concussion with a whipped cream dispenser, insists that she doesn't like dessert, and bids fifty thousand dollars for a date with me. Then all bets are off."

"Lucky me."

She slid her hand to the back of his neck, driving her fingers into his thick hair as their lips met in another hot kiss.

Sudden urgency flared between them. His mouth still locked to hers, Evan brought his hands up to cup her breasts, flicking his thumbs over her stiff nipples. Desire shot through Hannah. Her whole body arched toward him, pulsing with a need she was certain only he could satisfy.

He trailed his lips across her cheek, down to her neck, and bit gently on her collarbone. She pressed her hand to his chest, his heart thumping steady and strong against her palm. Then she stroked lower to the heavy bulge pressing at the front of his trousers. Dizziness swept through her at the thought of him assuaging the ache of need that had been building inside her for months…

The sound of laughter and loud voices crashed into her ears from the foyer. Evan lifted his head, muttering a curse beneath his breath. He pushed away from her, his hands loosely circling her arms.

"I guess it was too much to hope they'd all just go home," he said wryly.

Reality broke through the heat waves of pleasure still enveloping Hannah. She slipped past Evan, brushing loose strands of hair from her face as she regained her composure.

"I'm sorry," she said. "Your aunt hired me to work at the auction, not make ridiculous bids and then canoodle with you in the kitchen."

"Actually, my aunt would be glad to know I'm *canoodling*," he replied. "With Luke and Polly off together, Julia is likely to turn her matchmaking skills on me next."

"So you want to head her off at the pass?"

"No. I do want to kiss you again though."

Hannah tried to deflect the pleasurable rush his words evoked. Lack of sex aside, she couldn't even remember the last time she'd engaged in gentle flirting with a hot guy. With Evan, that flirting could so easily turn into more.

The warning light inside her flashed harder. With the pressure of the desserts, the whipped cream, the craziness of the bid, and Evan's irresistibly sexy charm…this night had clearly gotten the better of her. Time to pull herself together and finish her job.

"You'd better go." She nodded to the door. "They'll be waiting for you."

Evan opened the door, his gaze on her. Heat lingered in his expression, a smoldering fire that would flare back to life with one breath.

"You owe me $8.56, Lockhart," he said. "I intend to collect."

Her heart thumped with both wariness and anticipation as the reality of her mistake crashed in on her. Clearly she had a hard time controlling herself around him, and if he were to actually pursue her... Hannah suspected her debt would end up being a much higher price than she was able to pay.

CHAPTER 5

*E*van ran back up the beach toward his house, his lungs aching and his breathing fast. For the past two days, his usual three-mile morning run had been extra tough as he wrestled thoughts of Hannah Lockhart. His mind burned with the sharp memory of her warm, sweet mouth, the curves of her slender body, her full breasts...

Ah, he wanted her bad. He'd wanted her since he'd first met her at Wild Child and felt the clasp of her fingers around his. And now that he knew how sweet she tasted...he craved more of her, as much as he could get. He hadn't been thinking of anything but her at the auction—the flash of her smile, her insistence that she didn't like dessert, the collision of their gazes across the crowded room.

It had been a long time since he'd felt that hot, welcome rush of desire. Everything about his encounter with Hannah had diluted his unease over his upcoming doctor's appointment. Though his heart defect often dictated what he could do, he'd always had total autonomy in his relationships with women. He knew what he wanted and how to get it.

And right now, he wanted Hannah Lockhart. He could ignore

the fact that she was Polly's sister, almost his sister-in-law, and that Luke might not like him hooking up with her. Evan hadn't been with a woman in well over six months, and now that he was focused on running Sugar Rush in Luke's absence and finally securing the acquisition of Alpine Chocolates, he wasn't looking for anything serious.

Which also meant he should stay away from Hannah. If he started something with her, and it ended badly, that could screw up his relationship with Luke and Polly.

The Stones had been through a lot. Luke had worked hard to save Sugar Rush after their mother's death and again after a paternity suit had almost wrecked them. Evan would never do a damned thing to threaten their family relationships.

But Hannah was only in town for a few more months. And she was such a beauty with her long brown hair and blue-green eyes, not to mention her fiery, willing response to him...he ached to see her trembling naked beneath him, to hear her breathy little cries in his ear. Hell, he'd wanted to strip off her pants the other night and fuck her right up against the door, her mouth locked to his and her body shuddering around him.

Women had always been a constant in his life, but he couldn't remember ever having this sharp and intense a pull toward one as he did with Hannah. She had an intriguing mixture of innocence and experience. And she was adorable as hell—when she smiled at him, when whipped cream streaked her face, when her eyes widened with shock. He had to see her again.

That alone was a warning signal. One Evan wanted to ignore. In affairs and relationships, he controlled his heart. Not the other way around. He'd learned that as a teenager when rumors of his defective heart had spread and girls started calling him *Heartbreaker*— a nickname that had stuck and made him realize he had a degree of power over the often baffling female species. He'd liked finally getting attention for something more than his health.

By college, Evan had discovered he could have sex with any woman he wanted—whether she was attracted to him or his air of tragedy made no difference. And though heart issues could impair one's sexuality, for him it had always been the opposite. Sex was the one thing he could control. He'd learned quickly what women liked, how they responded, what would bring them pleasure.

They flocked to him for numerous reasons—because of his family's wealth, or because they had a caretaker complex, and often just because they liked him. Rarely had a woman been turned off because of his heart, though he didn't let them in too far.

Despite his sexual confidence, he disliked the idea of any woman—especially one he cared for—having to endure the uncertainty of being with a *heartbreaker*. Which was why his affairs and relationships didn't last long.

They were good, though. Hot. He liked taking a woman to the edge, seeing how far she'd go. To prove that he was no less a man just because he'd been born with a broken heart.

He pulled in a breath and came to a slow walk as he approached his bungalow on a private stretch of beach bordering Indigo Bay.

He took a tepid shower, trying to stop thinking about Hannah, and then got ready for work. His phone rang, and he picked it up from the nightstand.

His aunt Julia's number showed on the screen. If anything would kill his lustful thoughts, a call from his very fashionable and sharp-tongued aunt was it.

He lifted the phone to his ear. "Julia, what a surprise."

"Why didn't you tell your father about your doctor's appointment?" she asked.

Evan sighed. "It was just my annual."

"You still should have told him. I asked him yesterday what

tests you had done, and he said he hadn't even known you had an appointment."

"Yeah, he left a message giving me shit."

"No wonder. Why didn't you tell him?"

"Because I think he was going on a date. I didn't want him to worry all weekend about the test results."

There was a moment of silence on the other end.

"I beg your pardon?" Julia said. "Warren went on a date?"

"I *think* so. He went out with a woman, at least. Saturday night. I figured that was progress."

"What woman? Where did they go?"

"He didn't tell you?"

"I wouldn't be asking if he had," Julia replied crisply.

"It's why he wasn't at the auction. He told me he was heading up to San Francisco for a Santana concert. When I asked him if he was going alone, he said no, but he didn't give me any details. Then later he asked me about reservations for the Skyline restaurant, which is a total date joint."

"So who do you think he went with?"

"No idea."

"Are you sure it was a date?"

"No, but I think he took the Bentley. And I'm pretty sure he wasn't making reservations at the Skyline for him and his poker buddies."

"Well," Julia remarked. "I'll be damned."

His aunt's bafflement didn't surprise Evan. Since Rebecca Stone's death almost fifteen years ago, his father had been laser-sharp focused on his family and Sugar Rush. Just like Luke had been.

Family and business had always been Warren's excuse for not getting back out on the dating scene. After Warren had lost his high-school sweetheart, Evan suspected his father's pain would never fully heal.

"He deserved to have a good time," he said. "I'd planned to tell him about the appointment when I got into work, but thanks to you he already knows."

"Which is why you should have told him first. He needs to hear these things from you, not me."

"And neither one of you should make a big deal out of it." Irritation cut through his voice. He'd spent his childhood being watched over like a hawk, but when he'd turned eighteen he'd finally thought college would give him autonomy over both his life and his health.

In some ways it had—at least he'd been on his own, and the World of Women had opened up in front of him like a paradise— but after the car accident that killed his mother and left his sister badly injured, the Stones closed ranks like a fortress. Evan's health had taken on a heightened significance after the tragedy, especially with Aunt Julia.

His mother's younger sister, Julia had stepped in as the family matriarch in spite of her own grief. Both his aunt and his father would turn the world back on its axis to prevent anything bad from happening to any one of the seven Stone siblings.

It was the same reason Luke hadn't wanted Evan to direct Sugar Rush's Fair Trade Foundation, which had been Evan's idea. Overprotectiveness ran in the Stones' blood as powerfully as a love for candy-making did.

"I've gotta go." Evan shrugged into his suit jacket. "I'll call you later."

"See that you do."

After grabbing his briefcase, Evan headed out to his SUV. Ten minutes later, he pulled into the employee lot of the Sugar Rush headquarters, a sprawling campus of red brick buildings perched on a grassy hillside above Indigo Bay.

Even with his brother Luke's overhaul and expansion of the company twelve years ago, the culture hadn't changed. Sugar Rush was still a family-owned, synergetic company with a reputation for creativity and employee support. People who came to work at Sugar Rush tended to stay because of the supportive working environment, upward mobility, and excellent salaries and benefits.

In Luke's absence, Evan had taken over the CEO duties—a job he'd wanted to both prove he could do it and pave the way for him to take on a higher-level position at the company, one that would allow him to implement his own agenda on corporate responsibility. His brothers all had different roles at Sugar Rush, but even at thirty-three Evan still hadn't found his place.

He greeted the receptionist and walked to his office, where he checked in with project managers and reviewed the latest report for Alpine Chocolates, a Swiss company Sugar Rush was in the process of acquiring.

Despite his insistence on handling Sugar Rush business alone, there were times when Evan was tempted to call Luke for advice or to ask his opinion. After leaving for Paris three months ago, his brother had been—rather to Evan's surprise—hands-off about Sugar Rush business.

Occasionally Luke asked how things were going, but he hadn't butted in with orders or even advice. Instead he was doing what he'd promised to do, which was leave the company in Evan's hands and take a full leave of absence devoid of all things Sugar Rush.

Evan hadn't been entirely convinced his dedicated, workaholic brother could actually do that, but so far Luke had proven him wrong. And while Evan trusted himself and the other Sugar Rush executives to make the right decisions for the company, this was the first time in his life that he didn't have his older brother to turn to.

A knock sounded at the door, and Adam entered. At thirty-one, he was the third eldest Stone brother and the most global—though he did occasional work for Sugar Rush, his true calling was in the small adventure travel company he'd started a few years ago.

Adam stopped in front of Evan's desk and slapped a piece of paper in front of him.

"What's this?" Evan picked it up.

"Just heard about it. Apparently *The Guardian* sent a reporter to investigate Sugar Rush's new Fair Trade Foundation and is collecting evidence that contrary to our claims, we're sourcing palm oil from an Indonesian company that's destroying rainforests and orangutan habitats."

"The Singa Corporation? We cut ties with them a few years ago."

"Not according to the report," Adam said. "And since you wrote the foundation's statement of principles, *The Guardian* is going to call you for comment."

Irritation tightened Evan's neck—not at the idea of a reporter calling him but at the thought that the rumor was *true.* He'd been the one to come up with the idea of the Sugar Rush Fair Trade Foundation to solidify the company's commitment to sustainability, as well as ensure fair compensation to their suppliers and help with local infrastructures.

But instead of letting Evan spearhead the project, Luke had turned the directorship over to Vice-President Sam Walker because he'd been concerned about Evan traveling to remote areas of Africa and South America with little or no medical care —a requirement needed to get the foundation off the ground.

Though Evan understood his brother's concern—even agreed there were some things he just shouldn't do or risk affecting his health—that didn't make it any less frustrating to still be treated like "the sick one."

Hearing that his idea might already be corrupted was even less bearable.

"You want to call Luke?" Adam headed toward the door.

Christ. That was the last thing Evan wanted to do.

"No, I'll handle it. Thanks."

Evan turned to the computer and wrote an email to Sam,

demanding more details and warning him about *The Guardian* report. If he couldn't direct the Fair Trade Foundation, he wished Adam would—but Adam had always resisted full-time involvement with Sugar Rush.

Evan responded to several emails and calls, headed a short board meeting, and reviewed the latest acquisitions information for Alpine Chocolates.

At two, he told his assistant Kate to handle all calls, and then he drove back into Indigo Bay. He parked in the lot of the doctor's office and went inside.

"Hello, Mr. Stone." The receptionist smiled and typed a few keys on her computer. "I've got you checked in. Dr. Peterson will be with you in a moment."

"Thanks, Alice." Evan sank into a chair and checked his phone while he waited.

A few minutes later, the nurse led him back to the doctor's office.

"Come on in, Evan, and have a seat." Dr. Peterson, who had been treating him since he'd transitioned from pediatric to adult cardiac management, waved him toward a chair in front of the desk.

Evan had been with Dr. Peterson long enough that he could read the doctor's demeanor before he spoke. As Dr. Peterson walked around to sit at his desk, lines of concern creased his forehead and a solemn glint darkened his eyes—which confirmed what Evan had been thinking all weekend.

Smothering a rush of apprehension, Evan unconsciously rubbed his chest. "So what is it?"

"I have the blood test and echocardiogram results," Dr. Peterson said. "There's a problem with your mitral valve, which would explain your increasing headaches and fatigue. We need to replace the valve again."

Dread pooled in Evan's stomach. He'd spent most of his childhood hoping he'd be *done* with medical treatment when he was an adult.

Then his doctor had said he'd need ongoing check-ups and management, which had been uneventful for years. And while Evan had always known he might need further surgeries one day, he sure as hell didn't want one. Especially not while he was running Sugar Rush.

"When do I need the surgery?" he asked.

"I suggest within the next four or five months," Dr. Peterson replied. "You'll be in the hospital for about a week. Considering that you're in good shape, I'd expect the recovery to be about four weeks. I know you'll want to get back to work immediately afterward, but I'll be monitoring you closely."

He turned the computer toward Evan to show him the digital image of his heart. Evan had seen it countless times before. For him, pictures of his heart were practically part of his family photo album.

He left the doctor's office, his head crammed with new, unwelcome information. As he got back in the car, his phone rang with a call from Julia.

Evan didn't answer it. He didn't want to go back to the office. He didn't want to see his father or aunt. If he told them about the surgery, they'd be worried and upset. They'd try not to interfere, but invariably would because they loved him.

His phone buzzed again. His father, this time. Evan answered.

"How did it go?" Warren asked.

"Fine." The lie spilled out of him like water. "Tests are all okay."

"Good. Do you need to see Dr. Kumar?"

"Not anytime soon."

That was the truth, at least. He'd see his cardiologist when he scheduled the surgery. Four months from now.

Evan skipped over a few more details of the appointment

before ending the call. He started the car and drove out of the parking lot.

He knew the sequence of events as if it were a map leading him right back into the past. His father and Julia would pressure him to get the surgery done soon. Luke would find out and come home, even if Evan told him not to. Hailey would drive down from Stanford and probably miss her classes to be here. His father would insist he take time off work, which meant Luke and Warren would take over Sugar Rush along with the other executives.

And Evan would be the sick one again.

He tightened his grip on the wheel. Not this time. He was in control now. He intended to keep it that way.

CHAPTER 6

*H*annah had not done that. She was not a walking cliché—the hired help who'd gotten hot and heavy with the wealthy heir of the manor.

Except that she had. And she was. But now in the clear light of day when all cute talk about whipped cream and liking sex had faded into a memory, Hannah's anger toward herself mounted.

It annoyed her to no end that Evan Stone had gotten under her skin to the point that she'd not only succumbed to his charm, she'd bid for him at a bachelor auction, then let him kiss her in the middle of a damned kitchen when she should have been working.

Hormones or whatever, her body remembered everything— the way Evan had cupped her nape and tilted her head to just the right angle, the firm, insistent pressure of his mouth, the exquisite way he'd deepened the kiss, gliding his tongue over her lower lip as his fingers caressed the ridge of her collarbone.

She'd wanted him to keep going. Worse, she'd wanted to let him take the lead, and she'd wanted to simply follow wherever he planned to go. For a woman who'd been traveling independently for over a decade, it was a decidedly unnerving realization.

With a groan, she rolled out of bed and stumbled to the shower. For two days now, she'd battled the knowledge that she'd both encouraged Evan's attentions and wanted more of them. She couldn't even remember if she'd ever felt that way about a man before. She wasn't the girl who got all weak-kneed and sappy over men. She was the girl who could take them or leave them, who carved her own path, who set the terms of short affairs.

She turned her face up to the hot water, trying to let the spray ease the tension gripping her neck. Not only did she dislike the way Evan had gotten to her, he was a man who thought it was *no big deal* to drop fifty thousand dollars in less than half an hour. Yes, it was for charity, but it was also fifty thousand dollars. She hadn't even had *five* thousand dollars at any one point in time.

Restlessness seethed through her. She got out of the shower and dressed in loose cotton pants and a T-shirt. She poured a cup of coffee and sat down to check her email.

A message from Polly's friend Mia flashed on the screen—a photograph of her and Evan kissing, along with the words *OMG!! Tell me everything now!!*

Hannah's heart plummeted. If Mia knew, then Polly knew. She responded with: *Nothing to tell, sorry.*

A quick search led to the bachelor auction site, which included dozens of professional photos from the evening, and a local news report about the amount of money raised for the Rebecca Stone Foundation.

She picked up her phone, not bothering to calculate the time difference, and called Polly.

"My my," her sister answered. "That's quite a photo."

"It was a total mistake," Hannah said quickly. "I didn't mean to bid on him. It's a long story, but he's paying for the bid and taking someone else on the dates."

"Why aren't you going?"

"The last thing I want or need is to spend a weekend in Napa and a day on a yacht," Hannah replied. "Besides, it's a romantic thing, and I'm not romantic about Evan."

"That kiss sure looked romantic."

Hannah was certain she was mistaken. No way was that *hope* in her sister's voice.

Or was it? Polly had always wanted Hannah to stay in Rainsville, especially during the past four years as their mother battled leukemia. Though Hannah had returned from her travels, she'd never stayed longer than a couple of weeks—a pathetic fact that had only underscored her cowardice.

Their mother hadn't minded Hannah's absence, or at least she hadn't indicated that she had. Jessie Lockhart had always told Hannah how much she enjoyed her blog, how pleased she was that Hannah was so committed to seeing so much of the world like her father had always wanted to do.

Her mother's blessing had been one of the reasons Hannah had been able to justify leaving again. Polly had been another. She and Jessie were so close, always working at the bakery, taking trips, watching movies. Neither one of them needed Hannah, not really. And leaving was so much easier than having to watch her mother's health decline and be unable to do anything about it.

Just like she'd been unable to do anything about Andrew.

Coward, the guilt fairy hissed.

Oh, be quiet.

Hannah deflected the accusation. She was trying to correct her mistakes by staying in Rainsville to help her sister. She'd promised Polly she would run Wild Child while Polly finished her pastry-making course and internship.

Once that was over, Hannah's promise would be fulfilled and she could get back to her real life. Which was definitely not in a small farming town in inland California.

And it definitely didn't involve a man like Evan Stone, whose whole life was rooted so close by. If Polly was hopeful about something happening between Hannah and Evan, then best to squash those hopes right away.

"The whole auction thing was ridiculous," she said, keeping her tone light. "But we've worked it out. I just didn't want you to think anything was going on. He's cute and all, but since I'm leaving first chance I get, it would also be weird."

"What do you mean you're leaving first chance you get?"

Hannah's hackles rose at the faint disapproval in Polly's voice. She'd heard that tone countless times before when she'd left Rainsville, and it never failed to irk her. Just because Polly was a homebody didn't mean everyone else had to be.

"I have another job too," Hannah reminded her. "If I don't keep my blog updated regularly, I'll lose both readers and income."

"I know. But do you have to leave already?"

Hannah sighed. *Have to* was very different from *want to*, but she knew what would happen if she did leave. Even though Wild Child would be fine under Ramona's and Sophie's care, if Hannah left Polly would come back because Polly was all about home, traditions, commitment, and doing right by their mother's legacy. And once again, she would be disappointed in Hannah's lack of ability to just *stay* and be loyal, even for a few months.

Hannah would be disappointed in herself too. She just wished Polly trusted her more. She wished she trusted *herself* more.

"I might have to take a short trip or two," she admitted, but she bit back the urge to tell Polly about the Franklin Publishing editor's interest in turning *Lock Heart* into a book.

Though she was cautiously excited about it, there was no offer on the table. And if nothing came of it in the end, she'd have to tell Polly that she'd failed.

"But Wild Child is doing fine," she hastened to assure her sister. "More than fine. It practically runs itself. All I do is put out pastries, refill coffee, and take care of ordering and payroll. Now that we have Sophie working with the specialty cakes and Ramona's help at the counter, I'm barely needed."

"That's not true," Polly said. "Wild Child belongs to us. You're always needed when something belongs to you. I appreciate everything you're doing, Hannah. More than I can say."

"I know."

And helping her sister now was the least Hannah could do, especially after not being there for so long.

"Oh, I meant to tell you I've been experimenting with that pumpkin spice cake I mentioned last week," she said, needing Polly to know she was committed to her stint at Wild Child and wanted to contribute. "It's not at all sweet, but it has a nice, rich nutmeg flavor."

"That sounds delicious. It would be great to offer some less sugary pastries."

"I'll put out some samples and find out what people think."

After they talked for a few more minutes, Hannah ended the call and finished getting ready for work. She walked down the narrow staircase to the Wild Child Bakery. The two bakers were already busy getting muffins and croissants into the oven, and Hannah started prepping the front counter.

As the clock inched toward seven, Polly's friend Ramona came in for her shift—she'd started working at the bakery after the de facto manager, Clementine, moved away to be closer to her family. Though Ramona's help was supposed to be temporary, she'd taken to the work and appeared to have no interest in leaving.

They worked through the morning Declair rush—after capping their daily output at two hundred Declairs, the rush was a one-hour frenzy of activity that repeated twenty-four hours later—and Hannah set out samples of her freshly baked pumpkin spice cake.

She attended to several regular customers—a mother who came in with her two home-schooled daughters, two students from Hartford Community College, and one of the men from the company that had installed Wild Child's security system.

Hannah's friend and fellow nomad Dave Roland sat in a cushy chair by the wood-burning fireplace, one foot resting on the stone surround. He gave her a sheepish grin as she approached with a teapot and a basket of spice cake slices.

"Try this." She extended the basket. "Pumpkin spice cake."

He took a slice and bit into it, his eyebrows lifting. "Nice. Tastes like autumn."

"I've been trying new recipes." Hannah refilled his mug with macha tea. "Gives me something to do here. That'll be three fifty for the tea and the muffin you think I didn't see you take."

"Put it on my tab." Dave reached for another slice of cake.

"Your tab is over a foot long."

"That's what she said." His grin widened behind his beard.

Hannah narrowed her eyes. She disliked freeloading in any form, but she had an admitted soft spot for Dave. They'd met a couple of years ago after he had flunked out of college and made his way to Italy to learn how to be a vintner. After failing at that, he'd tried his hand at numerous other trades—tour guide, fruit picker, bartender, assistant souvenir hawker.

Hannah had found him camping at Prague train station where she'd just disembarked from Dresden—after he'd offered her half of a potato pancake, she'd taken pity on him and warned him that the police were ousting "vagabonds" from the station.

Since then, they'd traveled on and off together before Dave returned to the US to join a buddy on a Route 66 trip. Hannah had intended to go with him months ago after she'd first arrived back in Rainsville, but then the whole thing with Polly and the Paris pastry-making course had conspired to keep her here.

Dave had been coming and going for the past few months, still trying to convince her to go with him as he figured out his next move. Though there had never been anything romantic between them, not for Dave's occasional lack of trying, they had a friendship based on mutual love of spontaneous travel and bickering.

"If you don't pay your tab within twenty-four hours, I'm putting you to work," she said.

"Way to kick a guy while he's down, Banana," Dave muttered.

"You're so far from down you're practically airborne," Hannah replied.

That was one of the other reasons she liked his company. Everything was *all good* with Dave. She appreciated that nothing ever seemed to hurt him too much.

Hannah turned away. Movement caught her eye, and she glanced out the front window. Evan Stone was walking across the street toward Wild Child, his stride long and confident, a breeze whisking through his dark hair.

Her body surged with a remembrance of tunneling her fingers through his hair and surrendering to their hot, perfect kiss.

She tightened her grip on the teapot, steeling herself against the upwelling of heat in her chest. She needed to be cool and distant, to convey the message that the other night had been a mistake she had no intention of repeating.

"Dave." She leaned in closer to him as Evan approached the front door. "See that guy?"

He peered outside. "*That* guy? Yeah, I see him."

"If he talks to me, I need you to pretend to be my boyfriend."

Dave's eyes widened. "Wha...?"

"We kissed the other night," Hannah hissed, pinching his arm lightly. "But I don't want him to think it'll turn into more than that. So just go along with whatever I say, okay?"

"Will you forgive my tab if I do?"

"Yes."

"Okay, then, sweet cheeks." He waggled his eyebrows at her.

Hannah groaned inwardly as the wind chimes over the door

jingled. She straightened and started back to the counter, feeling rather than seeing Evan approach her.

"Hello." Her voice came out breathy and *girly*, not cool.

Evan nodded, his gaze moving slowly over her. "Hi, Lockhart."

Their eyes met. A hot, electric current crackled between them. She thought of blueberries, sapphires, forget-me-nots, robins' eggs. She remembered the warm feeling that had flourished inside her when he'd stood beside her decorating desserts with Reddi-Wip.

"What can I get for you?" she asked.

He turned his attention to the display cases. Hannah took the opportunity to drink in the sight of him.

In striking contrast to his "movie-star handsome" of the other night, Evan now looked corporate-handsome in dark trousers, a striped tie, and a wrinkled, tan shirt. He'd also lost the amiable, relaxed demeanor he'd had; now there was a tense set to his shoulders, a faint tightness around his mouth.

"Any Declairs?" he asked.

"You're too late. You know you need to be here by nine to get a Declair."

"Then you pick something for me." He dug into his pocket for his wallet.

"Hey, baby, you want to bring me a doughnut?" Dave called.

Evan slanted him a glance, his expression frosting over. Hannah smiled weakly.

"Just a sec," she told Dave, trying to send him a warning look that he didn't need to overdo it. "I'm helping a customer."

Evan turned his attention away from Dave and back to his wallet. Hannah selected the shiniest, fattest chocolate éclair from a tray and set it on a plate for him. She poured a cup of coffee and rang up the purchases. He nodded his thanks and walked to a table by the window.

She secretly admired the length of his legs in his trousers, which fit his hips and rear to perfection, and the evident muscularity of his broad back.

She caught sight of Mia looking at her with interest. Great. So much for secret admiration. All she needed was for Mia to text Polly that despite her protests, there *was* "something going on" with her and Evan. Which Mia was probably doing right now, given the way her fingers were whisking over the screen of her phone.

"I doughnut like waiting, baby," Dave remarked.

Hannah gritted her teeth and brought him a glazed doughnut. "Tone it down a bit, huh?"

"Hey, I'm a macha macha man." He reached out to pat her ass.

Hannah flicked his ear hard.

"Ow." He scowled.

"Hands off. Eat the doughnut."

Hannah went to the sink, filled the small watering can, and watered the plants scattered around the bakery. She still couldn't stop herself from casting glances at Evan. Instead of digging into the éclair, he was scrolling on his phone. His shoulders were hunched, his thick hair falling over a creased brow.

Something was wrong.

The knowledge bloomed in her with sudden force, as if she could feel his distress, like a crack right through his center.

She watered the ficus near the community bulletin board. Everyone had problems, right? Just because they'd gotten hot and heavy in the middle of a bachelor auction—and just because she'd stupidly bid fifty thousand dollars for him—didn't mean she needed to probe at his feelings.

Except she disliked the shadow that had fallen over him, darkening the charmer who had winked at her and informed her she'd lost her sweet tooth.

He frowned at his phone, his forehead wrinkling.

Though she was abandoning her resolve to be "cool and distant," Hannah grabbed a Declair from her stash in the walk-in refrigerator. She put it on a plate, dusted it with powdered sugar, and set it in front of Evan.

He glanced up in surprise. "I thought you were out of them."

"I have a secret stash I keep for emergencies," Hannah said in a low voice as she sat across from him. "Don't tell anyone."

"I qualify as an emergency?" Evan put his phone on the table.

"You seem a little down." She studied him, taking in the dullness of his blue eyes, the lines of stress bracketing his mouth. "Are you all right?"

"Yeah." He took a bite of the Declair, making a rumbling noise of appreciation that rippled over Hannah's skin.

"Hi there." Dave yanked a chair up to the table and sat, sticking his hand out toward Evan. "I'm Dave, Hannah's boyfriend."

Evan's eyes turned wintry. Ignoring Dave's outstretched hand, he set his gaze on Hannah. "Boyfriend, huh? Funny you didn't mention a boyfriend when I had you pinned up against the wall the other night."

"Whoa, does that mean what I think it means?" Dave's eyes widened.

Hannah sighed. "Never mind, Dave," she muttered.

He looked wounded. She felt Evan's penetrating gaze. A flush heated her cheeks.

"He's not my boyfriend," she admitted. "He was pretending to be because...well, just because."

"Because you thought I'd come here to hit on you?" Evan asked dryly.

"Because I make a good beard." Dave tugged at his beard and grinned.

At another glower from Hannah, he pushed his chair back and extended a fist to Evan. "Hey, no hard feelings, man, huh?"

Evan shrugged but allowed the fist bump. Dave retreated to his seat by the fireplace. A heavy silence fell between Hannah and Evan. She tried to squash her embarrassment.

"He's an old travel buddy," she explained. "He's deflected unwanted attention from me before, but he's never been a boyfriend. Never will be."

He gave a short nod. "Good."

The possessive tone in his voice made her feel hot and prickly in a good way.

"So why the 360?" Evan asked.

Hannah took a breath. She owed him the truth. Not only had she done her share of flirting the other night, but she'd let him kiss her senseless—hell, she'd practically begged him, at least in her mind—so it was only fair that she confess her new misgivings.

"I felt really stupid after the auction," she admitted. "I mean, you're Luke's brother, and first I sprayed you with whipped cream and then I accidentally bid a fortune for you, and then the kiss ended up on the website, of all places...I wasn't exactly behaving like myself. I'm sorry."

"I'm not."

She lifted her head to look at him. Heat jolted through her, reminding her all too clearly of what it had felt like to press her lips against his and feel the hard strength of his body—

"Best night I've had in a while." Evan took a bite of the éclair. "And worth every penny."

Hannah's flush deepened, even as pleasure curled through her. She cleared her throat and nodded toward the éclair.

"So do éclairs also date to the Renaissance?"

"Later than that." He licked a drop of chocolate from his lip. "They were first made for French royalty in the nineteenth century. Originally called *pain à la duchesse*."

"How do you know that kind of obscure fact?"

"I've spent a lot of time reading obscure fact books."

He'd also obviously spent a lot of time perfecting his kisses.

Hannah shook her head to dislodge the unbidden thought,

even though it was near impossible to look at Evan and not remember the seamless press of his lips against hers.

"How are things here?" He pushed his empty plate away and gestured to the bakery. "Do you have a new manager yet?"

"No. I told Polly she should just hire Ramona." Hannah tilted her head toward the other woman. "She's worked out great as a general employee, and she knows what she's doing."

"What about you?" Evan's gaze settled on her again, and Hannah felt as if she were standing outside on an overcast, blue-sky day when clouds drifted briefly across the sun and blocked its warmth. Then the cloud passed, and heat spilled down to spread over the grass, the trees, and her skin.

She loved days like that. Mutable, ever-changing.

"I don't want to be the manager." She ran her finger over a crack in the rustic wooden table. "I'm leaving as soon as Polly gets back. I wish I could leave now."

She hadn't meant to confess that last part, not wanting further word to get back to Polly of her restless discontent. Aside from the fact that she didn't want her sister to worry, it was selfish and petty to feel this way. There were far worse fates in the world than to work at a nice bakery for six months.

But there was also the reality of *Lock Heart*, which had been Hannah's only source of income, and success, for years. She couldn't let her blog die any more than Polly could have let Wild Child die.

Evan's gaze was still on her, like sunlight warming her bare arms.

"Polly told me you're a world traveler," he said. "You should talk to my brother Adam. He just got back from Mozambique."

"What was he doing there?"

"Sugar Rush business, though he's more of a freelancer than a full-time employee. He also runs an adventure travel company."

"I've always thought travel itself is an adventure."

"How many countries have you traveled to?" Evan asked.

"Over thirty. I took an au pair job the summer after my high school graduation and I've been traveling ever since."

"Sounds like a great life."

"It is." Her mouth twisted. "When I'm living it."

"Why have you spent so many years traveling the world?" he asked.

To escape.

Being back in Rainsville had sharpened the truths Hannah already knew, but she still had a hard time confessing her fear to herself. She certainly couldn't confess it to him.

"I have a lot of wanderlust," she said instead.

The word *lust* spilled from her mouth like a spicy mint. Evan's eyes slipped down to her lips. Hannah's blood quickened just from the brush of his stare, her skin tingling with fresh awareness of him.

God. This was just an after-effect of their hot encounter, something to do with neurotransmitters and hormone surges. Heightened awareness.

That was the reason Evan's scent still tickled her nose. It was why she noticed his bare forearm, corded with muscle and dusted with golden-brown hair. It was why she looked at his hand curled around the coffee mug and remembered the way he'd cupped the back of her neck, as if she were someone precious to him.

"Wanderlust," Evan repeated slowly. "That's a loanword."

"A what?"

"A word adopted into English without translation, like *café* or *ballet*. Wanderlust is from the German *wandern*, which actually means 'to hike,' and *lust*, which of course means 'desire.' Germans call that feeling *fernwah* now, the feeling of missing a place you've never been to."

"How do you know all that?"

"I studied linguistics as an undergrad. I did a thesis on foreign words that can't be translated into English but have significant meaning."

Ah. His studies explained why he also knew the origins of pastry-related words.

"So what's an example of an untranslatable word?" she asked.

"*Meraki* is a Greek word, meaning to do something with great creativity and leave a part of yourself in your work. *Lagom* is a Swedish word that translates to just the right amount of something. *Gigil* is a Filipino word that means the overwhelming urge to squeeze or pinch something very cute."

"Aw. Like a baby?"

"I guess so," Evan said. "But as a college kid, I always thought of that word when I looked at a pretty girl's ass."

Hannah laughed. He flashed her a smile that made his eyes crinkle at the corners, and for an instant she caught sight of the charmer who'd rescued her from homicidal whipped cream.

"Did you study linguistics because of Sugar Rush?" she asked.

"Partly, but I also like the science of figuring out how language is acquired," Evan said. "How it varies according to geography. The discovery of patterns. I majored in business, with the idea that studying language would help with Sugar Rush's international efforts at sustainability. That's also why I started the Fair Trade Foundation."

"The one Luke wouldn't let you direct?" She winced a little when he glanced up at her. "Polly mentioned it. She said Luke had his reasons, whatever that means."

"Yeah." A shadow passed across Evan's face. "He did."

"Well, I know sustainability in travel is a huge thing," Hannah said quickly, hoping to banish the shadow. "Even on smaller levels. I once stayed with a family in Mongolia who wanted to build half a dozen yurts near their lakeside village. They planned to offer tourists a chance to experience their lifestyle for a couple of weeks, helping with farming, making food and crafts, hiking…

basically as a way to help their local economy while also educating people about their way of life and maintaining it."

"Interesting. Maybe we should incorporate travel into the Fair Trade Foundation." He studied her for a moment, as if he were trying to figure something out. "What're you doing Friday night, Lockhart?"

"Baking muffins and cupcakes."

"Come out with me."

Hannah blinked. "You mean like a date?"

Amusement flickered in his expression. "Not *like* a date. An actual date."

"I can't do that."

"Why not?"

"Because you're not obligated to take me out on a date. You paid for the auction bid."

"This has nothing to do with the auction, but you did contribute $8.56 for me," Evan said. "You might as well get something for your money. A night out, at least."

Hannah tried to resist the *want* that bloomed inside her fast and hard—the desire to spend more time with him, to enjoy the attraction that crackled between them, to forget about her frustration over her blog and her selfish desire to leave. If the auction night was anything to judge by, spending an evening with Evan would be a delight. She hadn't had many *delights* lately.

Except she was supposed to be cool and distant, right? She was annoyed with herself for behaving rather wantonly when she should have been working. Plus, he was Luke's brother and—

"Stop thinking so hard, Lockhart." Evan squinted, as if he could read her thoughts. "Give me one night. You might even be tempted by the dessert I can offer."

Maybe even a dessert that didn't have any sugar but plenty of heat. Her blood sizzled with anticipation, even as she managed to say, "Not a chance."

"Is that a yes?" he asked.

She liked the light that appeared in his eyes again. It dispelled the lingering darkness of whatever was bothering him. And, unexpectedly, she liked that she might be able to help him forget his troubles. She'd never been a man's clear sky before.

"I'm not refusing," she admitted.

"I don't dislike double negatives." He lifted his eyebrows, his amusement deepening. "And this is not an unfavorable course of events."

"I can't say it is an unappealing offer."

"You ain't seen nothing yet, baby." Evan pushed back his chair and stood. "Do you have a blue dress?"

"Yes."

"Wear it."

CHAPTER 7

*S*he was the answer. The thought of going out with Hannah, of *her*, eased the tension in Evan's shoulders. Their encounter at the auction had obliterated his concern about his medical condition that night. Spending more time with her would keep the darkness at bay.

He still hadn't told his family about his need for another valve replacement surgery—in fact, he'd shoved it so far to the back of his mind that he had no intention of dragging it out for months.

Then there was the irrational but undeniable hope for a miracle. Somehow his heart would magically repair itself, and he wouldn't need the surgery anymore. Stupid how after all these years he held onto that childhood wish even though he knew it would never come true.

"Hey, man, you go on your date yet?" Adam asked.

He was sitting on the sofa in their father's living room, balancing a bowl of tortilla chips on his stomach. Across the room, the big-screen TV displayed the 49ers football game.

"Not yet," Evan said.

"Really?" Their youngest brother Tyler, slouched in a chair with his tablet, lifted his eyebrows. "The way you and that girl were playing tonsil hockey, I thought you'd be hitting that Saturday night."

Evan didn't bother responding.

"I was surprised she kissed you back, though," Tyler continued.

"What does that mean?"

"Nothing, don't get me wrong." Tyler shrugged, flipping his overlong hair away from his forehead. "She's hot if you like that type."

"What type is that?" Adam cracked open a beer.

"Kind of a wallflower."

Evan glared at his brother. "A *wallflower*?"

"Yeah." Tyler swiped at the screen of his tablet. "You should've seen her when the spotlight hit her. Looked like she was about to faint. I mean, don't get me wrong, bro. She's pretty and all. Just seemed a little dull, you know? She'd be perfect for Spence, not that he'd know what to do with her."

He shot a mischievous look at their other brother, one of the twins who preferred spending more time in the laboratories at Sugar Rush than he did on the social scene. Not even Aunt Julia could have wrangled Spencer into participating in the Cream of the Crop auction.

"That's the best you can do?" Spencer asked dryly.

"How do you keep a major nerd in suspense for twenty-four hours?" A sly grin crossed Tyler's face. "I'll tell you tomorrow."

Spencer sighed. "As Dr. Who once said, you are a classic example of the inverse ratio between the size of the mouth and the size of the brain. And I'll give you a hundred dollars if you can explain *inverse ratio*."

"I'm pretty sure it has something to do with the way your dick shrinks in direct proportion to a woman's fuckability."

"Boys." Aunt Julia walked into the living room, dressed in a well-fitted 49ers jersey and jeans so artfully ripped in various places that they probably cost a fortune. "I will not tolerate that kind of talk about women. *Tyler.*"

"You know I love women wildly." He turned his engaging grin on her. "By the way, I saw you chatting up that IT guy at the auction. Reeling in some cougar bait, Aunt Julia?"

She shot him a repressive look. "I love the sound you make when you shut up."

"I'm taking bets on whether Spencer could manage half a boner for the girl who bid on Evan."

Evan bolted from his seat in a flash of anger. Tyler barely had time to recoil. Evan grabbed the front of his brother's T-shirt and yanked him so hard Tyler's head snapped back.

"Enough," Evan snapped. "You keep your fucking mouth shut about Hannah. Got it?"

"Whoa, man, just joking around." Tyler held up his hands in surprise.

"Don't."

"Dickwad," Adam added, shooting their youngest brother a look of disgust.

"*Boys.*" Julia sighed.

Evan pushed Tyler back in the chair and went into the kitchen. He didn't often get physical with his brothers, not because he couldn't hold his own but because they'd always treated him with a degree of deference. Unfortunately his arrogant little brother knew how to push all their buttons.

He gripped the edge of the counter and looked out the window at the backyard. For years he'd had no major medical problems, and aside from Luke, his brothers seemed to have forgotten he even had a heart defect. That wouldn't be the case much longer.

He'd never wanted his heart to affect any part of his life, including his relationships with his brothers. They hadn't known his driven efforts at sports and school had been his way of compensating for his health—or if they knew, they hadn't made an issue of it. He'd always needed to prove he was as good as they were, for himself if no one else.

Only after their mother's death had Evan backed into the shadows. His father, Luke, and Aunt Julia had had enough to worry about with both Hailey's injuries and Sugar Rush's decline. Not to mention the corporate vultures circling what they thought was a company on the verge of collapse.

Evan couldn't give anyone reason to worry about him too, so he'd finished his MBA quietly and gone to work for Sugar Rush. For seven years, he'd worked whatever position Luke put him in —and probably still would be if Luke hadn't taken the Fair Trade Foundation away from him.

Then Evan had realized he'd done himself a disservice in flying beneath the radar, and it was finally time to do more. He just had to remind everyone of that.

He pulled his buzzing phone from his pocket. Speaking of reminding everyone he was good at what he did...

He pressed the button to accept the call from Luke, who asked immediately about Sugar Rush's relationship with the Indonesian Singa Corporation.

"We stopped working with them years ago," Luke said. "Why the hell is *The Guardian* asking about *our* involvement with deforestation and illegal sourcing of palm oil? And why would Singa claim to still be doing business with us?"

"Because Sam contacted them on behalf of the Fair Trade Foundation." Evan bit back the urge to remind his brother that he'd been the one to put Sam in charge of the foundation in the first place.

"The reporter told me they're talking to Greenpeace," Luke said, frustration threading his voice. "And we don't fucking need Greenpeace on our ass about deforestation. Not when social responsibility is part of Sugar Rush's philosophy."

"It needs to be more than a philosophy," Evan said. "We need to be leaders on the issue of sustainability, which is just one of the goals of the Fair Trade Foundation. Sam doesn't get it."

Luke didn't get it either. His brother was a powerful CEO who had revamped and saved the company, but he couldn't see past profits and a rigid corporate culture about social responsibility that was more talk than action. The Fair Trade Foundation was supposed to change that, to make a real difference.

"Is Sam still in Jakarta?" Luke asked.

"Yes, and I'm contacting legal to prove the Singa contracts were suspended two years ago."

"This could turn into a PR nightmare if we don't have proof we're not doing business with them."

"I already issued a statement about Sugar Rush's stance on deforestation," Evan said. "But if the controversy starts going viral, we're in deep shit."

"What's the strategy?"

"It's the first agenda item at the board meeting this afternoon. We're finishing due diligence on Alpine. Once we get the final contracts, I'll send them your way before the meeting."

Evan needed his brother to know he'd succeeded. He had reviewed all of Alpine Chocolate's financial documents, employee structure, customer base, taxes, real estate, and management issues. He knew how they would fit in Sugar Rush's expansion of the chocolate division and the company's overall culture.

And he had assured Luke he could close the deal. He couldn't let a public controversy get in the way.

"I've got this," he said, then changed the subject to get Luke off the topic of Sugar Rush. "Hey, how's Polly doing? Her sister said she's been getting some ideas to bring back to Wild Child."

"She's doing great. I think she's worried about Hannah, though."

"Why?"

"Last time they talked, Hannah said she wanted to leave Rainsville again."

"Why would she?"

"I don't know, man." Luke sighed. "Polly doesn't think Hannah will break her promise, but you know my girl. She wants to believe the best about everyone."

Evan tightened his grip on the phone. "So why would she believe differently about her own sister?"

"Because Hannah has disappointed her in the past. She's the one who told me Hannah is irresponsible. And it wouldn't be the first time Hannah has left Rainsville with little advance notice."

Like she's done countless times before.

Evan knew Polly had reason to be concerned. Even if he hadn't kissed her the other night, he'd have sensed Hannah's restlessness, like it was seething just beneath the surface of her lovely skin. She reminded him of the ocean, constantly moving in different directions, pushed by both the winds and the water's own undercurrents and riptides.

"I don't want Polly to be disappointed again," Luke said. "She needs to stay here for her classes, but maybe I should come back for a while. Make sure everything is okay."

Whoa.

"You want to come back?" Evan said.

"Just for a few days. We can strategize about Singa, and I can check in on Wild Child."

"And Polly is okay with that?"

"I haven't talked to her about it yet."

Evan's brain went into overdrive. He knew his brother. He and Luke had been close their entire lives. Even their arguments about Sugar Rush after their mother's death—when Luke had been determined to save the company from takeover—and Evan's frustration with Luke's overprotectiveness hadn't caused him to lose sight of who Luke really was.

If his brother returned sooner than he'd promised, then Luke would dive right back into the business of Sugar Rush. And intentionally or not, Evan would get pushed to the sidelines once again, cast under the force of his brother's powerful shadow.

No. Evan had been admittedly shocked when Luke agreed to take a nine-month leave of absence from Sugar Rush and let Evan take over as interim CEO.

It was Evan's one chance to prove he was capable of running the company, but if Luke came back right when he was trying to close the Alpine acquisition and deal with the rumblings about the illegal sourcing of palm oil—well, Evan would no longer stand a chance of "proving himself" because Luke wouldn't be able to help himself from taking over again.

Luke might be head over heels in love with Polly, but that didn't mean he'd gone soft. Sugar Rush was still the company Luke Stone had saved, and he'd never let it completely out of his control.

Evan pinched the bridge of his nose and sighed. He had to deal with the Singa Corporation and complete this acquisition successfully, and then maybe...*maybe*...Luke would finally make him the head of his own division.

Maybe Evan could finally be part of Sugar Rush because he was *good*, not because he was the entitled brother whose heart condition gave him a free pass.

"I'm handling the Singa issue," he said. "And I'll take care of Wild Child."

"How?" Luke asked.

"I'll make sure everything is okay with Hannah and that she's not planning to bail on Polly."

He wouldn't believe Hannah capable of breaking a promise, but he also couldn't let his brother come home. Not yet. Which meant he needed to find a way to ensure that Hannah stayed. It was far less a chore than it was a golden opportunity to see her again.

"I can't ask you to do that," Luke said. "Hannah isn't your problem."

Irritation rippled down Evan's spine at the definition of Hannah as a *problem.*

"She's not a problem at all," he said shortly. "And I go to Wild Child for the Declairs anyway, so it's not a big deal."

"Neither is my coming back."

"Look, man, you said you'd take the leave of absence," Evan continued. "You made a promise to both me and Dad. Remember he's making you use your vacation time. That means you need to stay in Paris. Don't you think Polly will be upset if you tell her you're coming back here? She's the reason you left in the first place. And she wouldn't be happy to hear that you're coming back because of her sister. Especially without her."

When Luke didn't respond, Evan had a faint rustle of hope.

"Hannah has been at Wild Child every time I've stopped by," he said. "She works twelve-hour days, if not more. She's not going to bail. And you could very well fuck up her relationship with Polly by butting in where you're not wanted."

That did it. Even the silence seemed to relent.

"Okay," Luke finally said. "Do whatever it takes."

"You tell Polly to enjoy her classes and work hard," Evan replied. "I've got everything covered here. I promise."

He disconnected before Luke could turn the subject back to Sugar Rush. For six more months, this was Evan's show, and he intended to keep it that way.

He ended the call and went into the office adjoining the living room. Walls of bookshelves, leather chairs, and a massive mahogany desk dominated one half of the room, while the other was dedicated to a long table strewn with model airplane and boat equipment—parts, glue, and paint. Shelves displayed dozens of intricate models, from clipper ships to WWII bombers.

Every time Evan stepped into his father's office/workshop, a combination of nostalgia and slight apprehension assaulted him

—the office had always been the place where he and his brothers were summoned to answer for one infraction or another.

And while Warren Stone had never physically disciplined them, his big, stern demeanor and grave disapproval had added layers of regret to punishments of grounding and extra chores. Warren's hard edges had been muted by grief after the death of his wife, but he still radiated an authority that even Luke couldn't refute.

The model boat and aircraft were the only external evidence of their father's lingering pain. He'd started the hobby while Hailey was still in the hospital, and in the years since it remained Warren's escape from the world.

His father stood at the window, the phone at his ear and his voice low. Evan stopped just as Warren turned to look at him.

"I'll call you back," he said into the phone.

He ended the call and tossed the phone on the desk. A faint flush colored Warren's neck. Amusement rose in Evan. His father was never embarrassed.

"Anything to do with your date Saturday night?" he asked. "Are you going out with her again?"

"No." Warren scowled. "What do you want?"

Evan knew when not to push an issue with his father.

"Didn't Mom once work with Greenpeace about scholarships for environmental research?" he asked.

"Yes, quite extensively. She wanted their input and ideas."

"Do you still have contacts there?"

"I don't, but I probably have names of people she worked with." Warren went to his desk and opened a file drawer. "I keep most of the conservation documents in the library at Sugar Rush, but here's a file of recent work. I'll go through email records too."

Evan leafed through the documents and briefed his father on what was going on with the Fair Trade Foundation and the Singa Corporation.

As he started to leave the office, he caught sight of the family portrait on the wall—the one taken when he and his brothers were teenagers, and Hailey was still in grade school. They were all smiling in a natural, unforced way, and his parents stood behind the children with their arms linked.

His father would carry his grief forever, but Evan wished the past twelve years had eased it somewhat. Maybe that was even the reason neither he nor any of his brothers had gotten married yet. It was tough to find the kind of love their parents had shared. Just as it was tough for Warren to move on.

Apparently Evan wasn't the only one in the family with heart problems.

CHAPTER 8

*H*annah fastened a lid to her take-out coffee and pushed through the glass door of the diner. A taqueria, a Chinese restaurant, the Cozy Coffee Café, an insurance agency, a bank, and several stores bordered the main street of downtown Rainsville. Residential neighborhoods, strip malls, and agriculture fields—lettuce, strawberries, broccoli—radiated outward from downtown.

As far as she could tell, nothing had changed here in the past decade. Not that she'd expected it to. Rainsville was like a dry, overbaked cake stuck in the pan.

Even the seasons failed to change—the temperature dipped in fall and winter, but the leaves remained mostly green and there was little actual *rain* in Rainsville. Blocked by mountains, the ocean breezes and fog didn't reach the town either, as if the wealthy residents of Indigo Bay were hoarding the coastal beauty for themselves.

Hardly a wonder that she'd been desperate to leave, even before Andrew had died. As a teenager, she'd found an escape in Indigo Bay half an hour west with its stone cottages, hidden courtyards, and the stretches of beach that hugged the rocky shoreline. She'd gone there to run on the beach. To smell the salt air, stare at the ocean, and imagine what was on the other side. To window-shop at the boutiques that sold French linens, Italian pottery, Turkish rugs, Scandinavian woolens, Japanese tea services.

Her plans with Andrew, the older boyfriend she hadn't told anyone about, had been grandiose and thrilling—they'd take off to see the world, carrying nothing but their meager belongings in backpacks. They'd work where they could, save money, meet people, and visit as many places as possible—all together.

Then a surfing accident had taken Andrew away, and the devastation that followed had incited Hannah's urge to flee. When she'd turned eighteen and graduated from high school, it had been so easy to leave. An au pair job, a cheap ticket to Rome, no other plan except to earn enough money to go to as many different places as she could.

A decade later, that plan hadn't changed.

She walked east to Rainsville Park, the only public place in town kept green by careful rationing of water. The Shingle Mill Creek, a narrow intermittent stream of water, ran through the town before joining a watershed farther south. A wooden bridge spanned the creek, leading to a playground and splash pad on the other side of the park.

Hannah sat on a shaded bench and pulled her laptop out of her bag, opening the browser to her blog. In the past three months she'd only managed two measly posts about Wild Child.

No wonder. There was nothing to write about around here. The bachelor auction was her only useful content to date, but she had no other ideas.

She needed to come up with something soon, though, or she'd start to lose both advertising revenue and readers—both of which she'd need once she was back to her real life. She could stick out her time in Rainsville, but *Lock Heart* would never survive six months of slow, tepid content.

She scrolled through her blog. During her trips back to Rainsville, especially when her mother was sick, she'd written posts on Indigo Bay, several local restaurants, a trip to San Francisco. What was left? A review of the Cozy Coffee Café? A description of broccoli-growing season?

She couldn't write when she was standing still. Being *on the move* always generated ideas, the physicality of traveling causing her blood to rush faster in her veins, firing her brain synapses to *create*.

As she navigated the crowded bustle of a market in Hong Kong, climbed to a mountainside tea garden in China, ate curry from a roadside stand in Bombay, she subconsciously wrote the narrative in her mind while taking photographs that captured both unexpected moments and her own carefully constructed compositions.

She pulled up the draft of her post about the bachelor auction and reread it. Though uninspired, at least it was something. She edited a few sentences, added several of the photos she'd taken, and hit the publish button.

A shadow fell across the keyboard. She looked up at a blonde woman who'd stopped a few feet away, her slender figure clad in jogging pants and a T-shirt. A second passed before Hannah realized it was Lucy Clements, Evan's ex-girlfriend.

"I thought that was you." Lucy approached, pulling her earbuds out of her ears. "You won Evan at the auction."

Unease rustled in Hannah, but she kept her voice polite as she said, "That's correct."

Lucy crossed her arms, her gaze narrowing. "I haven't seen you around here before."

Hannah blinked. "You live in Rainsville?"

"No, I live in Indigo Bay. My grandmother lives here, and I sometimes housesit and take care of her cats when she's away."

"Oh." Somehow this bit of information softened the image of the sharp-clawed, cheating ex Hannah had developed. "Well, nice to see you again."

"So have you and Evan planned your dates yet?" Lucy asked.

"No." A touch of irritation tightened Hannah's spine. "Not that it would be your business if we had."

Lucy shrugged. "I guess you two planned that bid in advance."

"Why do you say that?"

"I overheard Julia Bennett saying you own Wild Child. It's a nice place, but I'm pretty sure it wouldn't give you fifty K to throw away at a bachelor auction."

"Again," Hannah replied, "not your business."

"Evan was my business for six months," Lucy said, her lips compressing. "Everyone at that auction expected us to get together again."

Hannah had no desire to get dragged into a conversation about Evan and Lucy's failed relationship, but she also wasn't about to let the other woman have the upper hand.

"Evan would have to agree to that, wouldn't he?" she said.

"What did he tell you about me?" Lucy stepped closer, and the sunlight glinted off a sheen of tears in her eyes. "Did he tell you why we broke up? Is that why you two cooked up the bid so I wouldn't win?"

"First," Hannah said, shoving her laptop back in the case, "we didn't *cook up* anything. And second, if you really want to know, he did tell me you cheated on him."

"Did he also tell you that he strung me along for months?" Lucy snapped. "That I thought the whole time we were going to get married? And that I only found someone else after Evan said he didn't want to marry me?"

Pity rose in Hannah at the other woman's obvious distress, but she steeled herself against it because she still didn't want to be having this conversation.

"I'm sorry," she said. "But I don't know why you're telling me this."

"I'm telling you because if you expect your fifty-thousand-dollar bid is going to force him to commit, you're totally wrong." Lucy swiped at a stray tear. "I really loved him, and I thought we'd have a life together. But not only does Evan *not* want to have a life with anyone, I don't think he's even capable of love. And that's the biggest fucking irony of all."

Hannah picked up her bag and stepped away. "Thanks for the warning, but I need to go."

"Good luck with him." Lucy started jogging toward the Shingle Mill Bridge, then called over her shoulder, "There's a reason they call him *Heartbreaker*."

Whatever.

Hannah had always stayed away from cat fights and bitchiness, so it was easy enough to deflect Lucy's biting remarks.

Except her comment about Evan not being capable of love stuck in Hannah's mind like a burr. Why would Lucy say that? And why would she call it an irony?

Because she's a bitter ex-girlfriend who didn't get the big diamond ring she'd wanted. Simple as that.

She'd forget about the encounter. Evan's past relationships were none of her business, even if it had been the reason she'd spontaneously bid on him.

Well, one of the things. There was also the crackling heat between them, the way his lips turned upward when he winked at her, the ridiculously sensual way he'd fondled her earlobe—

And it didn't matter if he was capable of love or not, because she didn't want that from any man, much less one whose entire life and family revolved around the very area Hannah had sought to escape.

In fact, she was *glad* to know about Evan's emotional distance from relationships...it would be much easier to keep their date casual and free of expectations. Much easier to remind herself not to be caught up by his sexy charm and devastatingly hot kisses. She had no time for a *Heartbreaker*.

She walked back to her van and returned to Wild Child, stopping to hold the door open as a sharply dressed elderly man with a cane approached.

"Hi, Mr. Becker," Hannah said. "I saved the biggest croissant for you this morning."

"That's my girl. Why aren't you fifty years older?"

"Born in the wrong year, I guess," Hannah replied wistfully. "My loss."

She cleared a few magazines off the table near the bookshelves, which was Mr. Becker's favorite place to sit. After bringing him his croissant and a pot of Darjeeling tea, she lowered her voice to avoid being overheard.

"Any luck?" she whispered.

He shook his head, leaning toward her conspiratorially. "I've finagled a way to sit beside her at Bingo on Friday night. I'm going to bet her a cup of coffee that I'll win."

"What if you lose?"

"Then she'll have to buy me a cup of tea." He touched his finger to the side of his nose, as if he were imparting an espionage secret.

Hannah smiled. "Make sure you bring her here, either way. What's her favorite kind of cake?"

"Carrot, I think."

"I'll have two big slices waiting for you."

She patted his shoulder and silently sent up a wish to whomever was in charge of senior citizens' love lives to cut Mr. Becker a break with Miss Purdy, the white-haired septuagenarian whom he'd been trying to court for all the months Hannah had been in Rainsville. Either Mr. Becker was off his game or Miss Purdy really wasn't interested.

Hannah suspected it was the former—for all his awkward attempts to gain Miss Purdy's attention, Mr. Becker cut quite a distinguished figure in his well-tailored suits and ascots that put even the corporate Stone brothers to shame.

She made the rounds refilling tea and coffee. Several of the regular customers were there, including Polly's friend Mia, Mr. Singh from the Indian restaurant down the street, and Gavin Knight of Knight Security, the company that handled security for Sugar Rush and, at Luke Stone's insistence, had installed Wild Child's elaborate alarm system.

Hannah stopped by a cluster of cushy chairs, where four young mothers sat, one rocking a baby and the others supervising three toddlers playing with toys and puzzles from the children's shelf.

"How was the concert at the park?" Hannah checked to make sure their carafe of French Roast coffee was still warm.

"Only a two-tantrum event, so I'd say it was a rousing success." One of the mothers gave Hannah a rueful smile.

"And we're going to the circus this afternoon, so keep your fingers crossed for us," another one added.

"Sounds like you'll need a *petits fours* fortification."

Hannah filled a plate with a variety of the miniature cakes and brought it to the ladies. As she returned to the counter, her phone buzzed in her apron pocket.

She glanced at the screen, her nerves suddenly jumping to high alert. She indicated to Ramona that she was going into the back to take the call.

After inhaling a deep breath, she swiped the screen. "Hannah Lockhart."

"Hannah, it's Elaine Miller from Franklin Publishing. Do you have a moment to talk?"

"Yes." Her hand tightened on the phone.

"I apologize for not calling sooner, but I've gone over your manuscript several times. I really do think your blog has enormous book potential, especially given the love theme of so many of your posts, but I'm afraid the manuscript you submitted isn't going to work."

Hannah's heart began a slow descent to the pit of her stomach.

"I'm sorry to hear that," she said.

"This isn't an outright rejection," Elaine assured her. "Honestly, Hannah, I've been wrestling with this myself for a few weeks. Turning a blog into a book isn't just a matter of compiling posts. In print, I see this as travel essays and photography, but it has to focus on you, the single woman traveling alone. Maybe connect everything to the concept of freedom and feminism or your own personal philosophy."

She paused and made a clicking noise with her tongue. "I think that's the missing element we could incorporate, more about your feelings and experiences. I'm sure you've had a lot of boyfriends over the past ten years, but you don't mention any of them on the blog. Perhaps we could do that in the book. Write it as a memoir of a woman who wanted to escape, and in doing so indulges in cultural excesses of food and sex."

Hannah frowned, irritation scraping her insides. "That's not what I did."

"It doesn't have to be totally factual," Elaine persisted. "But it needs a personal angle, more about Hannah Lockhart than the love festival in China."

"I see."

"Think about it," Elaine suggested. "See if you can rewrite the manuscript or expand the content so that we have a stronger foundation. Food and sex always sell, and your photography is so gorgeous it's almost fuckable."

"Uh...thanks?"

"Fuckable photography with sexy essays," Elaine replied cheerfully. "We might be on to something there. See what you can come up with and get back to me, okay? I'll expect to hear from you before the end of the month."

Sure. Hannah thanked her and ended the call. She wasn't about to fictionalize her entire experience of traveling. And yes, she'd had boyfriends but she purposely didn't discuss them on the blog because the blog was less about her than it was about the universality of love customs throughout the world.

At least Elaine hadn't given her a full rejection, though the "end of the month" gave her only four weeks. She had to come up with a brilliant, fresh idea fast...while being unable to do the one thing that fed her inspiration.

She returned to the front counter, where Mia was leaning against the counter, checking her phone.

"She did it." Mia held up her phone triumphantly in Hannah's direction. "Made a perfect crème caramel that Monsieur Lacroix said was *pas mal.* Polly says it was like receiving a benediction from the pope."

Hannah looked at the photo of a radiant, smiling Polly holding a plate displaying the golden-brown custard decorated with spun sugar. Her heart softened and ached at the same time.

"Good for her."

She kept her tone light, though she couldn't suppress a needle of hurt. Polly had never sent *her* pictures of Paris or the pastries, not that Hannah deserved them. It wasn't as if she'd ever made an effort to keep in touch with Polly over the last ten years. She'd never been there for her sister—well, not until now.

"Polly emailed me a list of French pastries she wants to add to the menu," Ramona said, flicking one of her dreadlocks over her shoulder. "Kind of a hippie-French thing."

"She's going to try a croquembouche next." Mia scrolled through her phone. "She and Luke are thinking of going to Switzerland over the holidays. He's going to teach her how to ski. He probably has a villa in the Alps, don't you think? Has Polly even seen the snow before?"

"I don't know."

Probably not. Her little sister had spent her twenty-five years of life either on the commune of Twelve Oaks where they'd lived before their father died, or in Rainsville. Aside from one year at college in San Francisco, this was the first time Polly had ever been anywhere.

Hannah rounded the counter and collected a few cups and dishes left on the tables. She wouldn't do anything to screw up Polly's adventure. She couldn't. If that meant losing a book deal, then so be it. She'd spent enough years being selfish, and it was time to buckle the fuck down and keep her promise.

"Hey, Hannah, do you want to go out for drinks and dancing tonight?" Mia sat at a table with a fresh cup of tea. "A few of the girls and I are thinking of heading up to a blues club in San Jose."

"Thanks, but I'm..."

Busy? No, she wasn't. Not a dancer? She actually loved to dance. Too tired? She was going for a run after work to get rid of this excess energy. Not a fan of the blues? Everyone was a fan of the blues.

"I have other plans," she finished lamely.

Mia shrugged, though a flash of hurt crossed her expression. Hannah put a dirty mug into the bin and went back to the kitchen, deflecting a surge of guilt.

Mia and *the girls* were Polly's friends, not hers. And Mia was the kind of childhood friend with whom you shared giggles, clothes, and secrets.

Hannah didn't have or want that kind of girlfriend. Her friends were fellow travelers who sent her emails every now and then with updates on where they were going next and suggested that if she happened to be traveling in the same direction, maybe they could connect. Or not. No big deal, either way.

She set the dishes by the sink and returned to the front. She'd keep her promise, but she didn't want to get chummy with Mia or any of Polly's other friends. She didn't want to give herself any reason to regret leaving Rainsville. Everything here, from the people to the studio apartment above the bakery, belonged to Polly. Hannah was just looking out for everything until her sister returned.

Besides, she needed to devote her spare time to "coming up with something" for her book proposal. Something to accompany fuckable photography.

"Oh, wow." Mia flipped her long blond hair over her shoulder and rested her elbow on the back of the chair, a move that rounded her breasts under the fabric of her well-fitted sweater. "The Slingshots are playing at Club Sphinx on Friday. I really need to find a date."

She shot a meaningful glance at Gavin Knight, a handsome but stoic man of few words who had, somewhat inadvertently, given Polly the name for the Declairs.

While installing the Wild Child security system, the men on Gavin's team had also developed a penchant for the pastries, and their appreciation had greatly helped spread the word.

Gavin and the Knight Security men still stopped by Wild Child on their breaks, though they spent most of the time working on their sleek laptops or having low-voiced conversations on their phones.

Mia, it was quickly apparent to Hannah, had a schoolgirl crush on the impassive Gavin Knight—a crush probably related to the fact that her flirtatious charms were lost on him. The harder Mia tried to attract Gavin's attention with her suggestive moves and flippant remarks about dates, the more he ignored her. Hannah didn't know if he even knew Mia's name.

"A date," Mia mused. "I guess I'll have to call an old boyfriend to go with me."

Gavin squinted at his computer screen. Mia scowled at him. He didn't glance her way.

Hannah smiled sympathetically at Mia. She couldn't help

admiring the girl's boldness, even if it wasn't getting her what she wanted.

Hannah had never flirted with men so overtly. Or at all, really. She'd always been forthright and clear because the fewer unknowns anyone had, the better. She liked unknowns in travel, but not when it came to relationships.

And she couldn't ignore the fact that Evan Stone was a rather large—not to mention delectably sexy—*unknown*.

She groaned inwardly as an image of him flashed in her mind —over six feet of pure, hunky male with those crystal blue eyes and devastatingly sexy grin. Just the thought of him heated her from the inside out. What would it be like to strip off his clothes and run her hands over his...and that had to stop. Right now.

Hannah shook her head. She would set things straight on their date tonight. She didn't need him charming her with talk about love. She didn't need him intriguing her with his knowledge of untranslatable words or the history of sweet things.

And she most certainly didn't need him distracting her with his hot kisses that made her blood run like thick syrup and pooled so much heat between her legs she ached to writhe against him and—

Cancel the date.

I can't cancel. That would be rude.

Right. As if breaking up with him before you've even gotten together is all kinds of polite.

Oh, be quiet.

It wasn't even a date, not really. Just dinner or something with an acquaintance. She would tell him where things stood so he would know pursuing her was a fruitless endeavor. With that resolved, Hannah returned to the kitchen to try a recipe she'd found for jasmine rice pudding that might be a good alternative to Wild Child's sugar-loaded desserts.

She collected the ingredients and got to work. Once she put Evan out of her thoughts, all she had to do was wrestle her way through a new book proposal that she had no clue how to even start. Then she had to get through the next few months without losing her blog and her sole source of income.

As goals went, her stint in Rainsville was turning into her own personal Mount Everest.

CHAPTER 9

The blue dress was a draped, open-back jersey dress that Hannah had bought after she'd started making a bit of extra money through her blog. She had never been one for spending money on clothes, but the soft, cornflower-blue dress with the cowl neckline and cloth belt had both fit her to perfection and felt like a dream.

After lacing the ties at the back of her neck, she looked at herself in the mirror. The skirt fell just above her knees, revealing the length of her legs, and the color brought out the blue in her eyes. Though she loved the dress, she hadn't worn it often—it wasn't practical for travel, and she didn't often have the need or desire to get dolled up for a date.

Except for now. Despite her attempt at cool, distant resolve, there was no question Evan had an effect on her that was hard to withstand. And since he'd covered for her costly impulsiveness at the auction, she had to be gracious about going on a date with him.

Gracious also apparently translated to "making an effort." She brushed her hair until it shone, applied make-up, even spritzed some of Polly's floral perfume on her wrists.

At five, a knock came at the door, and when she opened it, her heart bumped against her chest at the sight of Evan in dark trousers and a navy blue shirt open at the collar to reveal the strong column of his throat.

"Damn." His gaze tracked over her, his breath expelling in a rush. "You take my breath away, *Sahnehäubchen*."

Hannah smiled. "What does *Sahne*…whatever mean?"

"Look it up." He grinned and extended a bouquet of wild-flowers.

"Thank you." She took the flowers, suppressing a shiver as their fingers touched. "Come in, and I'll put these in water."

The scent of the blossoms filled her nose as she rummaged in the cupboards for a vase. Somehow he'd known she would appreciate wildflowers—daises, asters, bluebonnets, passion-flowers—more than a bouquet of perfect red roses.

"This is a nice place." Evan glanced around the one-room studio with its shabby-chic furniture and breakfast nook.

"It's all Polly's."

Hannah set the vase of flowers on the windowsill. Her sister's mark was everywhere—the prints of Paris on the walls, the glossy cookbooks of French pastry-making, the photographs of Polly and their mother.

Even though the studio was old and rundown, Polly had turned it into a little haven of warmth. Hannah hadn't bothered changing anything for her stay here; the only evidence of her presence was her tattered suitcase beside the bed, her laptop, and camera bag.

"I'm sure Polly will move out when she and Luke get back," she said.

Her sister would likely move into Luke's house, which she'd told Hannah was some sort of massive, gated mansion on a cliff overlooking the ocean. Evan probably lived in a similar sort of luxury with housekeepers, expensive cars, and elaborate security systems.

"Much as I love the sight of you in that dress, you'd better bring a sweater," Evan said. "We're going to be outside."

"Outside where?"

"You'll see. It'll be a good surprise."

She slipped into a knit cardigan and picked up her bag containing her camera and personal items she brought with her everywhere. They went downstairs to his SUV. She'd expected him to take her to a fancy restaurant in downtown Indigo Bay, but instead he guided the car onto the interstate heading north.

The reddish gold of sunset spilled over the ocean. The rocky cliffs of the coastline gave way to farmlands and low, rolling hills, then they returned to the coast as they drew closer to Santa Cruz. He pulled the SUV into a parking lot across from the beach boardwalk.

"Really?" Hannah looked dubiously at the amusement park where roller coasters and a Ferris wheel rose like constellations above the adjoining beach. "Our date is at the boardwalk?"

"Yes, it is. When was the last time you were here?"

"I can't even remember."

"That's why we're here. Because it'll feel like the first time."

Well. That sounded rather…special.

She couldn't help being charmed by his boyish anticipation; even his steps got quicker as they crossed the street to the admissions booth. A few wetsuit-clad surfers rode the waves like sharks in the distance, and people who had spent the day on the beach still dotted the sand. The grungy, free-spirited vibe of Santa Cruz with its coffee houses, street performers, hipster restaurants, and microbreweries seemed a part of the air itself.

"Do you come here often?" Hannah asked.

"I haven't since I was a kid," Evan said. "My father used to drop me and my brothers off here for the day, partly to keep us occupied but also sometimes as a reward if we'd done all our chores."

He indicated that she should extend her arm so he could

fasten the wristband to her wrist. Again the light brush of his fingers gave her pleasant little shivers. She'd really have to bring out her inner Iron Woman to resist his sex appeal.

They entered the park, which bustled with the start of a Friday night crowd. The scents of fried funnel cakes and popcorn mingled with the sea air.

"You could have warned me that a dress wasn't exactly practical for roller coasters," she remarked.

"We're not going on any roller coasters." Evan's gaze slid over her like a touch, full of heat and promise. "And I really wanted to see you in a blue dress."

"Well," Hannah huffed, flinging her hair back. "If I catch a cold, it's your fault."

"I'll bring you chicken soup. Come on, let's go on the train ride."

Despite the impracticality of wearing a dress to an amusement park, Hannah felt him watching her as she climbed on to the train ahead of him. The fabric stretched over her ass, and though the length was modest enough, it rode up her thighs when she maneuvered in and out of the ride.

Thanks to Evan's intense attention, Hannah began to enjoy showing off a flash of thigh or drawing his gaze to her bare legs by tugging her skirt down. Aside from being flattered by his obvious interest, it served him right for asking...okay, *ordering* her to wear a dress without telling her they were going to an amusement park.

They went on the cyclone spinner, the high swings, and the haunted castle ride. Every time Hannah climbed into a car, the brush of cool air under the hem of her dress reminded her of the thong she wore underneath. Yet the heat generated by Evan's attention was more than enough to keep her warm.

Rather...dramatically warm. Every time he touched her, whether accidentally or to help her off a ride, her body surged with desire. Sparks traveled through her from the point of contact, and more than once she resisted the urge to move closer to him, maybe tuck herself against his side and feel the weight of his strong arm settle over her shoulders as he pressed his lips to her temple...

She was no fool. This was getting dangerous. For all her talk about setting things straight and keeping her distance, being with Evan was almost irresistibly easy and *good*, like putting on pajamas warm from the dryer or indulging in a long stretch.

Smoldering looks aside, she just liked being with him. She liked the movement of his muscular body beside hers, the brush of his hand against hers as they walked. And despite her snarking a little about the dress, she liked that he'd taken her to the board-walk rather than somewhere fancy like the theater.

As they started toward the historic carousel, he paused by a cotton-candy stand where the vendor was swirling a fresh thatch of candy onto a paper cone.

Hannah made a face. "That's like eating sugar right out of the bag."

"Exactly." Evan dug into his pocket and handed the vendor a few bills.

Though it was fun to watch the threads of sugar spin into a fluffy cloud, she let Evan take the lion's share. For his sake, she pulled a piece off and ate it. The sticky sweetness clung unpleasantly to the inside of her mouth.

"Machine-spun cotton candy was invented by a dentist in the late nineteenth century." Evan pulled off another piece.

"Hah. No wonder, if he knew what it would do to people's teeth."

He ate more of the candy, drawing Hannah's gaze unwillingly to his mouth. Only he could make her want to kiss the sticky strands right off his lips. She wanted to press her hands to his jaw and guide his mouth down to hers, to feel his large, warm hand on her back beneath her sweater. Lord, she so desperately wanted to slide her body right up against his and—

"Hey, check it out." Evan extended the cone. "Shaped like a heart."

Hannah jerked out of her wayward thoughts. She looked at the mass of cotton candy, amused to see that he was right. In pulling off bits of sugar, the fluff had formed a heart.

"Hold it up." She took her camera out of her bag and lifted it to her eye. She adjusted the lens and took several pictures of the cotton candy, both with Evan in the frame and close up.

"It's also called sugar glass and fairy floss," Evan said. "Sugar Rush cotton candy has different flavor combinations, like strawberry and orange. Want some more?"

He waggled the cone in front of her. Hannah shook her head.

"You don't find it too sweet?" she asked.

"Sure, but cotton candy tastes like summer to me." He polished off the candy and tossed the cone into a nearby garbage bin. "And sometimes excess is a good thing. After all, if you hadn't bid fifty thousand dollars for me, we might not be here now."

A flicker lit in the center of Hannah's heart. "What other excessive things do you like?"

"Owning too many books and not enough shelves. Swimming so long in the ocean you're pruney and shivering when you get out, then taking a long hot shower that feels like paradise. Gigantic ice cream sundaes. All-night sex marathons."

Hannah snorted, even as her blood heated at the thought of an all-night sex marathon with Evan.

"*All* night?" she repeated. "That's such a guy lie."

"Is that a challenge?" Evan shot her a look simmering with repressed heat.

"You wish."

"Indeed I do, *Sahnehäubchen.*"

Truthfully, so did she.

So much for keeping her distance. She couldn't stay away from the man with whom she'd shared her first perfect kiss *ever*.

A man she also liked a lot. A man who found hearts in cotton candy.

A Heartbreaker.

An unwelcome image of Lucy Clements appeared in Hannah's mind. She pushed it ruthlessly aside. Bitter ex-girlfriends were very unreliable sources of information, not that she wanted information about Evan that she hadn't divined herself. And though it was easy enough to dismiss Lucy, Hannah couldn't quite forget the other woman's comment that Evan was incapable of love. *"And that's the biggest fucking irony of all."*

It made no sense. Why would that be ironic? And of course it was silly to think Evan was *incapable* of love. A man who knew how to give a perfect kiss couldn't possibly be incapable of love. Maybe he was wary after a bad breakup, but he seemed like the kind of man who would love the right woman deeply and loyally and—

Well. She didn't need to be thinking about all the ways in which Evan would love a woman.

She excused herself to use the restroom, taking the time to collect her wayward thoughts. If there was anything she hadn't expected to find during her stint in Rainsville, it was a man. Especially a man like Evan, who was already smoothing over all her bad memories about Rainsville. He could probably even make her *not dislike* it here.

After washing her hands, she returned to where she'd left him near the cotton-candy stand. She first saw him, her gaze going like a magnet to his broad back and the glow of lights against his thick hair.

He looked as if he were speaking to someone, but only when he moved to sit on a nearby bench did Hannah see the young boy, his body supported by a wheeled walker.

Evan lowered his head to be eye-level with the boy and continued talking as the boy both listened and responded animatedly. The man and woman with the boy, probably his parents, were smiling at both of them.

Hannah stopped. Something fierce and tender flared inside her. Evan extended his fist, and he and the boy exchanged a series of fist bumps.

He took a business card out of his pocket and handed it to the father, then ruffled the boy's hair. The parents couldn't seem to stop beaming as they thanked Evan and guided the boy down the midway. Evan watched them go, his smile fading.

No. She didn't want his smile to fade. She wanted the untroubled, charismatic Evan who found hearts in cotton candy.

She approached and reached out involuntarily to thread her hand through his hair. "What was that about?"

The creases on his forehead cleared as he glanced up at her. "I was just inviting them to a tour of Sugar Rush."

"Did you know them?"

He shook his head. "Sugar Rush has a lot of programs for kids, but we go the extra mile for special needs children. Whenever I get the chance to invite a kid to Sugar Rush, I do. It's not much... a tour, some candy-making lessons and a lot of tasting, but they always seem to have a great time. And I tell the parents about my mother's foundation, which has a division focusing on services, financial assistance, and wish-granting for special needs children."

"That's incredible. What a wonderful gift."

Evan shrugged. "At least it's something."

The mixture of regret and sorrow in his expression told Hannah that his reaching out to special needs children was more than just a charity for him and his family.

For some reason, it was personal.

"Come on." She tugged him to his feet. "Let's play some games. Maybe you can win me a ridiculously big stuffed animal."

They walked to the game booths and tried their hand at balloon-popping and ring toss.

"Does your aunt Julia plan a lot of events for your mother's foundation?" Hannah asked, aiming to throw a ring onto the neck of a soda bottle. "Like the auction?"

"Yeah, it's her pet project." Evan tossed a ring that landed on a bottle. "Her way of keeping my mother's legacy alive. She even gets Adam involved when he's in town."

"Do you ever go on trips with his travel company?"

Evan shook his head, collecting three more rings from the vendor. "I've always traveled conventionally. Hotels, taxis, mostly big European cities. The best travel I've done was spending a year in Copenhagen during college when I was working on my thesis."

"Did you learn Danish?" Hannah threw her last ring and stepped back to watch him, admiring the quick flex of his wrist as he tossed.

"Some, yeah." Evan eyed the bottles and took aim again, landing his second ring. "I wrote a section in my thesis on the word *hygge*. It conveys the idea of the emotional contentment that comes from enjoying life's little pleasures. Like sitting by a fire, or walking into a warm house after being out in the cold. A type of happiness."

He tossed a third ring, hooking it around the bottle.

"Three is a win!" The vendor gestured to the array of stuffed animals. "Anything from the second tier."

"You pick." Evan stepped back to let Hannah approach the prizes.

She selected a big-eyed stuffed elephant, tucking it under her arm as they walked to another game booth. A warm pleasure rose in her. Being on the boardwalk with Evan made her long for a nostalgic youth she'd never had. She wanted to share ice-cream sundaes with him, hold hands at the movies, kiss in a parked car by the ocean.

"So do you have a favorite moment that brings you *hygge*?" she asked.

Evan was silent. She glanced at him. His eyes were so blue, like the clear cobalt of Icelandic waters.

"Right now," he said, "is definitely one of them."

She smiled. He could pull a smile from her like no one else ever had.

"For me too," she said.

a cold wind swept in from the ocean. Evan watched Hannah take a picture of an old-fashioned Love Tester machine. The sleeve of her sweater had ridden up her arm, revealing the goose bumps prickling her tanned skin.

Was she that same golden-brown tone all over? She'd taste like warm things—honey and spice cake, apple crisp, cinnamon.

She turned, focusing her camera on sights he wouldn't have thought were photogenic—a creepy jester on the side of a game booth, a crumpled funnel cake wrapper, a few pigeons flocking around a bench.

Curious girl. A wanderlust photographer who found beauty in strange places other people wouldn't think to look. What other secrets did she have? She was like a present wrapped in bright shiny paper that he couldn't wait to tear open.

When she lowered her camera, Evan shrugged out of his jacket and put it around her shoulders. She slipped her arms into it without hesitation, as if it were natural for him to give her his jacket, as if she'd expected he would do no less.

"You ready to head home?" he asked.

"Just about." She put the camera back into her bag and zipped up the jacket, murmuring a noise of pleasure that went straight to his blood.

He gathered the length of her hair in his hand and tugged it free from the collar, barely restraining himself from running his fingers through the thick strands. His fingertips brushed her warm neck. His teeth clenched with the urge to slide them lower, to trace the elegant ridge of her spine and follow the path with his mouth.

She stood very still, her back to him. Evan pulled his hand away from her, forcing a casual note into his voice.

"Any other rides before we leave?" he asked.

"No, I'm good."

She hitched her bag over her shoulder. Even in the multicolored lights of the boardwalk, a visible flush colored her cheeks. Blushing was, he'd noticed, the most telling sign of her emotions.

He kept a distance between them as they walked to the parking lot. His *want* for her was like a rubber band stretching tighter by the second. One day soon it would snap, but before that happened he had to tell her the truth.

As a child, he hadn't been able to hide his heart defect, but it became easier to do when he was older. His childhood surgeries had repaired the problems well enough that he was able to live a relatively normal life.

Of course there was no hiding the scar on his chest when he took his shirt off, which meant he'd always been upfront with his girlfriends about his condition. He'd never balked at the confession either—sometimes they'd already known about it, but if they hadn't, he'd just told them the straight truth and answered whatever questions they had. A simple enough way of dealing with a complex issue.

But Hannah was different. He trusted her not to cut him off—though a couple of women had in the past, he wouldn't believe Hannah capable of that—but he didn't want his damned heart to get in the way. He didn't want to think about his upcoming surgery. If he was lucky, he'd have a short time with her. He didn't want her to look at him differently.

"I was in Paris when they had the Ferris wheel on the Place de la Concorde." Hannah paused by his SUV to look at the Ferris wheel lit against the dark sky. "It was amazing to see the city all stretched out below like a magic carpet."

Evan could imagine her high above Paris, the wind blowing through her long hair and her cheeks flushed with cold. He could imagine her anywhere in the world—hiking up a mountain in Cambodia, drinking sangria in a Barcelona cantina, navigating a Mexican marketplace. Her evident ease in the world was just one of the things that pulled him to her.

"Of all the places you've traveled," he said as they got into the SUV, "what's been your favorite?"

"Iceland."

"Iceland?" he repeated. "Not a tropical island?"

"I've seen some amazing tropical islands, but Iceland is magical."

"Because of the Huldufólk?"

"You know about the Huldufólk?" She glanced at him with raised brows.

"The hidden people." He started the engine and headed out of the parking lot. "Like elves or fairies, who live in the lava rocks. I've heard you shouldn't walk over lava fields so you don't hurt them."

"There's also a tradition that you should leave food for them on Christmas," Hannah said. "And sometimes if you keep an eye out, you see little wooden houses that people have built for them to live in. The landscape of the whole country seems to support this belief in the supernatural. When you're there, it's not even all that strange. Of course the sea has monsters, and trolls live on the black sand beaches. It's just the way it is. There are good and bad things in the world we can't always see."

Good and bad. Just the way it is.

Evan guided the SUV on to the freeway. His scar twinged. He rubbed his chest.

What happened when a scar was sliced open for the fourth time? Did the scar tissue ache forever? And what would happen when they stopped his heart again? What if it didn't restart?

Fuck. He deflected a stab of fear. He'd deal with it. He'd hide his fear, act like it was nothing. Then when he could no longer keep the surgery a secret and had to tell his family, maybe Luke wouldn't come back, and maybe his father wouldn't keep him away from Sugar Rush.

And if they still did, at least Evan's calmness might make it easier for his family to watch him go under the knife again. He just had to *be* fucking calm about it first.

After taking the exit to Rainsville, he pulled up in front of Wild Child and got out to walk Hannah up the narrow stairs to her apartment door. He stopped behind her on the rundown landing and breathed, inhaling the scent of her—sea salt, perfume, cotton candy. Desire pulsed through him, washing away his apprehension.

Hannah lowered her head to dig into her bag for her keys. Her hair parted at the nape, revealing the sweep of her golden skin.

Evan couldn't resist. He moved forward, clutching her hips with both hands the instant before lowering his mouth to the back of her neck.

Her gasp of surprise bolted through him like fire. He pressed his lips to her warm, soft nape, right at the top of her spine. His fingers flexed on her hips. Her ass nudged against his thighs. Her breath increased. He darted his tongue out to taste her honeyed skin.

He lifted his head, his breath rasping against her nape. He tightened his hold on her hips and turned her so she was facing him. Her eyes were wide and luminous in the porch light, her full lips unbearably tempting. No lipstick or gloss, just a beautiful, pale pink mouth he ached to kiss, touch, lick.

He slipped his hand under her chin and lifted her face. Kissed her. Gently at first, gauging her response. He had no doubt about her intense attraction to him, but she was skittish, wary, uncertain of exactly what he—or she—wanted. He wouldn't scare her away, not when he needed her so badly. She needed him too. She just didn't know it yet.

"Open," he whispered against her mouth.

A tremble coursed through her. Her bag dropped to the floor. She parted her lips, letting him inside. Their tongues touched.

Christ in heaven. He was hard already, and he'd barely gotten started. Naked together, they'd be combustible.

A low murmur escaped her. He pressed closer, easing her up against the door. She was still wearing his jacket. He yanked the zipper down and pushed his hands into the opening.

Ah, fuck. He touched Hannah's warm, soft curves encased in that blue dress that had been driving him crazy all night. He'd go there again too, a thousand times over, if it meant he could look at her and touch her as much as he wanted.

He slid his hands up to her breasts. She moaned, her tongue sweeping across his, her hands fisting in his shirt. He ached to drag her dress down and kiss her breasts. He moved one hand lower, edging his fingers under the hem of her dress to her smooth, bare thigh.

Her lips broke from his, her breath hot against his jaw. She trailed her mouth across his cheek to his ear. The scent and feel of her consumed him. His heart jackhammered, pumping hot blood into every corner of his being.

He slid his hand to her inner thigh and up higher... higher...*ah, shit*...a flimsy thong met his touch, the scrap of fabric already damp with her arousal. His cock throbbed like a fucking engine. She gasped, her head falling back against the door.

"Evan..."

The sound of her voice—throaty, pleading—intensified the haze of lust, even as part of his mind knew he was pushing this too far, too fast. He wanted to make her come while she was writhing naked underneath him, not standing on a decrepit porch outside her one-room apartment.

He forced his hand away from her, but couldn't stop himself from stroking it around to cup her smooth round ass. He brought his other hand to her hair, tugging her forward. His mouth crashed down on hers again.

She whimpered, a little pleading noise like a preview of all the sounds she'd make in bed. She loosened her grip on his shirt-front. Her hands moved under his shirt, and then she was stroking his bare skin, her touch hot and cool at the same time.

"You feel like I thought you would," she whispered, tracing the ridges of his abs with her fingers. "So warm and hard."

He wanted her naked. He wanted her soft body arching full against his, her breasts pillowed on his chest, her legs opening and wrapping around him—

Her palms moved higher toward his chest. A sudden chill snaked through him. He lifted his head and circled his hands around her wrists, stopping her upward exploration.

Hannah froze, pulling her head back. She stared at him, her chest rising and falling, her lips reddened.

Regret stabbed him. Her pulse hammered against his finger-tips. He dragged air into his lungs, willing his hard dick to calm the hell down.

Before he could speak, Hannah slipped away from him, her hair falling forward to conceal her profile.

"I...I need to go in," she stammered.

Fuck.

"Hannah, I have to explain."

"There's nothing to explain." Her voice was composed now, but her hand trembled as she picked up her satchel and resumed the search for her keys.

"Yes, there is." Anger twisted through him. He put his hand on her arm. "I have to—"

"I should have listened to myself." She shook her head, freeing her keys from her bag and turning to the door. "I'd made all these promises that I would stay away from you after the way I behaved at the auction. Clearly I have trouble keeping promises."

Evan frowned. "If you wanted to stay away, why did you agree to go out with me?"

"You seemed upset about something the day you asked me." Hannah opened the door and stepped inside. "I thought maybe it would help if we had a good time."

His jaw tightened. Bitter cold pierced him. He slapped his hand on the door, keeping it open.

"You agreed to go out with me to make me *feel better*?" he snapped.

"Well, yes." Hannah put her bag on a chair and slipped out of his jacket. A line appeared between her eyebrows as if his faintly hostile tone of voice baffled her. "What's wrong with that?"

"I'm not accustomed to having a woman agree to date me out of pity." Evan stepped into the apartment, letting the door slam shut behind him.

"It wasn't pity." Her eyes darkened. "After the Dave debacle, you seemed less...troubled, and I liked the idea that it might have been because of our conversation. So when you asked me out, I didn't want to say no."

"Is that the same thing as wanting to say yes?"

"Um...yes?"

He folded his arms across his chest, lowering his head to look her in the eye. She met his gaze unflinchingly, the striking aquamarine of her irises giving nothing away.

He liked that about her. With the exception of her desire, which blazed in her expression and movements like a beacon, he had to work to figure out what she was thinking, to get behind her guard. It made him trust her more. Women who didn't control their emotions were a lot less likely to keep other people's secrets.

But he didn't want Hannah going out with him, or keeping his secret, because she felt sorry for him. No fucking way.

"Make no mistake, Lockhart," he said, his voice low. "Pity, sympathy, whatever…that's not what I want from you."

Her throat worked with a swallow. "What…what do you want from me, then?"

You.

If he told her that, she'd run. With her bristling urge to leave Rainsville and her futile attempts to deny their attraction even when everything about her signaled a hot *yes*, she would try even harder to resist him if she knew how determined he was to have her.

"I want…" he straightened, not taking his gaze from hers, "… Moroccan coffee."

Hannah blinked. "What?"

"You told me Moroccan coffee is so good you learned how to make it yourself. That's what I want from you."

For now.

"Oh." An intriguing mixture of relief and disappointment lit in her eyes. "All right, then. Have a seat."

Evan watched the sway of her hips as she walked into the kitchen. Lust fired his blood again.

Hands off, Stone.

Hardest fucking order he'd ever have to follow.

CHAPTER 11

"The coffee grounds are brewed with spices, kind of like chai." Hannah handed Evan a cup of the fragrant coffee and settled beside him on the sofa. "Cinnamon, pepper, ginger, cloves. I first had it when an acquaintance invited me to her mother's house in Marrakesh. I liked it so much I asked her to show me how to make it, though I've experimented with the recipe over the years. Took awhile to find the blend that was perfect for me."

Evan took a sip. "Not bad. Could use sugar, though."

A smile tugged at her mouth. For him, of course. Where Evan was concerned, the "perfect blend" always seemed to include sugar. The literal kind, as well as the figurative kind that involved hot kisses and touching.

Warmth swept through her. He was sprawled out on the narrow sofa, his big, muscular body incongruous and yet completely at home against the floral print upholstery.

Hannah sipped her coffee, both annoyed and vaguely impressed by how casual he was now after having kissed her and touched her to the point that she'd been devoid of all thought and focused on pure sensation.

After an evening of Evan's sizzling glances, her body had been primed and ready to let him take her on that delicious ascent toward release—even standing out there on the old landing with its peeling paint and cobwebs.

She exhaled slowly. Lingering arousal coursed in her blood. She told herself it was a good thing that Evan had stopped her exploration of his bare chest and broken their kiss. Not a good thing for her body, which still ached with thwarted lust, but for her sensibilities.

She rose to pour them more coffee. Evan picked up a framed photo from a nearby shelf and looked closely at it. "Is this you?"

Hannah leaned over to look at the photo. She'd never bothered really looking at the photos scattered around the apartment, assuming they were all of Polly, their mother, and Polly's friends.

A strange, bittersweet feeling rose in her. She was maybe twelve in the photo, wearing shorts and a T-shirt, with both of her arms around a smiling, seven-year-old Polly. Behind them, her parents stood, also smiling, with the buildings and orchards of Twelve Oaks stretching in the background.

"That's me, Polly, and our parents."

"Great picture." Evan set the photo on the table. "You were a cute kid."

"I've never seen that picture before. I don't even remember who took it."

"Was that the commune where you grew up?"

"Twelve Oaks," Hannah said. "I loved it there. But after my father died, my mother moved me and Polly to Rainsville so she could open Wild Child."

"And you hated it."

She nodded, seeing no point in denying the truth.

"Is that why you started traveling?" Evan asked.

"Partly." Hannah ran her thumb over the edge of her mug. "I also had a boyfriend...an older guy in his twenties who'd dropped out of high school. He was a surfer with grandiose dreams of finding the perfect wave. I never told my mother about him...I don't think she would have told me to break up with him, but she wouldn't have thought he was appropriate for a seventeen-year-old girl. And he hadn't wanted to tell anyone because he thought he'd get in trouble being with a minor.

"We had all these plans for traveling the world after I graduated. He wanted to hit all these famous surfing spots, and I just couldn't wait to leave Rainsville and see as much of the world as I could.

"Then right before graduation, Andrew was killed in a surfing accident. It was awful. I didn't even know until three days later when one of his friends told me. I couldn't go to his funeral because none of his family knew about me. I was really lost for a while before I decided that I still wanted to go away somewhere. Maybe Andrew would have wanted me to. So after graduation, I left Rainsville."

They were both silent for a moment. Old grief simmered in Hannah. She'd loved Andrew in an intense, puppy-love way, but even more she'd loved the carefree life and freedom he'd promised.

And though the spontaneity of traveling had soon become part of her, she knew her wanderlust stemmed from the fear of loss. Her father. Andrew. Her mother. Maybe even Polly, who'd never had the older sister she deserved.

"I'm sorry," Evan said. "Tough thing for a young woman to deal with. Is that why you haven't come back to Rainsville often?"

"Maybe. But I could have come back more." A flush of shame swept over her. "I used my blog as an excuse." She picked up her phone from the table and scrolled through it. "I have a travel blog...well, it's mostly a travel blog but it also deals with love."

She pulled up the blog on her browser and handed him the phone. *"Lock Heart: The Things We Do For Love."*

"Love, huh?" Evan squinted at the screen. "Interesting topic for a woman who doesn't like sugar."

Hannah wasn't all that sure she liked love either, not after several failed attempts at actually experiencing it. She was a reporter, an impartial observer who wrote factually about the world's love customs while sprinkling her posts with personal descriptions of her travels.

"How long have you been writing?" Evan asked.

"Ten years. I started it mostly as a way to let my mother and Polly know where I was, just a general travel blog. It's still about the places I visit, but the theme eventually became about love traditions throughout the world."

"How did that start?" He scrolled through the posts.

"The summer I first left, I visited the Milvio Bridge in Rome where people put locks with their names on it, signifying their love. Turned out the tradition came from an Italian novel about two teenagers who put a padlock on the bridge and threw the key into the Tiber as a symbol of their eternal love.

"The padlocks reminded me of my last name *Lockhart*, and I was still grieving the loss of Andrew, so I planned my next trip to see other 'love lock' bridges in the world.

"As I traveled, I started looking for other romantic traditions, like throwing coins into the Trevi fountain, kissing under the Bridge of Sighs, the Qixi festival in China which celebrates a love story in Chinese mythology. I took pictures and started writing posts about those things. And it became a niche for the blog."

"That's quite a story." He handed her the phone. "You're probably the only person who can say she travels the world looking for love."

Hannah smiled wryly. "That's not what I do. I'm kind of a reporter. I report about love."

"So tell me which *report* above love traditions is your favorite."

"I like an old Welsh custom where young men present their beloved with an elaborately carved wooden spoon as a symbol of their devotion," Hannah said. "The lovespoons are such works of art. Of course, I also have a soft spot for the padlocks on bridges."

Evan ran his finger across the tattoo decorating her upper arm. Her breath caught at the light, warm touch.

"When did you get this?" he asked.

"The summer I started traveling." She looked down at his finger tracing the outline of the compass with the tiny paper airplane right at the north point.

She half expected him to ask her about the airplane. Though she hadn't ever told anyone about it, she'd probably tell Evan. Just like she'd told him about Andrew, as if it were the most natural thing in the world to give him her secrets.

"You know, I'm only here for a short time," she heard herself saying. "I agreed to stay until Polly gets back from Paris."

"I know. Six more months, right?"

Something about his tone of voice hinted at determination, as if he had plans for her, for *them*, during those six months. A note of apprehension struck her.

"Maybe." She forced her voice to sound offhanded. "I wish I could leave sooner."

He glanced at her, faint tension lining his mouth. "Why?"

"Not many people realize that my blog is actually my job," she said. "I spent years building up a readership before I made even a penny from it. Now I'm able to fund my travels through advertising revenue and partnerships, but if I don't update with new content regularly, I start to lose traffic, which affects my income. And unfortunately, there isn't much to write about here. Certainly nothing to include in a blog about love traditions."

She was almost tempted to tell him about her conversation with Elaine Miller of Franklin Publishing, but then something flickered across his expression that she couldn't quite read.

"Is that why you want to leave?" he asked.

Hannah nodded. "First chance I get."

"No."

"What do you mean, no?"

"You can't leave."

Hannah welcomed the prickle of irritation at his flat statement, as it mitigated the soft feelings she'd been experiencing all
evening. "Why can't I?"

"If you leave, Polly will come back," Evan said. "And Luke will
come with her. No way can he come back before I've finalized
the acquisition of Alpine Chocolates and dealt with the Fair
Trade Foundation."

"I thought someone else was doing that."

"Sam Walker, yeah. But I just found out the foundation might
still be involved with a company known for large amounts of
deforestation…a company we cut ties with years ago."

"So what does that mean?"

"It means that the Fair Trade Foundation could not only have
ethical and financial issues, but it could also end up a PR disaster." Evan's mouth compressed. "And it means that if Luke comes
back and gets involved, he'll take over. It was hard enough
convincing him I could handle it. I need to fix this by myself."

Hannah didn't understand why Luke wouldn't believe his
brother was capable of taking care of Sugar Rush. But she didn't
ask because it wasn't her business, and she didn't want another
avenue into knowing more about Evan Stone.

He turned toward her, resting his arm along the back of the
sofa. "We can help each other here, Lockhart."

"With what?"

"We have three dates from the auction," Evan said. "Two
nights in Napa, a boat trip on the bay, and a date of our choice.
You agree to go on those three dates with me, and I'll prove to
you that you don't need to travel the world to report about love.
There are plenty of romantic things right in your own backyard."

Hannah eyed him skeptically. "What if you fail?"

"I won't."

"That confident, are you?"

"I've lived in the Bay Area my whole life." Evan leaned
forward, his blue eyes gleaming. "I've also had a lot of girlfriends.

Believe me when I tell you I know how to bring the romance in these here parts."

Hannah smiled, though she did not love the idea of Evan taking her places where he'd already taken "a lot" of other women.

"You're not obligated to take me anywhere," she reminded him. "You paid for the bid. You can take anyone you want."

"I want you."

The phrase rumbled over Hannah's skin, leaving a trail of fire in its wake. She tried to ignore the feeling, to muster up some irritation over his charm.

Unfortunately, being irritated with Evan Stone was like turning down a second helping of steamed mussels at a Prince Edward Island fish shack. You couldn't do it.

"I need you to stay in town," Evan said.

"So I just have to go on three more dates with you?"

"To start with," he allowed. "But there are plenty of other places I can show you. Enough to fill a book about *The Things We Do For Love*. Maybe even an encyclopedia."

A shiver trickled down Hannah's spine. She suspected all those alleged girlfriends would do many things for Evan Stone's love.

And she certainly needed enough content for a *book*. Maybe letting Evan show her the romance of the Bay Area would inspire her with an idea for her revised manuscript.

But she couldn't let it turn into a real romance. She couldn't let him kiss her and touch her the way he had at the auction and on the landing. Given her uncontrollable response to him, he'd have her naked before they even got to the second date. He'd have her *feeling* things for him that she couldn't afford to feel.

Not even for $8.56.

"Okay," she said slowly. "But we need to set some ground rules. This can't be the start of an affair."

Evan winced. "So much for showing you the mechanical bed at the Love Hurtz Motel."

Hannah smothered a chuckle. "I'm serious. It's not a good idea."

"You forget." He leaned forward, fixing his gaze on hers. "Less than an hour ago, I slid my hand between your legs and felt how wet you were from one kiss. No way you can tell me fucking wouldn't be a goddamned brilliant idea."

Heat flared in her chest. "I mean...with you being Luke's brother, and me only here for a few more months..."

"This isn't about Luke or Polly, or about you leaving," Evan said, still holding her captive in that blue spell. "It's about you denying what you want because you're still blaming yourself for hating Rainsville and not being here for your family."

Hannah's chest constricted. "Are you trying to guilt me into having a fling with you?"

"No. But I won't let you say it's because of Luke or because you're only here for a few months. I'm not looking for a relationship. I like you, and if you want to have a good time while you're here, I'm all in. It's as simple as that."

Except that it wasn't. Because she was already feeling all sorts of warm, squishy things for Evan that she'd never felt for another man before, and if she were to mix that up with what would surely be mind-blowing, explosive sex...well, that would result in more complications than she could handle.

She couldn't even bring herself to go out for drinks with Polly's friends for fear of establishing ties here. How could she have an affair with this mouth-watering, hunky male who kissed her as if she were the only woman in the world...and then leave?

"But if you think that's all I want, I'll prove you wrong," Evan said. "I won't touch you all weekend."

She ignored a flash of disappointment. "And you still think you can bring the romance without sex?"

"Is that a challenge?" He narrowed his eyes. "I can bring it, baby. I'm full of romance."

"You're full of something," Hannah muttered.

"I'll keep it platonic." Evan crossed his finger over his chest. "But just so you know, you're welcome to break the rules."

Hannah scoffed, although breaking the "no-sex rule" with Evan would be as easy as slipping thread from a needle.

"No sex," she said. "And no bringing me to places you've brought a dozen other women."

Satisfaction glinted in his expression. He turned his attention back to his coffee.

"Get ready, *Sahnehäubchen*," he said.

"For what?" And what the hell did *Sahne-whatever* mean, anyway?

"Evan Stone's Operation Romance." He shot her a smoldering glance. "It's irresistible."

That was exactly the problem. How could she resist the irresistible?

CHAPTER 12

*H*annah expected to have to make plans and arrangements. She thought she'd have to revise the Wild Child work schedule, complete a bunch of paperwork, and get everything in order.

Instead, when she told Ramona that she was going away for two nights with Evan Stone, the other woman waved her hand and said, "Go, go."

"But I have to figure out the schedule."

"Go," Ramona insisted. "I've got things covered here."

"What about the special orders?"

"Sophie's taking care of them."

"You're sure it's okay if I leave?"

"More than sure." Ramona peered at her knowingly. "And I won't tell Polly you're taking a trip."

The guilt fairy cackled in Hannah's ear. She winced.

"I shouldn't go," she said.

"Hannah, you haven't missed a single day's work in three months," Ramona reminded her. "You're entitled to a couple of days off. And it's Napa, not Tibet. You can be back home in three hours, if needed."

That was true, even if Rainsville wasn't *home*.

So instead of making arrangements for Wild Child, Hannah made them with Evan, who told her to be ready at four on Friday afternoon. She packed her backpack and travel bag with routine efficiency, but her jitters reminded her there was nothing routine about going away with Evan Stone. Or any man, for that matter.

She'd traveled with men before, but she'd never been whisked away on a romantic weekend trip whose sole purpose had been designed as a "get to know you" date. And though they'd established the terms of this weekend, there was no pretending she didn't want to *know* Evan Stone on much more intimate level.

She closed her backpack and did another quick check of herself in the mirror—black cropped pants, a navy blue tunic (which she tried to convince herself was not for Evan's benefit), and black flats.

Through the window, she saw his SUV pull up in front of the bakery. Despite her nervousness, a familiar and welcome anticipation rose inside her at the thought of getting on the road again, even if it was only a few hours north.

She grabbed her bags and went downstairs, rounding the side of the building as he approached. Sparks lit inside her at the sight of him—tall and handsome in worn jeans that hugged his long legs and a forest-green button-down shirt.

"Hey." He reached out to take her bags, his gaze moving over her appreciatively. "I was going to come up and help you with your stuff."

"That's all I have." Hannah indicated her bag and backpack.

"Really? Most women would bring a massive suitcase."

"I'm not most women."

"Just one of the many reasons I added you to my list." He put her bag in the back of the SUV and opened the passenger side door for her.

"What list?"

"The list of things I like."

The spark turned into an outright glow. "Do I fall between Christmas Eve and steak?"

"You're tied with sex right now." He grinned and strode around to the driver's seat. "Maybe even a cut above."

"Be still my beating heart."

Not that her heart bothered to listen. Instead, as Evan settled beside her and started the car, it pattered in a quick, happy rhythm, like an eager puppy scrambling across a hardwood floor.

They started out of Rainsville, and the months-long tightness in her chest eased. She was heading toward a place she'd never been before, which, ironically, had always been the only thing that made her feel at *home.*

"If you're hungry…" Evan gestured to a paper bag resting on the console.

Hannah opened it to reveal an array of Sugar Rush candy—Chocolate Crunchies, Fruit Bon-Bons, Honeybee Toffee, Cocoa Nibblers, Jelly Rolls. She picked up a grape-flavored Sparkle Pop.

"Is this the surprise lollipop you were telling me about?" she asked.

"It's a burst of hot flavor, baby." He gave her a sidelong glance. "Try it."

Hannah shook her head, unthrilled at the idea of candy exploding unexpectedly in her mouth. "Not a fan, sorry."

He frowned. "Don't think I'm giving up."

"I'd be disappointed if you did."

Just like she'd have been disappointed if he hadn't pursued her after the auction, much as she'd tried to convince herself she hadn't wanted him to.

"Polly really likes these." She opened the box of toffee and ate one of the little squares. "And the Cocoa Nibblers."

It occurred to her that Sugar Rush candy had been part of her and Polly's childhoods—in fact, part of the childhoods of almost everyone she knew. Fruit Bon-Bons showed up in birthday party goodie bags, a package of Chocolate Crunchies was a treat on the beach, and friends shared multi-colored Licorice Twisters during recess. Halloween was a windfall of Sugar Rush treats, especially the once-a-year Ghostly Gumdrops, Voodoo Corn, and chocolate witches.

Unexpectedly and despite her distaste for candy, Hannah liked the idea that she'd had a connection to Evan for years, even if it was just through his family's company.

They continued driving north. Music drifted from the media player as they passed through San Jose and Fremont toward Napa County. Late afternoon sunlight streamed through the windshield.

She appreciated that Evan didn't find it necessary to talk all the time—one of the reasons she preferred traveling alone was that she was never forced to make conversation when she didn't want to. But with him, compatible silence felt both comfortable and natural.

She was reminded of traditional coupling practices that historically took place in some Native American cultures. According to folklore, before a couple was engaged, they would spend time together in silence to see if they were comfortable with each other naturally and without awkwardness.

Hannah certainly felt that way about Evan. She cast him the occasional glance as they drove, taking in the stretch of his muscular thigh beneath the denim of his jeans, the loose grip of his long fingers on the steering wheel, occasionally tapping in time to the music, the watch band curled around his strong wrist.

He had an understated, quiet masculinity that was all the more powerful because of his complete self-possession—there was nothing leashed or forcibly restrained in him, nothing that could break loose without warning. Nothing he couldn't control.

She looked out the side window. Evan was also different from the men she usually gravitated toward—the youthful college boy backpacking through Europe for the summer, the wandering hippie on a pilgrimage to various ashrams and temples, the dedicated traveler who, like her, was happy to spend a couple of weeks together before parting with vague promises to "keep in touch."

Those men were pleasant, unassuming, and never inspired this intense mixture of desire, warmth, and unease that billowed inside Hannah every time she looked at Evan. He might exude self-control, but the feelings he evoked in her were edged with raw wildness—and that fact alone was enough to scare her senseless.

But she could ignore that since she and Evan had agreed this trip would be platonic.

And if you think that's going to be an easy agreement to keep, Hannah Lockhart, I've got a bridge in Moscow to sell you.

"So where are we staying?" she asked, realizing she knew nothing about the actual sleeping accommodations.

"A historic inn in the heart of Napa," Evan said. "Private cottage with two bedrooms."

"Did you choose it as part of your date package?" she asked.

"No. My aunt and her staff put together the date packages and matched them to each bachelor."

"Why did she match you with Napa Valley?"

He shrugged, though a faint tension tightened his mouth. "Guess she thought I was suited to the low-key weekend."

Hannah remembered his brother Adam had had the *Walk on the Wild Side* motorcycle package, and his other brother Tyler had been auctioned with the *Fall For Me* skydiving date.

"Did you want one of the other ones?" she asked.

"No, I couldn't do them anyway."

He hadn't been into roller coasters at the boardwalk either. Maybe he just wasn't an adrenaline junkie.

"What about your other brothers?" she asked. "The ones who weren't at the auction?"

"Carson is out of town, otherwise he'd have been there. Spencer isn't the type to let himself be auctioned off."

"What about your sister?"

"She's up at Stanford."

"Is she going to work for Sugar Rush when she graduates?"

"I don't know. My parents never had expectations that we'd all work for Sugar Rush, though sometimes it seemed inevitable. For me, at least."

"Why for you?"

"I didn't have as many choices." Evan pulled into a gas station. "I'll get us some water."

He got out of the car and walked to the convenience store. A breeze threaded through his thick hair and flattened his shirt over his broad chest.

Hannah remembered his remark about needing to prove himself at Sugar Rush. How could anyone, especially his family, think he was somehow lacking?

Evan exuded capability, assurance, and confidence. Heck, if he'd said he was running for president, Hannah would have asked about his stance on foreign policy.

But she knew better than most that family dynamics were weird and complicated. So for whatever reason, and intentionally or not, Evan's family had set him on a narrow path with narrow expectations. And out of love, loyalty, responsibility, or all three, Evan had stayed on that path.

She couldn't be the one to help him break free of it—not when she was fighting her own restraints—but she hoped being with her helped him forget about it for awhile.

He returned to the car with two bottles of water and continued driving. Soon he navigated off the main highway, and the landscape shifted to scenic rolling hills and lush vineyards.

Perched on at least two-dozen acres of land, the luxurious Mediterranean-style Castillo resort overlooked the sprawling beauty of the valley. Luxurious rooms opened onto stone terraces, sweeping staircases led to a crystalline swimming pool surrounded by white cabanas, and employees glided about with quiet deference.

A touch of anxiety wound through Hannah as they walked into the pristine, hushed reception area. She was not accustomed to high-end hotels or travel, but thankfully Evan handled everything with the ease of a man who'd grown up with wealth and luxury.

"Please take advantage of our all-inclusive spa facilities." The receptionist extended a creamy sheet of paper with a list of available services. "I especially recommend the Himalayan salt stone massage and the grapeseed crush exfoliation. We also have lovely spa packages for couples, if you'd like to indulge together."

"Oh, we like to indulge together," Evan deadpanned, shooting Hannah a mischievous look that made her smile.

She turned to pick up her bag just as a bellhop swooped past to take it from her.

"Allow me, miss. I'll show you to your private *maison*."

They followed him to the courtyard, then along a pathway lit by glowing little lanterns. Hannah tried not to be captivated by the place—she'd always taken pride in being suited to low-budget travel and roughing it—but this was straight out of a fairytale.

Nestled in a grove of olive trees, the *maison* boasted smooth hardwood floors and ceilings, warm earth tones, a full kitchen, wood-burning fireplace, and French doors leading out to a private terrace. Overhead fans circulated the breeze, and the windows all displayed an incredible view of the valley.

Hannah stepped on to the terrace, her chest tightening at the panoramic sight, the evening sky blooming with fluffy red-gold clouds.

She'd always been so convinced that landscapes were prettier, more majestic, and *better* elsewhere in the world. But this had been right in her backyard all along. It made her wonder what else she'd missed because she had only wanted to look forward, not around.

She wandered through the rest of the cottage. French doors led from one of the bedrooms to an enclosed terrace displaying a huge sculptural bathtub. A high wall on one side held a rainforest showerhead.

Between the his-and-her spa treatments and outdoor bathing arena, this place was clearly meant to bring the sexy. Too bad it was wasted on her and Evan. Not that she was disappointed about that.

Not *much*.

She returned to the living room, where Evan was closing the front door behind the bellhop. He approached, and she took in the sight of his ruffled hair, his long, easy stride, the way he looked directly at her as if she were his destination.

"This is amazing." She spread out a hand ineffectually, trying to encompass everything.

"It's a nice place." He reached for one of three bottles of wine that had been left beside a fruit and cheese platter on the wooden table in front of the fireplace.

"Have you been here before?" Hannah asked.

"A few times."

With a woman?

He glanced at her, faint amusement rising to his eyes. She realized with a start she'd spoken that question aloud.

"Sorry," she said quickly. "Obviously it's none of my business."

"I've stayed in rooms up at the main building," he said. "Twice with a woman, the same one, not lovely Lucy Clements, and another time for a Sugar Rush conference."

He uncorked the Shiraz and poured two glasses before handing her one.

"Speaking of Lucy Clements…" Hannah sank into a chair and sipped the wine, which probably cost a fortune. "I ran into her last week in Rainsville Park. But don't worry, neither one of us got hurt."

Her attempt at a joke fell flat. Evan straightened, his mouth tightening.

"And?" he asked.

She hesitated, belatedly questioning the wisdom of bring up the unpleasant encounter. But she'd been enjoying the relaxed, easy way Evan was around her, and she didn't want any unspoken negative history to come between them.

"She was upset." Hannah took another sip of wine. "Trying to justify her actions. She said she cheated after she found out you didn't want to marry her."

"That's a version of the truth," Evan admitted, turning his gaze to the wineglass. "Our families go back about a decade. There was a time last year when my aunt was hounding me about dating. Lucy was...convenient. She knew from the start I wasn't looking to get married, but she had a complex about me and thought she could change my mind. When I didn't, she tried to make me jealous by fucking another guy. It didn't work."

Hannah processed that. Lucy's and Evan's "versions of the truth" weren't so very different—the difference was in their perspectives.

"What kind of complex did she have?" she asked.

"Not a good one." He picked up his phone, his forehead creasing. "I'll order us some dinner."

Hannah set her glass down. Lucy's words echoed in her head. *"There's a reason they call him Heartbreaker."*

How many broken hearts had Evan left in his wake? As much as she liked him, Hannah had to ensure her heart wasn't one of them.

"Tomorrow we're scheduled for a breathtaking hot-air balloon ride just after dawn," Evan said, scrolling on his phone, "an art gallery tour, and wine-tasting at several renowned wineries. Then tomorrow night we have dinner reservations on a nineteenth-century restored train that will take us on a forty-mile journey through the spectacular scenery of Napa Valley."

He held up the phone. "According to the date brochure written by Aunt Julia."

Hannah shook her head slowly. "Is this normal for you? I mean, do you take women on dates like this all the time?"

"Not all the time."

"You date a lot though, right? Based on what I saw at the auction, you're quite a catch."

"Only with the right bait." He winked at her.

Hannah smiled, glad her mention of his ex-girlfriend hadn't cast a pall on their evening.

She excused herself to change into a nicer outfit, not that she had very many of them. She washed and slipped into a gray sundress, taking extra care with her hair and makeup. By the time she emerged, two resort assistants were setting up a linen-draped table on the terrace, along with tapered candles and a bouquet of creamy flowers.

The multi-course dinner was exquisite and elegant. Oysters, steak, red wine. Thyme, lemon, the faint bitter taste of rosemary. Crispy *pomme frites* laced with tarragon herb butter. *Haricot verts* fresh off the vine.

And Evan. Candlelight gleaming on his sharp-edged features, lighting a fire in the center of his blue eyes. His hands, big and capable, as he cut the steak and lifted the fork to his mouth. Swift, economical movements, no wasted energy.

The sun sank on the horizon—the same one Hannah had seen in dozens of other countries, and yet here its red-gold colors seemed somehow more vibrant, the sunset glow caressing Evan's hair with the warmth of a lover's touch.

After dinner, she accepted his offered bit of crème brûlée, agreeing that it was indeed smooth and creamy even if it didn't give her the same feeling of bliss that spread across his face. She didn't tell him that watching him enjoy the dessert was better than eating it herself.

"So where was crème brûlée invented?" she asked.

He broke off a piece of the hardened caramel topping. "I think the recipe was first recorded in a French cookbook in the late seventeenth century. It was also known as *burnt cream*. There's a Catalan dish that's also similar."

"How do you know all that?"

"In addition to liking obscure facts, I dated a historian a few years ago. She was writing a book about the history of royal cuisine. We talked a lot."

Hannah couldn't help chuckling. "How dorky. And romantic. But mostly dorky."

"I strive to throw a little dorky into my hot romanticism."

"You succeed admirably. So why don't you have a girlfriend?"

"You sound like my aunt."

She winced. "I didn't mean it that way. I meant...well, with your family and your good looks, not to mention your encyclopedic knowledge of pastry history, you have a lot going for you."

He shrugged, digging his spoon back into the dessert. "That's part of the problem. Sometimes I can't tell if a woman wants to be with me because of my family's money or because of me. Which I realize is stupid because what a problem to have, right?"

"Just because you have money doesn't mean you're not allowed to be wary," Hannah said. "Everyone has to protect his or her own heart."

A touch of bitterness flashed across Evan's features.

"Is that what you've done, Lockhart?" he asked. "Why don't you have a boyfriend?"

"I've had my fair share. They just don't stick around."

"Because they don't want to or because you don't want them to?"

"Both."

"Why?"

"Because even when they do, they don't." Hannah folded and unfolded a corner of her napkin. "They find someone else. They go back home. They want to go somewhere else. They..."

Her voice trailed off. She was painfully aware she wasn't just talking about men. It was *her* too. Maybe more her than them. She'd done the same thing with Polly and her mother—detached herself instead of trying to fit into their world.

"I always seem to end up alone," she said, "which is actually how I like it, so it all works out in the end."

"Or is that what you've been telling yourself?"

Hannah frowned. "What does that mean?"

"You don't write about love because you don't believe in it." A perceptive glint appeared in his expression. "You can talk all you want about being a reporter who just dishes out the facts, but you write about love because you know it's the one concept everyone in the world has the capacity to feel—at any time, anywhere, regardless of who they are or what else they believe. That's the reason people in dozens of different countries have traditions celebrating love. Everyone knows how powerful it can be."

"Love isn't the only thing we all feel. What about fear?"

"People don't want to be afraid. They do want to love."

"Why haven't you been in love then, Heartbreaker?"

"I've been in love. Best feeling in the world. And when it's over, the worst."

"Exactly."

The air crackled with energy. Candle flames glowed in his eyes, but the fire came from inside him. In spite of his charm and his love for whipped cream, Evan Stone was a danger to Hannah's self-control and maybe even her heart.

"Why haven't you stayed in love?" The question escaped her on a single breath.

He broke eye contact, pushing his dessert plate aside. "I can give a woman a lot. But there are some promises I can't make."

"Like the promise to stick around?"

"Exactly."

That was all right. That was what she wanted.

Wasn't it?

The light carved shadows on his strong features. A warmth that had been building all day slid through Hannah's blood, hot and thick.

"What are your secrets, Heartbreaker?" she asked.

He smiled faintly. "How do you know I have any?"

"Everyone does. History does. There are always secrets to discover when you travel."

"Like what?"

"Stonehenge, Easter Island, the pyramids. There's still so much we don't know. We may never know."

"But some things we've always known."

Evan leaned forward, his eyes glittering as he slid his hand around to cup the back of her neck. Warmth traveled down her spine. He was so close that she could see the flecks of silver in his irises.

"Maybe I'll tell you my secrets one day, *Sahnehäubchen*," he said. "It's up to you."

He eased away from her, his gaze still locked to hers, his thumb brushing gently against her cheek. Faint dizziness swept through Hannah's head. She wanted to drown in the deep blue of his eyes, to sink against him and feel his solid body pressing against hers. She wanted to strip off her clothes and invite him into her bed, into her body.

Evan stood slowly. Hannah admired his broad shoulders, the expanse of his chest, his biceps hugged by his shirtsleeves. Her arousal intensified at the evidence of what she was denying herself. She swallowed hard and imagined unzipping his trousers, sliding her hand into his boxers or briefs and closing her fingers around his...

"Go to bed, Lockhart." He curled a lock of her hair around his finger and gave it a gentle tug. "We need to be up early tomorrow."

He turned and left the room, closing the bedroom door

behind him. Hannah stared after him, her body pulsing with unfulfilled need.

She slowly pushed away from the table and went into the second bedroom. She paced to the windows and looked out at the star-sprinkled night. She pictured Evan taking off his shirt, unfastening his belt. His actions would be swift and fluid, edged with the economy of movement that was such a part of him.

She shivered. An emotion curled inside her, something hollow and yearning. It was a moment before she could put a name to it. Knowing Evan was so close by and yet they were purposely distancing themselves from each other, Hannah was struck with loneliness.

CHAPTER 13

"Swirl the wine in your glass," the vintner said. "*Swirl* it."

Hannah sloshed the wine around in her glass, hoping that was the same as swirling. She enjoyed wine as much as the next person, but she'd never understood all the hype about *terroir* and tannins.

"Now sniff," Mr. Benson ordered. With his neatly trimmed white beard and bushy white hair, the vintner was perfectly suited to this sprawling stone villa with its acres of flourishing vineyards.

Obediently all ten people crowded around the wooden table lowered their noses into their wineglasses and inhaled a series of sniffs that made it sound as if they all needed a tissue.

"I sense a strong grassy flavor," one woman remarked.

"Mmm," said another. "I'm getting mushrooms."

"I smell dampness and leather," a man announced.

"Now sip and savor," Mr. Benson said.

Hannah wasn't sure she wanted to drink something that smelled like old leather, but she took a small mouthful.

"You should taste hints of oak and blackberries," the vintner said. "And perhaps a bit of raspberry as well."

The other wine-tasters murmured and nodded. Beside Hannah, Evan took another sip of the burgundy. She sipped again, attempting to pick out blackberries and oak. As she'd been told, she sucked the wine noisily through her teeth to aerate the flavors. She ignored Mr. Benson's dictate to spit the wine into a bucket and swallowed it instead.

Evan picked up the bottle and poured more into her glass. "Are you getting the blackberries?"

What she was *getting* was a bit tipsy, but she didn't bother telling him that. Instead she nodded.

"Oak and raspberry, too. It's like a wooden fruit basket in my mouth."

She took another sip of wine. Evan's gaze went to her mouth as she pursed her lips and shifted them from side to side, then sucked the wine through her teeth. She swallowed the mouthful, enjoying the taste as it slid down her throat.

"You're supposed to spit," Evan admonished.

"I always swallow after I suck." She shot him a sideways look.

His eyes darkened. "Bad girl."

"Yes."

Evan breathed out a curse, turning his attention back to the bottles. Hannah grinned to herself, even as she told herself to be careful. Emboldened by the wine though she might be, she couldn't lead him on after they'd come to an agreement about this being a platonic weekend. A rather weak agreement, truth be told, but an agreement nonetheless.

Not that Evan was making it easy on either one of them the way he kept touching her. At first, she'd thought it was accidental brushes of his body against hers, but when she'd felt his hand on her ass as she'd climbed into the hot-air balloon, she'd realized he was deliberately touching her.

And she'd let him. Because Evan's touches were like fireflies, inciting bursts of heat in her blood. His hand on her back. His bare forearm grazing hers. The quick stroke of his fingers against her wrist.

And *him*. Even if he wasn't touching her, Hannah felt his presence with every fiber of her being. She caught herself staring at him multiple times throughout the day—the length of his muscular legs beneath his cargo shorts, the sheer breadth of his chest and shoulders in his short-sleeved shirt. The hollow of his throat. Every time she got close to him, she caught a whiff of his delicious scent of maleness and spice.

She'd never felt so...*dizzy* around a man before. She'd also never had such a good time. Yes, the whole day was a romantic cliché with the soaring over the valley in a hot-air balloon, bike ride through country lanes, hillside picnic lunch, and wine-tasting in a historic villa, but being with Evan was anything but cliché. In fact, it was the opposite.

It was unique. One of a kind. Special.

Hannah set her wineglass down. A few drops had spilled down the side of the glass, forming a shape that looked vaguely like a heart. Clearly Evan's cotton-candy heart was having an influence on her. She picked up her camera and adjusted the lens before taking several pictures of the wine heart.

After the tasting concluded, Evan purchased several bottles and stowed them in the back of his SUV before he drove to downtown Napa. They visited shops, art galleries, and a historical museum. As Hannah stopped to take pictures, Evan disappeared into a bakery and emerged with a frosting-loaded cupcake.

"You really live the whole Sugar Rush philosophy, don't you?" Hannah asked.

"It's chocolate." Evan wiggled his finger, coated with a dollop of chocolate cream, under her nose. "What kind of crazy woman doesn't like chocolate?"

"I don't hate it," she said. "It's what makes *mole* sauce so good, right? I think the Mayans were on to something with their hot chocolate and chili mixture. Then the Europeans had to add milk and sugar to it."

Evan narrowed his eyes at her. He stuck his finger in his mouth and sucked off the chocolate. "You're messing with me, Lockhart."

"I am not. It's a scientific fact that some people have less interest in sweet things. I'm one of them. I'm just not that into it."

Evan scooped another dollop of chocolate frosting off the cupcake. The way he kept doing that made Hannah a little tingly inside. She took the cupcake from him and scraped off a bit of frosting with her finger, then brought it to her mouth, as if she were about to eat it.

Just as Evan's expression turned smug, she extended her finger to him in invitation. He blinked, his gaze going from her face to the chocolate offering.

He grasped her wrist. Hannah's heart thumped. His fingers pressed against the pulse beating wildly just beneath her skin. She parted her lips to draw in a breath as he slowly and deliberately pulled her hand toward his mouth.

And then his tongue flickered out to lick the chocolate from her finger in a movement so sensual and warm that Hannah bit her lip to stifle a moan. Her breathing increased. Her nipples tightened, a current of heat sliding right down to her sex. Evan licked all the chocolate from her finger and lifted his head, his eyes gleaming with blue fire.

His grip tightened on her wrist. Without breaking his gaze from hers, he tugged her closer, so that a mere inch separated their bodies. Heat radiated from him, sinking into her skin.

Her body thrummed with the hot anticipation of feeling his chocolate-laced mouth press against hers. She ached to delve her fingers into his thick hair, to feel her breasts crushing against his hard chest. She wanted to part her lips, taste every inch of him, and sink into the swirl of heat and lust she hadn't felt in—

"Hmm." Evan's mouth was so temptingly close to hers that he

only needed to lean forward to initiate the kiss. "We'd better get back to the hotel."

Yes. Yes, they definitely had to get back to the hotel straight away because stripping naked right here on the street would be a very bad idea.

Evan drew away from her, turning his attention to his watch. "We have the dinner train ride at six, so if we want to change, we should head back now."

Hannah blinked. The world came slowly back into focus. Evan released her wrist and stepped away from her.

"Player," she muttered, still throbbing from the anticipation of hot contact.

"Tease," he murmured, though his eyes lingered on her mouth and heat crested his sharp cheekbones.

She was still holding the cupcake in her other hand. She held it out to him.

"You want this to satisfy your sweet tooth?" she asked.

"Lockhart." Evan flashed her a devastatingly sexy grin. "You *are* my sweet tooth."

He was on the edge. Hell, he was halfway over it. Every time Hannah's bare arm brushed against his, or he caught sight of her nape, his body jolted with awareness. And Christ in heaven, that little tank top she wore with the scooped neckline that revealed the barest hint of cleavage...he wanted to grab the stretchy material and yank it down along with her bra, exposing her breasts for the pleasure of his mouth and tongue.

He wanted to see her naked breasts. Hell, he wanted to see her naked *everything.* He wanted to know the color of her nipples, the way her skin felt under his hands, the scent and taste of her...

His cock twitched. He groaned inwardly.

It was his own fucking fault for touching Hannah as much as

he had. At first, he'd wanted to tease her a little, prove their chemistry was hot and electric, give her a hint of what she was missing with their *no sex* dictate.

Instead he'd incited a raging fire in his own body, one he couldn't smother. His blood simmered hot even as he sat on a bench, waiting for Hannah to finish taking pictures of the bridge connecting the train station to the boarding platform. Dozens of padlocks engraved with hearts and names were attached to the wire fence of the bridge, all left by lovers and tourists from around the world.

Hannah was bending over, adjusting her camera to take pictures of a cluster of locks. She had a perfect ass. It rounded the fabric of her skirt and looked so squeezable and tempting that Evan wanted to grab her waist and pull her ass right up against his groin. Then he'd slide his hands up to cup her warm breasts and—

Fuck.

He rested his elbows on his knees and turned his attention to a row of ants marching across the dirt near his feet. Industrious little creatures.

"Okay, I'm done." Hannah's hand settled on the back of his neck.

Electricity jolted down his spine. He lifted his head, willing his erection to subside. "So am I."

In more ways than one.

"Are you all right?" Hannah frowned, sliding her hand around to his forehead. "You feel a little warm. And you look flushed."

"I'm fine." *Just ready to yank your skirt up and drive into you so fast and hard the world spins.*

He stood and stepped away from her. Her touch would only make his inner fire burn hotter.

"Not bad, huh?" He nodded toward the bridge. "You should choose one of the padlocks and speculate about the couple who left it there, like you did with your post about the Milvio Bridge."

"How did you know I did that?"

"I read your blog."

Hannah looked at him with bafflement. "You read my blog?"

"Not the whole thing. Not yet, anyway. But yeah, I started it. Why are you looking at me like that?"

"It's just…" Hannah shook her head. "I guess I didn't think you'd go back and start to read it from the beginning."

"It's like a book," he said. "You have to read it from the beginning to know the whole story."

He wanted to know the whole story, all right. The whole story of Hannah Lockhart.

She concentrated on putting her camera back in the case. A crease grooved her forehead, as if she were either confused or thinking hard.

"Do you not want me to read it?" Evan asked.

"No." She glanced up. "I mean, yes. It's fine if you read it. I guess I'm just surprised. I…" She hesitated, and then said, "I have some interest from a publisher to turn *Lock Heart* into a book."

"Really? That's great, Hannah. Congratulations."

"Thanks, but it's not a done deal yet. The editor didn't like the manuscript I submitted. She said it has to be more than a compilation of travel blog posts. Apparently it has to be more personal or something. She didn't even seem to know what was missing, but she wants me to find it. I'm supposed to come up with a new idea and resubmit the manuscript."

"Whatever it is, I'm sure it's already in your writing," Evan said. "An editor wouldn't be interested in a book deal if your blog doesn't already have what she's looking for."

She looked mildly surprised, as if she'd never considered that. "Well, you were right about Napa. The train trip suits my *love traditions* theme perfectly. When romantic couples come to Napa Valley, they take the Wine Train. Not that we're a romantic couple," she added hastily.

Evan stepped closer to her, curling a lock of her hair around his finger. "We can be."

She bit her lower lip. The edge of her teeth made little indentations in her lip. He wanted to stroke them away with a sweep of his tongue.

"There's a village in Brazil where men compete for women's favors by bringing them gifts, like a basket of fish," Hannah said.

"Oh."

"It's interesting to me how cultures all over the world have customs that are so similar. Even the bachelor auction is like a courtship ritual in Africa where men strut their stuff in front of a group of women, hoping to entice them."

"Do you want me to strut my stuff and give you a basket of fish? Because I will, if that's what it takes."

She smiled. "You already did strut your stuff, and the flowers are more than sufficient. My point is that people everywhere often do the same things in their search for...companionship. It's a universal human need."

"Yes, it is. So why do you fight it so hard?"

Hannah didn't respond. Frustration rose in Evan. It made no sense—this beautiful, warm, curious woman deserved to be loved and cherished. And though he wasn't the man who could give her what she deserved, he hated that she was closing herself off to even the possibility.

She turned her attention to the train on the other side of the platform. The evening light shone on her brown hair, which shifted around her bare shoulders. Her eyelashes were dusky feathers around her intense, blue-green eyes that had the ability to hold him under a spell.

He took her camera from her. He peered through the lens and adjusted the focus, then snapped several pictures of her.

"You don't have a lot of pictures of yourself on your blog," he said.

"That's because I'm always on the other side of the camera."

"Not this time. Smile for me."

She faced him again, giving him a smile that he wanted to wrap up with a bow. He lowered the camera. A shadow slanted across her bare shoulder, a union of dark and light in the shape of a heart.

CHAPTER 14

*I*t was too quiet. No traffic noise, no voices outside the window, no barking dogs, no sirens in the distance.

Restless, Hannah paced the elegant bedroom of the *maison*. She turned the TV on, scanned the channels, and turned it off again. She checked her phone.

She wondered what Evan was doing. Was he sitting in the living room? Was he eating leftover dessert? Had he gone to bed?

Pushing aside the curtains, she looked at the terrace, where the sculpted bathtub sat glowing marble-white in the darkness. She'd never taken a bath outside before. She went out to turn on the bathtub faucets, then returned to the bedroom.

She stripped out of her clothes and put on a big, fluffy robe from the closet. After pinning up her hair, she selected lavender-scented bubble bath and lotion from the array of complimentary bottles in the bathroom. She walked out to the terrace, leaving the French doors open behind her.

A breeze drifted on the air. The valley stretched out like a tapestry below, lit with garden lights and the hazy light of the moon. Aside from the faint rustling leaves and chirping crickets, silence covered the landscape.

Hannah poured a generous amount of bubble bath into the water and tested the temperature. She slid out of the robe, the cool air prickling her skin with goose bumps before she stepped into the steamy hot depths.

A low groan escaped her as the water enveloped her in a rush of heat and scented bubbles. She sank lower, letting the water cover her all the way to her neck. The tension of the past few months slipped away. She rested her head on the edge of the tub and looked up at the sky, the black night sprinkled with stars like sugar.

Sugar.

Her heart thumped. Evan. Eyes filled with blue fire. Wickedly beautiful mouth. Ridiculous penchant for desserts. Gorgeous body with hard muscles she ached to feel beneath her hands…

She rested her hand on her thigh, rubbing it slowly beneath the water. A delicious tightness coiled in her lower body. She parted her legs and let her fingers slip into her cleft, her own touch filling her with a rush of heat.

She closed her eyes and eased her fingers deeper. The fantasy bloomed with sudden force in her mind—no gentle, prolonged seduction, but a vivid image of her spread naked on a bed, her hands beneath her thighs as she opened herself for the smooth, slow entry of Evan's cock…

She shuddered, slipping her forefinger into her body. The evening air caressed her damp neck, the scent of lavender swirling upward from the bubbles.

"Hannah?" Evan's deep voice drifted out to the terrace through the closed bedroom door.

Her eyes flew open, her heart crashing against her ribs.

"I…I'm outside," she called. "Sorry, did you knock? I didn't hear you."

"I didn't knock. Can I come in?"

"Um…I…" Hannah tried to muster up her resolve, but every part of her, including her thoughts, felt loose and liquid. She hastily arranged the bubbles over her body, concluding that the soapy suds were thick and copious enough to be more concealing than a terrycloth robe.

"I'm in the bathtub," she said. "But I'm decent. You can come in."

There was a brief hesitation before the doorknob turned. Evan stepped in, a plate in one hand. His gaze zeroed in on her like an arrow landing on target. Energy charged through Hannah's body.

"Ah." He approached with a slow, relaxed stride. "A mermaid."

"I couldn't resist." Hannah gestured to the valley, though the sight of Evan walking toward her was far more exhilarating than the nighttime view.

"I don't blame you." He paused, his gaze sliding over the frothy bubbles hiding her naked body. "I brought you another offer you can't resist."

He extended the plate. Topped with whipped cream and chocolate shavings, a round chocolate mousse cake sat amidst decorative swirls of vanilla. Hannah looked at Evan with amusement.

"You don't give up, do you?"

"Not when it comes to dessert." He pulled a chair up beside the bathtub and sat down. "To appeal to your penchant for spice, this is a Mexican chocolate mousse cake with Kahlua and ancho chilies. Decadent, spicy, and sweet all rolled into one. I had the hotel chef make it for you."

Hannah narrowed her eyes. "You did not."

"Okay, I didn't have him make it for you," Evan said, reaching into the breast pocket of his shirt for a fork. "I had him make it for *us*."

Oh...

The area around her heart softened in a way that was both sweet and painful, like a melting snowflake.

Evan dug the fork into the cake, bringing up a large portion of creamy mousse and crushed-cookie crust. He extended the fork to her. She obediently opened her mouth. He watched the movement of her lips as she closed them around the fork.

She tasted almost nothing—okay, thick, airy chocolate and the pleasurable bite of chili—but instead of indulging in the cake, all of her senses converged on *him*. The heat in his eyes. The small but evident increase in his breath. She wanted to press her mouth against his, feel him, taste him, eat him.

Hannah lifted a soapy hand to wipe a crumb off her lip. "It's… it's good."

"*Good?*" Evan frowned and sank the fork into the cake again. "It's more than good."

He ate the bite, half-closing his eyes as a groan of pleasure rumbled from deep inside his chest. Hannah shivered, acutely aware of the ache still burgeoning between her legs. The hot fantasy still flickered at the back of her mind.

She shifted, rippling the water around her. The bubbles slid like silk against her skin. Her blood pulsed.

"More?" Evan held out another forkful of dessert.

Hannah opened her mouth—not because she desired the cake, but because she loved the way he was looking at her as if he were about to devour her. At the same time, she knew to her bones that he would sit there forever and just *look* at her if that was all she wanted him to do.

How incredible to feel so reckless and protected at the same time.

She pushed herself upward a little, making sure the bubbles still concealed her breasts. Water splashed over the edges of the tub, and the bubbles shifted and resettled around her body.

Evan took another bite for himself and extended one to her. Hannah ate it, enjoying the bittersweet taste of chocolate followed by the fire of the chili. The steam from the bath flushed her skin, and damp tendrils of hair clung to her neck. She was warming from the inside too, the heat of the chilies seeping into her veins.

"It's…it's awfully warm, isn't it?" She rubbed the back of her neck.

"Indeed it is." Evan's gaze moved lower to where the bubbles had slipped to reveal the curve of her breast and the hard, rosy peak of her nipple.

A breath escaped him on a hiss. He started to push the chair back. "I need to go."

She held out her hand. "Give me the cake."

"Ah." He handed her the plate and stood. "I knew I'd find your sweet tooth."

"Not for me." Hannah's heart raced. Despite her nomadic life-style, as a rule she didn't take a lot of risks. She knew how to be on guard, cautious, watchful. She knew how to protect herself. She never ignored her own internal warnings.

Until now.

Certainty snapped inside her like a lock clicking into place. Not only did she trust Evan completely, the crackling heat between them was impossible to withstand. As long as they both knew what they were getting into, why was she resisting so hard? Why couldn't she just take what he was offering and stop thinking so damned much?

Ignoring the fork, she scooped up some of the cake with her fingers and held it out to him. He stared at her, intense desire rising to his eyes.

"Come on, dessert lover," Hannah whispered, her heart pounding so hard she heard the beat inside her head. "Take a bite."

He moved forward, his gaze never leaving hers as he closed his mouth around her fingers and sucked off the chocolate mousse. Hannah gasped. Arousal bolted to her core.

He curled his hand around her wrist, an unmistakable message that it was too late for her to retreat now, not that she wanted to. He licked her fingers with slow, easy strokes before sliding his tongue to her palm.

When not a speck of chocolate remained on her fingers, Evan lifted his head. Tension coiled through him, leashed and potent. He stood, not letting go of her wrist.

"Are you breaking the rules?" he asked, his voice husky.

Hannah bit her lip. "If we agree that this is a temporary fling, we can have some fun."

"Fun, huh?" He trailed his finger over the ridge of her collarbone. "If we start this, Lockhart, it'll be more than just fun. It'll be hot and dirty."

She pulled in a breath. "I like hot and dirty."

His gaze slipped to her breasts. Her nipples tightened further, as if his look were a touch. His mixture of gentleness and sheer masculinity had her both off balance and wildly excited.

"Are you sure?" he asked.

"Positive."

And she was. Finally.

Hannah braced herself on the side of the tub and allowed him to pull her to her feet. Nervousness wound through her. Water and foamy bubbles cascaded off her body, and the cool night air raised goose bumps on her skin. She longed for Evan to touch her breasts, then slide his fingers into her until she was gasping and writhing against him. Until she was begging for more.

But instead of touching her right away, he stepped back and looked at her. No, he *devoured* her with his eyes. He raked his hot blue gaze over her body as if he were memorizing every detail of the soap clinging to her curves, the water dripping down her belly.

"I love that you don't wax or shave down here." He stepped closer, running one finger over her mons. "So fucking sexy."

He slipped his finger into her cleft. Hannah gasped, her hips jerking involuntarily forward as he rubbed her clit and stroked down to tease his finger around her opening.

She gripped the front of his shirt to steady herself. This close, she felt the heat of his body. Though she didn't look down, she didn't need evidence to know a heavy bulge pressed against the front of his trousers.

"Evan." His name escaped on a breath. "I'm getting so hot."

"I know."

He brought his other hand underneath her chin and lifted her face toward him. His mouth came down on hers with an exquisite warmth and tenderness that was a striking contrast to the possessive way he was fingering her.

She arched toward him, pressing her damp breasts against his chest. He deepened the chili-chocolate kiss, his tongue tracing the seam of her lips until she opened to let him in. Their tongues licked, danced, tasted. His breath warmed her skin as he slid his mouth over her cheek, down to her neck.

"Evan, I'm..." Hannah glided her hands to his biceps, the pressure in her lower body expanding like rippling circles in a pond. "I'm going to come already."

"Good." He bit gently on her collarbone before lifting his head to cover her mouth with his. "Ah, fuck, that's it...I know how much you want it, honey..."

Hannah cried out, his words triggering an explosion of heat. Vibrations shuddered through her, pleasure peaking with a force that arched her body full against his. He eased away from her for a second, and then he was wrapping her in the big, fuzzy robe before sweeping her into his arms.

He carried her back into the bedroom and lowered her onto the bed, his eyes hot. He opened the robe and revealed her naked body again. Hannah squirmed, her skin still flushed with heat and longing.

"Kiss me again," she whispered, twining one hand around his neck and bringing him down to her.

Evan kissed her thoroughly, resting one hand on her breast. Hannah fumbled to get her hand between them so she could work the buttons on his shirt and finally touch his taut, bare skin. She wanted to run her hands over the slopes of his chest, trace the ridges of his abdomen, follow that secret trail of hair leading straight to his beautiful cock.

Fresh excitement flared inside her at the thought of exploring all the facets of his body. She hastily worked the first two buttons on his shirt before he suddenly pulled away from her. He grabbed her wrists.

Hannah flashbacked to the night of their boardwalk date, when he'd also stopped her from touching him. The sudden restraint in his expression made her heart stutter.

"Evan?" She frowned. "What's wrong?"

Lines of tension bracketed his mouth. He tightened his grip on her wrists.

"I have to tell you something," he said.

She swallowed. "Okay."

"I have a scar." He released her right wrist and drew a line down the center of his chest. "Right here. I was born with a congenital heart defect. When I was a kid, I had three heart surgeries, both to repair it and because of complications."

Disbelief raced through her. "*Three* surgeries?"

He nodded. "It's not a big deal…the scar, I mean. I don't care about it. Other women have seen it, of course. But before we take this further, you should know the deal. I had a rough start, went into heart failure twice, was back and forth to the ER for months. The repairs were successful and I've lived as normal a life as I can, but I've always been at risk for health problems. I always will be. My family knows it, and every woman I've been with has known it too."

Hannah didn't know what to say. It almost didn't make sense —that tall, strong, handsome Evan Stone could have any defects at all, much less one involving his heart. His pain twisted inside her like a corkscrew.

Feeling him watching her, she took hold of his shirt and pulled him closer. She unfastened the buttons and pushed the folds of material aside to reveal his chest. As she'd known it would be, his torso was beautiful—the slopes of his pecs led down to a six-pack abdomen, and every muscle was sculpted to perfection.

Hannah pushed his shirt off his shoulders, gazing at the golden-brown skin of his shoulders, the corded hardness of his biceps and forearms. She reached out a hand and touched his smooth shoulder, shivering with tactile pleasure as she stroked across to his chest.

She ran her finger over the scar, a jagged, vertical line extending over his breastbone to the top of his ribcage. Even touching the evidence, it was hard to imagine a surgeon cutting into Evan to repair his heart.

"Does it ever hurt?" she asked. "Your heart, I mean."

"Not physically." He looked at the sweep of her finger back up to the top of the scar. "Most of the time I don't think about it. And I don't know life without it or the scar. It's just how I am."

"I like how you are." Hannah trailed her fingers down to the ridges of his abdomen. "I like everything about you."

He captured her hand as she ran her fingers up his chest again. He leaned in to kiss her. Hannah let her other hand glide to the front of his trousers, and she gave his zipper an ineffectual tug.

"Hurry," she whispered.

Evan moved away from her only long enough to remove his pants, revealing the thick ridge of his cock pressing against his boxer briefs.

Hot anticipation swept through Hannah. She shifted to the edge of the bed, palming his erection that seemed even bigger than it had the last time she'd touched him.

"Take it out," Evan ordered.

His husky command sparked a fresh rush of desire. Hannah hooked her fingers in his boxer briefs and pulled them down, her eyes widening. She curled her fingers around him, the smooth, veined shaft pulsing against her palm.

When she started to lean forward, certain this was what he wanted, Evan curled his hand into the length of her hair and pulled her to a stop.

"Don't you want..."

"Yes." His chest heaved with a breath. "But first I want you."

He moved them both back onto the bed. Hannah shrugged the open robe over her shoulders and tossed it to the floor. A twinge of apprehension wound through her as he moved over her. Their eyes locked.

How long had it been for him? As long as it had been for her?

He bent to kiss her, his lips a surprisingly tender contrast to the rigidity coiling through his body. He moved his hands over her breasts, stroking down to her belly and between her legs.

"Open," he murmured.

Nothing could make her resist his gentle command. She parted her legs, quivering as cooler air brushed against her sex. Evan worked his finger into her, his touch still light and almost teasing. The combination of that touch and his hard, muscular body above her had Hannah panting and squirming with urgency.

"Evan, I'm ready." The plea escaped her on a moan.

"I know you are."

He shifted lower, sliding his hands under her knees to lift them. Hannah had never been so aroused and nervous at the same time—sex for her had never been like what she read about in novels. It was pleasant with a frequent side of *good*, but it never made her feel as if she were poised on the edge of control, a bird ready to plunge into soaring flight.

"Wider, honey." Evan pressed her thighs open.

Hannah bit her lower lip, forcing her muscles to relax and open for him. Evan's muscles gleamed with a sheen of sweat, and a flush darkened his face beneath his stubble. With that feral look in his eyes and his hair falling over his forehead, he looked like some sort of demigod laying claim to her.

She wiggled, her breath coming faster as he trailed his finger over her labia. "Evan, I don't have any condoms."

A grin pulled at his mouth. He leaned over to open the night-stand drawer. "This resort is fully stocked."

He took out a condom packet, moving away from her only long enough to roll on the condom before positioning himself between her legs. His hot gaze collided with hers as he began to slowly push his cock into her. She gasped, her body instinctively resisting the invasion.

"Relax," he said, his voice tense. "I'll go slow."

She took a deep breath. Silly to be nervous. She wasn't a virgin. She wasn't inexperienced. But something about Evan—his control, his quiet but indisputable dominance, his sheer size... maybe even her discovery of his scarred heart...all elicited a trep-idation that wound through her like wire.

"Hannah."

She opened her eyes, her breath catching at the sight of his face right above hers, his blue eyes burning like twin flames.

"Okay?" he asked.

The wire loosened, changed into something soft and silky like a ribbon.

"Yes," she whispered.

He kissed her between the eyes. He shifted to ease into her, and then he was filling her with delicious slowness, smooth and oh so easy, his muscles flexing with restraint, his breath rasping through the air.

Hannah pressed her head back onto the pillows. She ached everywhere, but in a lush, erotic way—her nipples hurt for atten-tion, her legs trembled from the strain of being spread so wide apart, her blood pulsed with the sweet pain of arousal.

"Ah, fuck, you're so goddamned perfect." Evan groaned, seating himself inside her with a final thrust of his hips. "Like you were made for me."

With a grunt, he pulled back, a slick glide that fired all her nerve endings. At first he moved slowly, letting her adjust to the size and feel of him. Then Hannah pushed upward to match his thrusts, a cry tearing from her throat as he plunged deep inside her, hitting an exquisitely tender spot.

"That's it," she gasped. "Right there...oh, harder..."

"Tighten around me," he ordered, his breath stirring the hair at her temple. "I want to feel you come."

Time folded in on itself. They rocked and thrust, the world distilling to the rasp of skin on skin, the collision of their bodies, the smack of his flesh against hers. Their mouths crashed together, open and hot. He sucked her nipples, drove his hands into her hair, gripped her ass. She raked her fingernails over his back, sank her teeth into his taut shoulder, moaned his name.

She came first, a flame bursting through her, lighting her blood. She cried out, locking herself around him as if he were the only solid, secure element in the world. He murmured a steady, low stream of words into her ear—*ah, so good, baby...ride it out... just like that...you're so fucking incredible*—and when she was sliding down the other side, his deep groan of release echoed through her.

Panting, they rolled away from each other and onto their backs. Hannah pushed her hair back from her damp forehead. The air hung heavily over them, drenched with the smell of sex.

"Wow," she remarked. "Why didn't we do that sooner?"

A chuckle vibrated through him. Hannah shifted onto her side. He was lying with his arm across his face, his chest still heaving. He lowered his arm and curved it around her, pulling her against him.

His heart beat steady and strong against her ear, like a rhythmic knocking on a door.

In response, her own heart softened, as if it wanted to answer.

CHAPTER 15

*H*e woke to everything Hannah. Her sandalwood scent, her long hair sliding on his chest, her breasts pressed against his side. A loose, comfortable sensation streamed through him, a feeling of rightness as unnerving as it was welcome.

For a few minutes he lay there absorbing the feel of her before climbing out of bed. He pulled on his shorts and went into the living room. He opened all the curtains to let in the view of the sun-drenched valley.

He checked his phone, ignoring a message from Luke. Tomorrow he'd be back in the business of Sugar Rush, but until then he intended to focus on Hannah.

Room service attendants arrived, pushing a cart laden with croissants, muffins, and fruit. Evan poured a cup of coffee and returned to the bedroom where Hannah still slept.

He rested his hand on her hair, brushing the dark strands away from her face. A fierce, tender possessiveness rose in him. He tried to suppress the feeling. He was careful to keep his emotions guarded and cautious with women, but if he let her,

Hannah could breach his guard. She might be the only woman in the world who could.

She shifted. Her thick eyelashes fluttered open.

"Oh, hi," she murmured huskily, pushing to one elbow. The sheet slipped down to reveal her naked breasts, the sight of them sending a jolt of heat straight to Evan's dick.

He held out the coffee. "Morning."

Hannah took a sip of coffee and closed her eyes on a groan of bliss. "Oh my God. What is this?"

"French Roast, I think. Some exclusive blend." He ran his hand over her warm, smooth shoulder to her hip.

Hannah scooted to sit up and lean against the headboard, unselfconscious in her gorgeous nudity. It was like finally surrendering to their attraction had unlocked something in her, as if she could now revel in the freedom to indulge in the time they had together.

He stroked his hand through her hair, watching the thick strands slide through his fingers.

"*Cafuné*," he said.

"Is that the brand of this coffee?" She took another sip.

"It's a Brazilian verb. It means *to run your fingers through a lover's hair*."

"Really?" Her mouth curved with a smile. "That's lovely."

"So are you." He brushed his lips across hers. "Now I'm going to walk out of here before I climb back into bed and do things to your body that have no words in any language."

"Promises, promises." Hannah winked at him as she set her cup down and climbed out of bed, sauntering to the bathroom.

Before he followed the hypnotic sway of her ass, Evan returned to his own room to shower and dress. When he came out again, Hannah was eating at the table, picking apart a croissant with her fingers and popping strawberries into her mouth.

Her green tank top revealed her smooth, tanned shoulders and arms, and her ponytail draped down her back. She was so damned sensual—everything she did, from taking photographs to sipping coffee, set his blood on fire.

She glanced at him as he stopped beside the table. "You're spoiling me with all this food."

He liked spoiling her. He wanted to do it more, partly because of her and partly because she didn't seem to expect it. Most women, knowing his family business and wealth, had a set of expectations that he'd become accustomed to fulfilling. Not Hannah. Her unaffected nature intensified his desire.

"Ah." She held up a strawberry. "Shaped like a heart."

She arranged the strawberry on a white plate and picked up her camera to take a few pictures of it. She set her camera down and passed him the strawberry.

After eating it, Evan sat down and brushed his fingers across the tattoo decorating her upper arm. A small, colorful compass with the four cardinal directions labeled in cursive letters, the tattoo suited her perfectly. A little paper airplane hovered over the north point.

"Why a paper airplane?" he asked, reaching for the coffeepot.

Hannah glanced down at the tattoo, a faint shadow coloring her features. "My father used to make elaborate paper airplanes. When we lived at Twelve Oaks, he'd make them for all the kids there, each designed to their specifications. And when we'd work at the farmers' market, he'd sit beside the booth folding airplanes for anyone who wanted one. So I wanted the tattoo in honor of him."

She turned her attention back to her plate, picking the stem off a strawberry.

"You miss him," Evan said.

She nodded. "He died when I was thirteen. I inherited my wanderlust from him. After he got together with my mother, they traveled the US in an old van...classic hippie style. They ended up at Twelve Oaks, and like most people they only intended to stay for a few weeks. Then my mother got pregnant with me, and they decided not to leave."

Her mouth twisted. "Well, I think my mother decided that. She wasn't as big a traveler as my father was. So I grew up at Twelve Oaks, and then Polly came along...my father always talked about wanting to take us around the world one day, but he never got the chance. Instead he became the paper airplane man."

And when Hannah had the chance, she'd taken off to see the world. She'd probably thought about her father every day for the past fifteen years. Maybe she'd even blamed herself for preventing his travels.

"My father started making model boats and airplanes after my mother died," Evan said. "I think it gave him something else to focus on besides his grief, especially after Luke took control of Sugar Rush. And when Hailey was in the hospital, my father didn't want to leave her side, so he'd sit in her hospital room for hours working on models. Everything from pirate ships to jets."

"Does he still build them?"

"Yeah, he turned half his office into a workshop."

"What does he do with them?"

"Nothing. They sit on a shelf." An odd sadness washed over Evan. He'd never before realized that his father spent so many hours working on intricate models that had no purpose except for display. At least Hannah's father had made people happy with his paper airplanes.

Hannah sat back and lifted her arms for a stretch, the movement shaking off the sudden pall that had descended over both of them.

"So are we heading back right now or do we have more on the itinerary?" she asked. "Ramona told me she'd cover the bakery today too."

"We can go into town for a couple of hours," Evan said. "Check out those art galleries you wanted to see, then head back."

A touch of uncertainty lit in her aquamarine eyes. "So what happens when we're *back*?"

Tension threaded his shoulders. If it were up to him, he'd take her home and keep her in his bed, by his side, for the next six months. Or four, if the doctor had been right about the timeline for his surgery.

"Whatever you want." He cleared his throat, forcing his voice to sound casual. "I'm not going anywhere."

"For a few more months, neither am I." She leaned over to press her lips against his, resting her hand on his chest right over his scar. "So until then, I'm all in too."

His blood filled with the scent and taste of her, but she lifted her head before he could deepen the kiss.

"Was it related to your heart?" she asked. "The complex Lucy had about you."

"Yeah." He put his hand over hers, knowing she could feel his heartbeat increase. "She had all these ideas about how she was going to take care of me since I was sick. She wasn't the first one to think that. Other girlfriends have wanted to be my caretaker or healer rather than my partner. They didn't last long. I get enough overprotectiveness from my family."

"You're lucky to have so many people care about you, though."

He nodded, drawing her hand to his mouth. He pressed a kiss to her palm.

"Thanks for coming here with me," he said. "Did you get good material for your blog?"

Hannah nodded, a thoughtful expression crossing her features. "It's funny, but I've never really been part of all the things I've written about. I watch it all from the sidelines."

He knew a lot about being on the sidelines. "Sometimes you have to put yourself back in the game."

Hannah pushed back her chair. "I guess that's what we're both doing."

She walked back to the bedroom. Evan's gaze skimmed over

the curves of her hips. He had no intention of losing the Sugar Rush game. But it was the Lockhart game he really wanted to win.

The drive back to Rainsville took longer than Evan had anticipated. Hannah kept wanting to detour and take pictures of roadside oddities—a giant statue of a man crushing grapes, a robot museum, the world's largest outdoor Monopoly board.

Not only did he not mind the frequent stops, he found himself wishing for more of them. He loved Hannah's curiosity and enthusiasm for seeking out unique attractions, her openness to whatever happened to be nearby.

He knew it would be the same no matter where she was in the world. In addition to famous monuments, she'd want to see the Ramen Museum in Japan, the megalithic stone jars in Laos, the Gnome Reserve in England. And he tried to smother the wish that he could one day go with her. It was like his childhood wish for a whole heart—useless and stupid because no matter how hard he wished, reality always kicked him in the ass.

By the time they got back to Hannah's apartment, the sun had already sunk behind the horizon. Evan set her suitcase beside the bed and got a bottle of water from the fridge.

"I need to do a load of laundry." She emerged from the bathroom, tying her hair into a ponytail. "Do you want to stay the night?"

Her upraised arms pushed her breasts out against the fabric of her stretchy shirt. Evan's dick hardened at the thought of sliding his hands under her shirt and cupping her tempting breasts in his palms while he pressed his mouth to hers and—

"Evan?" Hannah lowered her arms with a slight frown. "Where did you go?"

"Sorry." He shook his head. "I was thinking about fondling your tits, maybe rubbing my cock between them."

"Oh my God." A flush rose to paint her skin a becoming pink. "You aren't too tired from all that driving?"

He looked down at his erection outlined against his jeans. "No."

Hannah's gaze followed his, her breath escaping on a heated rush. "Good. Because neither am I."

Electricity sizzled through the air. They both moved forward, their bodies and lips colliding at the same instant. Evan grabbed her hips and tumbled them both onto the bed. Within seconds, they were both naked.

Time collapsed. Nothing existed except the heat of Hannah's body, the taste of her lips, the glide of her skin against his. After they were both spent and exhausted, they fell into a sweat-drenched sleep, their limbs twined together like the vines of a plant.

He woke at dawn the next morning and dragged himself reluctantly away from a still-sleeping Hannah. He kissed her forehead before heading back to his house on the beach. He'd have to bring her there soon; instinctively he knew she'd like the beachfront bungalow with its worn furniture and deck over-looking the sand dunes. She'd find dozens of things to photo-graph, too.

By eight, he was at Sugar Rush headquarters, getting his head back in the game. He worked through the morning, fielding calls from both a reporter and the legal department, who'd issued proof to the media that Sugar Rush had severed contracts with the Singa Corporation years ago.

Shortly before lunch, a sharp knock on his office door announced his aunt's arrival.

"Ah, you're back." Julia strode across the room, her perfectly made-up features not concealing the curiosity in her eyes. "How was your weekend?"

With Julia, a simple question was often not *a simple question.* Evan eyed her warily.

"Great. Thanks for asking. See you later."

"I'm surprised you took Hannah." Julia settled her hands on her hips. "After all, you paid for the bid. You could have taken anyone."

"I wanted to take her." Evan unwrapped a Sparkle Pop and narrowed his gaze on his aunt. "And don't give me your rich maiden aunt crap about Hannah not being suitable for the second son of Lord Stone."

In truth, he'd be surprised if that was her attitude, considering Hannah was Polly's sister. Julia had a distinctly archaic sensibility about the women she considered right for her nephews, but Luke's relationship with Polly had put a dent in her haughtiness.

Despite their antagonistic beginning, Julia and Polly had gotten all sorts of chummy over the past few months, a relationship that had culminated in Julia taking Polly on a whirlwind shopping excursion in Paris *"because that girl can make a heavenly pâte à choux, but she cannot choose her wardrobe to save her life."*

As far as Evan knew, Julia hadn't spent much time with Hannah, but the sisterly connection should have softened her attitude.

"It's not about her being *suitable,*" Julia replied. "And it's not about me disliking her, although she's quite a bit less charming than Polly. But Polly told me she's only in town for a short time, so..."

Her voice trailed off. Evan didn't have to hear the rest—*why waste a fifty-thousand-dollar date package on Hannah?* He'd never tell his meddling aunt it was the best money he'd ever spent.

He sat back and studied her. As always, Julia was a vision of lovely perfection with her sleek, blond hair, elegant features, and tweed Chanel suit. She'd always been part of their lives, but after their mother died, Julia had taken on the role of the Stone family matriarch with a vengeance.

And beneath her sharp tongue and fashionable beauty, her heart beat with fierce overprotectiveness and love for her nephews and niece. She was a lioness guarding her cubs, and if her frequently abrasive, over-the-top interfering was a pain in the ass, any one of the Stone brothers would defend her to the death if needed.

Not that it had ever been needed. Julia was more than capable of taking care of herself and those around her. Even when they didn't want her help.

"Hannah knows about my heart," he said. "And we both knew before I told her that we're just having an affair."

Julia crossed her arms, her eyes narrowing. "That is precisely my point. In case you forgot, women don't call you *Heartbreaker* solely because of your heart condition. And I've had my eye on Hannah. She's not Polly, but she's working hard to do right by her sister. She's making an effort. And I do not want to see her hurt at the end of your fling."

Huh.

Never before had Julia been worried about him hurting a woman.

"I'm not going to hurt her," he said. "She's leaving anyway. She probably already has plans. How could I hurt her?"

A faint sigh escaped Julia's perfectly red lips. "You're easy to fall in love with, Evan. And if Hannah is anything like Polly... which I suspect she is, at her core...she'll give herself fully to a man she loves."

"Christ." Evan groaned and dragged his hands over his face. "Love advice from my aunt Julia. Just what I need."

"I'm not telling you this for you, you fool," she retorted. "I'm protecting Hannah."

"By telling me not to have a fling with her?"

"By telling you to be careful. Even if you both made the terms of your arrangement clear, there is nothing to prevent feelings from getting involved."

She straightened and stepped toward the door. "If you end things badly with Hannah, that could affect her relationship with Luke and possibly even Polly. Then what would happen with you and Luke? I will tolerate many things, Evan Stone, but a rift in this family is not one of them. And if you do anything to screw up my seating arrangements and plans for the holidays, I will never forgive you."

She turned and swept out of the office, closing the door behind her. Evan resisted the urge to thunk his head on the desk. One of the things he'd always disliked about being part of a big family was how difficult it was to have anything solely to himself. Even a relationship.

He got back to work, trying not to think about what his aunt had just said. He didn't believe Hannah would, or could, fall in love with him. But he'd also known her relationship to Polly could be problematic since their affair had an end date. And as Julia had correctly pointed out, family events and holidays always brought them all together.

With Luke and Polly engaged, Hannah was part of the Stone family now. If she came back to Rainsville, she'd be included in whatever event or party Julia hosted.

The thought was both unsettling and reassuring. Because Hannah had roots here, something to bring her back. But she might very well not want to come back. Not once the world took hold of her again.

He shook off his musings and focused on a slew of emails about Sugar Rush's connection to the Singa Corporation. After several tries on the phone, he got ahold of Sam Walker, the VP whom Luke had put in charge of the Fair Trade Foundation.

"Sugar Rush barely uses the freaking palm oil," Sam said, his voice distant and crackly due to the static on the line. "You'd need a microscope to find it in our products. And it's way more cost effective to get our supply from them."

"That's not the point," Evan retorted. "We stopped doing business with Singa years ago. We're not starting up with them again. And the point of the Fair Trade Foundation is to ensure that both Sugar Rush and the companies we deal with adhere to a set of responsible procurement policies based on sustainability."

"Yeah, and how expensive is that going to get?"

"This isn't about cost," Evan snapped. "Social responsibility needs to be at the core of Sugar Rush's culture. Not just as a long-term investment, but because consumers want it and because it's an inroad into new markets and partnerships. And it's the right thing to do. We can't have an old partnership, which was severed years ago, ruin what we're trying to do now."

"Singa started the Palm Oil Initiative," Sam argued. "Ten companies are part of it now, committed to sustainable practices and certification."

"And those companies have all continued to destroy rainforests and peatland," Evan said. "You need to review the Fair Trade principles I drew up. I will not sign off on doing business with any company we know is involved in destructive practices."

"Your brother is going to have issues with that, at least once he sees the expense reports."

"Luke isn't in charge. I am."

Evan dropped the phone back into the receiver. He logged on to his computer. Four VPs had forwarded him social media posts about Sugar Rush's involvement with the Singa Corporation. One of them was titled "Sugar Rush's Un-Fair Trade Foundation."

Shit.

Evan hit the button on his intercom. "Kate?"

"Yes, sir," the executive assistant replied.

"We need an emergency board meeting about this palm oil issue. All the VPs and the media liaison. ASAP."

"Yes, sir. I'll make calls right away. The boardroom is available at two. Sue Rendell has a meeting at one-thirty, but I'll see if she can postpone it. I'll call catering to prepare snacks, and I'll make copies of all the sustainability documentation."

Not until Kate had started working temporarily for him had Evan understood the value of a ridiculously efficient assistant.

He thanked her and stood, rolling his shoulders back to ease the tension. Part of him wanted to call Luke and hash this out. He'd always relied on his older brother when the going got rough. But he'd committed himself to handling this alone.

Strengthening Sugar Rush's social responsibility was the mark he needed to make on this company. He couldn't do it directly through the Fair Trade Foundation, but he sure as hell wouldn't allow anyone else to mar the company's reputation for good, ethical business practices.

His cell phone buzzed with a call from Hannah.

"Hi," she said. "I L B L eight."

"What?"

"Tonight," she said. "I L B L eight."

"Are you eating something? You sound garbled."

"It's a text abbreviation."

Evan picked up a pen. "Say it again."

"I L B L eight."

"Oh. You'll be late."

"Yes. I have to work until six, so I'll be late for dinner."

"Why didn't you just text that?"

"I wanted to call so you could hear my voice."

A slow grin spread across Evan's face. "You remembered."

"Of course."

"U R," he said, "a Q T."

"Good one."

"What are you doing?" he asked.

Her laugh puffed into his ear like a dandelion. "Coming from the Heartbreaker, I'd have expected you to ask *what are you wearing?*"

"What *are* you wearing?"

"An apron covered with gooey dough," Hannah said wryly.

"I'm trying to make a rhubarb lavender pie. It has not been successful."

"You got me thinking about you wearing nothing but an apron," Evan said. "By my estimation, that is a rousing success. And I do mean *rousing*."

She chuckled again. He could see her standing in Wild Child's kitchen with her hair tied back in a tangled ponytail, her face dusted with flour, the scooped neck of her shirt revealing her elegant collarbones.

"I gotta go," she said. "H and K. B four N."

"C U L eight R," Evan replied. "L H six."

"L H six? What does that mean?"

"Look it up."

He ended the call, only half remembering what he'd been doing before talking to Hannah.

A few seconds later, his phone buzzed with a text: OMG. LOL! OK.

Evan turned back to his computer, unable to stop smiling. A feeling rose in him that he didn't recognize. Something intensely good.

Forelsket. The euphoria of starting to fall in—

He blocked the thought. No way could he let his heart go there.

CHAPTER 16

*R*eturning to Wild Child after the weekend away with Evan was like reentering the atmosphere. Hannah felt as if she were in a dream-like fog, one she'd experienced before when immersed in an unexpected wonder of the world—the canopy of green trees and temple silhouettes in Burma, the crashing majesty of Victoria Falls, a herd of gazelles leaping over the golden-brown plains of the Serengeti.

Except then she'd always been alone. She'd chosen to be alone. Much less risk of getting hurt.

She smothered her unease over the acknowledgement that she didn't feel alone with Evan. She'd been upfront with him from the start about leaving as soon as Polly returned. She didn't have to feel guilty about enjoying his company.

She did think about his health, though. Part of her was still in disbelief that her big, strong Evan could ever have so much as a cold, much less a serious medical issue. His heart defect explained why he hadn't gone on roller coasters at the board-walk, why his mother's foundation helped special-needs children, why he disliked girlfriends with a caretaker complex, why he'd reacted angrily to Hannah's remark about wanting to make him "feel better."

The knowledge of his condition also intensified her feelings for him—she liked him even more for trusting her with the truth, and her admiration for him increased tenfold. She tried to set aside a newfound fear, focusing on the fact that Evan was much stronger and more capable than men with no medical issues at all.

He had also been right about Napa—the romance of the valley and all its offerings had given Hannah quite a bit of material for her blog. She started writing posts about the bike trips, the Wine Train, and the station with its own "love lock" bridge.

But as she worked, Hannah still drew a blank when it came to compiling a new manuscript for Elaine Miller of Franklin Publishing. She would not rewrite her history into a "sex-starved woman abroad" memoir, and she didn't want to dredge up her own romantic history, or lack thereof, to add a personal flavor to her essays.

All she had to offer was her photography and her reporter's posts about love traditions. If that wasn't enough for Franklin Publishing, then *Hannah* wasn't enough.

The *blank* was the only thing marring her thoughts, especially now that Evan came into Wild Child every day during his lunch hour.

Sparks of happiness flared inside Hannah whenever she turned and saw him standing on the other side of the counter, his hands in his pockets, his gaze on her, and his beautiful mouth curved into a smile.

She started setting aside his usual order of a ham-and-cheese croissant sandwich, followed by a Declair from her secret stash and a cup of coffee. Sometimes, if it wasn't too busy, she'd sit with him for a few minutes and ask about how things were going at Sugar Rush. He'd then return after work to either take her out or spend the evening in her apartment, which invariably led to very hot and satisfying overnights.

Four days of this routine passed before Hannah realized that her thoughts of *leaving* had lessened. They hadn't gone completely silent—thinking about *where to go next* was such a habit for her that she doubted she'd ever be rid of it completely—but now her mind had shifted to *when will I see Evan next?*

She even caught herself glancing at the clock after the morning Declair rush was over, calculating how long it would be before he walked in the door. She felt silly about her reaction, but she also rather liked it. She'd forgotten how good it felt to have a crush on a boy. A real "*like* him like him" crush that went beyond physical attraction.

Though she was certainly physically attracted to Evan. In truckloads, if her body's reaction was anything to judge by. Her breath shortened every time his fingers brushed hers when he handed her the money for the Declairs. She watched the movement of his mouth as he chewed, remembering the sensation of his lips on hers.

Her gaze drifted over the strong column of his throat exposed by his unbuttoned collar, and then down over the breadth of his chest. Little tingles washed through her as she imagined the sensation of his warm, taut skin beneath her palms.

For the first time in more years than Hannah cared to think about, she was content. She couldn't stay in town, of course, and this thing with Evan would burn out like her affairs always did, but she was happy to enjoy it while it lasted.

"So I invented a cake recipe this morning," she told him, setting a cup of coffee on the table.

His eyebrows lifted. "*You* invented a dessert?"

"You and all your *sugar-rushness* got me thinking more about savory desserts. Wait here." She went into the kitchen and returned with golden-brown cake. "When I was in Greece, I tried olive oil cake, which isn't too sweet. So this is a riff on semolina olive oil cake, which I flavored with bergamot, orange, and basil."

Evan looked at the cake a bit skeptically. "Sounds like a perfume."

"It's a *dessert*." She sliced a piece and put it on a plate for him.

"Where's the frosting?"

She tweaked his ear. "Eat it."

He took a bite and spent a rather inordinately long time chewing and swallowing.

"Well?" Hannah regarded him expectantly. "What do you think?"

"It's good. Zesty. It could use frosting, and I think I'd call it more of a snack than a dessert, but you did good, *Sahnehäubchen*."

She smiled. "I'm not sure if that was a compliment or not, but I'll take it."

"I don't want you to get a swelled head."

"Hmm. I kind of like it when you get a swelled head."

He flashed her a grin as he dug his fork into the cake again. "Let's have dinner at L'Etoile tonight. They're known for their profiteroles. No way will you be able to turn them down."

"Challenge accepted." Hannah picked up the cake plate. "I'll be ready at seven."

This would be the second time this week he'd taken her out to a fancy restaurant. Come to think of it, they'd only ever gone to outrageously expensive or luxurious places that Hannah could never have afforded on her own. When she was traveling alone, they'd also never held much appeal for her.

Of course, with Evan everything was appealing, and she was both flattered by and grateful for his generosity, but even though they'd only been "together" for less than a week, it had all been on his level of rare wines and caviar. Soon they'd end up at his custom-made mansion with its waterfall swimming pool and five-car garage.

And six months from now, when she was sharing a room with

half a dozen fellow travelers in a low-budget hostel, she'd think of Evan in his huge house and remember the world of luxury she'd lived in for a short time.

She wouldn't long for that world, but she might very well long for him.

An ache pushed at her. The wind chimes over the door jingled. Hannah turned, welcoming the distraction from the thought of pining for Evan.

A bearded man and a woman with short, curly hair entered, both dressed in jeans and T-shirts with backpacks hitched around their shoulders. Hannah's brain stuttered for a second before she recognized them.

"Hey, Hannah." The man grinned as they approached the counter.

"Peter." Hannah looked from him to the woman. "And Laura. What in the world are you both doing here?"

"We were in San Francisco and remembered your post about working at Wild Child," Laura said. "So we thought we'd drive down and see if you were still here."

"And we heard about the famous Declairs, too," Peter added. "Any chance of us getting one?"

"Sure, hold on. I have a secret stash in the back. Have a seat."

As they moved to sit down, Hannah hurried into the back to get a couple of Declairs. She poured two cups of coffee and brought them over to her friends' table along with the Declairs. Aware of Evan watching her, she turned and gestured to him.

"Evan, these are my friends Peter and Laura," she explained. "We connect on the road sometimes. Peter does archaeological volunteer work, and Laura is a writer."

They exchanged greetings. Evan turned his attention back to his laptop. Hannah pulled a chair up to the table.

"How long are you staying here?" she asked.

"Just a couple of days." Laura bit into the Declair with a noise of appreciation. "There are discounted tickets to the UK through SFO right now, and we were thinking of heading to Ireland."

"We were wondering if you wanted to go with us," Peter added.

Hannah's heart skipped a beat. "Go with you?"

"There's that County Clare Matchmaking Festival later this month," Laura said. "I was there a couple of years ago in this little town where there are also a bunch of spas. The town match-makers help single people find partners. And there's a horse race and music and stuff."

"We figured you could write about it for your blog," Peter added. "Unless you already have."

Hannah shook her head slowly, unable to look in Evan's direction though she felt him watching her.

"No," she said. "I haven't."

"Great, then come along." Laura beamed. "Lowest price tickets we've seen in a while. When can you be ready?"

"I...I don't know."

"Okay, well, we were planning to leave on Thursday," Peter said.

"Can I think about it and let you know?" Hannah asked. "I promised my sister I'd run her bakery, so she wouldn't be thrilled about the idea of me running off to Ireland."

"You could always take a couple of days to visit her," Laura said with a shrug.

"I'll let you know," Hannah repeated, pushing her chair back.

She returned to the front counter and started rearranging the baskets to give herself something to do. Restlessness seethed through her veins. With its emerald-green hills and sweeping vistas, Ireland pulled at her.

But Evan pulled at her harder. The sky over the Cliffs of Moher were no match for his blue eyes. The heating effects of Irish whiskey were nothing compared to the warmth of his smile. Her heart would never dance at the sight of a historic castle the way it did when Evan walked through the door. Her love for the savage beauty of Connemara paled in comparison to her love for—

She shook her head. Her jaw tightened against a sudden sting of tears.

Silly girl. Her defenses were down. All these months stuck in Rainsville had weakened her. She'd find her old self again once she got back on the road. And a matchmaking festival in Ireland...well, if that wasn't a *sign* that she needed to travel abroad right now, she didn't know what was.

The wind chimes over the door jingled again. Hannah looked up, her interest piquing at the sight of Mr. Becker holding the door open for an attractive, elderly woman wearing a peach-colored suit. As he guided the woman to a table by the windows, he caught Hannah's eye and winked.

She gave him a discreet thumbs-up and hurried to make a fresh pot of Darjeeling tea. She went to their table as Mr. Becker held out the chair for his lady friend.

"Welcome to Wild Child," she said pleasantly. "We have fresh-baked cranberry muffins, and the pastry chef is just putting the finishing touches on our tiramisu flan and our orange-carrot cake."

"That all sounds lovely, dear." Miss Purdy smiled at Hannah as she patted Mr. Becker's hand. "You choose."

"Two pieces of the carrot cake, please." Mr. Becker almost glowed with happiness.

"Coming right up. I have a fresh pot of Darjeeling almost ready for you."

She fetched their order and brought it to their table on a tray. They were whispering like two teenagers, unable to take their eyes off each other.

How sweet. Clearly they'd made the match themselves the old-fashioned way. A lovely tradition in its own right, but one she'd never actually written about.

She approached Laura and Peter as they stood to leave.

"Hey, thanks for the invitation," she said. "But I can't leave Rainsville...at least, not yet. I promised my sister I'd stay until she returns, so I have to keep my promise."

"Okay." Peter shrugged, accustomed to last-minute changes of plan. "Just let us know if you change your mind."

"The ticket sale lasts until the end of the week." Laura gave Hannah a hug. "Great to see you again."

Hannah watched them leave, experiencing a sudden and forceful wave of relief. Almost as if she hadn't wanted to go to Ireland in the first place.

Well, of course she'd *wanted* to go. She just couldn't. She was keeping her promise to Polly, like any good sister would.

She pulled out a chair at Evan's table. He glanced up from his laptop, his expression unreadable.

"You're not going?" he asked.

"I can't. Promises and all." She picked up a few packets of sugar and started building a little house with them. "Plus we have two more dates, right?"

"We do. I've booked the yacht trip on the Bay for this weekend. We'll take a town car up to San Francisco, stay the night at the Four Seasons."

"That sounds lovely, but..."

Evan frowned. "You don't want to go?"

"Yes, I want to go. But not because of the yacht or the Bay." She cleared her throat, her cheeks heating. "Because of you."

"Good. I want to go because of you, too."

"Then you won't mind if we don't go at all," Hannah said.

A crease appeared between his eyebrows. "Now you don't want to go?"

"Ever since we...got together, we've been having expensive dinners and doing things that I could never afford if I were traveling the way I'm accustomed to," Hannah explained. "A yacht trip on the Bay is definitely one of those things."

When he didn't respond, she added, "I've enjoyed every minute of it, but what if we skipped the yacht trip in favor of something else? I want to show you how I do things."

Evan leaned forward, a glint firing in his eyes. "Oh, you've shown me how you do things, Lockhart."

"I *mean...*" Hannah tweaked his nose. "Come with me on a weekend road trip done my way. It'll be our third date, the date of our choice."

"What's your way?"

"Low-budget. Cheap food. We take the bakery delivery van. No fancy hotels or hot-air balloon rides. We have to make our own good time."

A smile tugged at his mouth. "Don't we always?"

"I mean, we have to rely on ourselves. Can't fall back on paying for something or someone to show us how to have fun."

"Where are we going?"

"I have no idea. We leave Friday night and just go."

Intrigue appeared in his eyes. "You can take time off again?"

Guilt pricked Hannah. "If we go the weekend after next, it should be fine. Better than going to Ireland, right? Are you in?"

"I'm in. But what should we do about the yacht trip?"

Hannah glanced toward Mr. Becker and his lady friend, who were laughing merrily at a private joke.

"I have an idea," she said.

CHAPTER 17

*H*annah and Evan's *Lock Heart* Road Trip. Every time she thought about it, excitement spiraled through her. She couldn't wait to travel with Evan in her unplanned, spontaneous style, as if by doing so they would close the circle of their knowledge about each other. She'd experienced his world; now it was time for him to experience hers.

Three days before they planned to leave, she sat in her apartment and tried to make some headway on her book proposal for Franklin Publishing. She reviewed the *Lock Heart* archives, struggling to come up with whatever elusive element the book editor needed to tie the whole thing together. Two fruitless and frustrating hours later, she pulled on a jacket, packed her camera, and headed to Indigo Bay for a change of scenery.

She parked in a lot near the pier and walked to the sand, enjoying the cold ocean air against her face. The beach was deserted, the sand peppered with bits of shell and driftwood. The red-gold colors of the sunset glowed on the water, but the wind whipped white caps on the surface.

Even though turning her blog into a book was proving to be

more difficult than she'd anticipated, Hannah had discovered a newfound pride in what she had been doing for the past decade.

She wasn't just an irresponsible vagabond who roamed the world with no purpose or destination. She earned a solid income with her writing and photography. She had a readership, a strong online presence, interest from a publisher. Wanting to leave Rainsville didn't mean she was running away. It meant she was making a living.

She walked along the ocean's edge, pausing to focus her camera and adjust the lens on various sights—a smooth, gnarled piece of driftwood, a sand crab scuttling into a hole, the brush of the water against the sand.

The smell of salt and seaweed filled her noise, and the ocean stretched out endlessly in front of her. Cypress trees stood on rocky cliffs, waves crashed against natural rock outcroppings, and pockets of sand created both private and public beaches.

A few cars passed on the streets of Indigo Bay beyond the rows of oceanfront cottages and shops. Hannah continued walking. She reached a hillside where rocks cascaded out into the ocean. Gray storm clouds gathered on the horizon, casting a metal-colored shadow over the water.

She started to go back in the opposite direction, but then turned toward the rocks. A memory of her childhood flashed in her mind, a time when she'd spent many happy hours exploring tidepools with her father. They'd picked their way over the rocks as the sun and sea air surrounded them. Just the two of them. Back when it felt as if nothing would ever change.

Then it had.

A low wave crashed against the rocks, sending up a spray of salty water. Though it was mid-tide and the clouds were growing darker, it was still light enough to see, and the water wasn't too rough.

She put her camera around her neck, found a handhold on a large rock and hauled herself up, taking care to step in shallow grooves as she made her way slowly out onto the ledge. Water pooled in the depressions, creating miniature ecosystems filled with tiny fish, sea anemones, crabs, and sea stars.

Out on the ledge, the wind gusted harder. She hiked out carefully, pausing to crouch and take pictures of the tidepools. Another wave crashed against the rocks, splashing her.

She shivered as the cold penetrated her jacket. Rain started falling. She poked gently at a sea anemone and watched a crab scuttle along the sandy bottom of a tidepool.

The cold intensified, more waves washing over the rocks and wetting Hannah's shoes. She stood, tucking her camera into the case.

"Lockhart!"

The familiarity of the deep voice, carried on a gust of icy wind, lodged inside her. Her body warmed down to her bones. Hannah turned, squinting through the gray fog. Evan was running across the beach toward her, his face shadowed by a black hoodie.

She started back to him, her rubber-soled sneakers slipping over the rocks. Another wave, heavier and stronger, splashed against the base of the ledge.

Evan shouted her name again. He reached the rocks and started to climb, his steps quick and certain despite the increasing rain. He moved as if he'd climbed these very rocks countless times before and knew exactly where to grab hold of them.

Hannah hurried toward him, trying to maintain her balance on the rocks. Waves slammed with increasing force against the ledge, the water spraying high overhead. "Hannah, look out!"

His words crashed into her ears the instant before a rogue wave blasted against the rocks. The freezing water flooded her in a terrifying rush.

A cry lodged in Hannah's throat. She went down, her knees

hitting the stone hard. She scrambled to gain a foothold, a hand-hold, anything...

Evan's hand clamped around her wrist.

"I've got you." His voice was gritty and certain.

He hauled her toward him, dragging her away from the last currents of the ocean. The wave receded in defeat.

Shaking and coughing, Hannah struggled to her feet and followed him toward the slope leading to the other beach. He tightened his grip on her wrist as he led the way over the rocks and back down to the sand.

He turned to face her, pushing the hoodie off his head. His dark hair was damp with rain, his eyelashes spiky around his sharp blue eyes.

"Are you all right?" he demanded, his expression flashing with something resembling anger.

Hannah was momentarily startled. She'd never seen him angry before.

"I'm...I'm fine." She coughed to rid her throat of the sting of salt water. "What...what are you doing here?"

"What am I doing here?" His mouth compressed. "What are *you* doing out here in a storm?"

"I didn't know a storm was coming. I just came down to take some pictures."

"The National Weather Service issued an alert that goes until tomorrow night," Evan said. "The beaches all along the coast have a high probability of sneaker waves and long shore currents. There's also a steep grade right at the end of that ledge that creates abnormally large waves. Even on a nice day it's not safe."

"I'm sorry. I didn't know."

"Obviously." He heaved a sigh, some of the anger seeming to drain from him as he tracked his gaze over her again. "You need to come in and dry off. The storm isn't going to let up for another hour at least."

He led her toward a rustic bungalow nestled among the trees

with a rickety deck overlooking the beach. The wood siding of the house was weather-worn, the windows smudged. She followed him inside, glancing around at the tiny kitchen with a worn Formica table, peeling paint, and linoleum stained with age.

Surely this wasn't Evan's house. The Stones were mansion people, not beachfront shack people. *She* was beachfront shack people.

Water pooled from her clothes onto the floor, and a shiver rocked through her. Her teeth rattled uncontrollably.

"Is...is this your house?" she stuttered.

"Yeah." Evan's eyebrows drew together. "You need to shower and change. You'll catch a cold if you don't."

"I don't have any spare clothes."

"You can wear mine."

He strode down a narrow hallway, returning a few seconds later with a blue T-shirt and a pair of cotton pajama pants. "These will be too big, but at least they're dry. I'll show you where the bathroom is."

Hannah pushed off her tennis shoes so she wouldn't soak the carpet and followed him down the hallway to a small bathroom. She started unfastening her running jacket, but couldn't get her numb fingers to work the zipper.

"Need some help?" Evan tugged the zipper down, then peeled the wet jacket from her body. His gaze heated as his eyes lingered on her hard nipples poking against her T-shirt, but he remained businesslike and he reached for the hem.

"I can take it from here," Hannah assured him, more embarrassed by her stupidity in being out during a storm than by his attentiveness.

"Clean towels are in there." Evan pointed to a white cabinet. "Get yourself warmed up."

He left, closing the door behind him. Hannah tugged off the rest of her clothes, peeled off her striped knee socks, and turned the water on. She got into the shower, groaning with relief as the hot water cascaded over her and her blood started flowing.

She found a bar of soap in the holder and worked up a lather over her body. The scents of sage and cedar filled her head, evoking memories of burying her nose against Evan's throat and inhaling his delicious scent. She'd thought it was from some expensive aftershave, but no. He was all soap and maleness.

She washed the lather off, then briskly dried herself with the towel and slipped into the clothes Evan had given her.

Her bra had been soaked through, but as Evan had predicted, the shirt came almost to her knees. It was also baggy enough to provide her with some modesty, and it was dry and warm. She tugged the drawstring pants on and folded the waistband over a few times before tying it so she wouldn't trip.

Only when she was brushing the tangles from her long hair did she realize she was wearing Evan's well-washed, soft T-shirt and pajama pants. And she had nothing on underneath, not even her panties. Which meant the material tucked between her thighs had once touched his…

Heat spooled through her, like an uncoiling thread.

Girl. Not the time or place. Besides, I think he's still mad at you.

She gathered her wet clothes and hurried out of the bathroom. Evan was in the kitchen, still soaked, though he'd removed his hoodie and shoes.

"Sorry if I took too long," she said breathlessly.

"It's okay." He reached out to take her clothes. "Your shoes are probably ruined, but I'll put your clothes in the dryer. There's a drink for you, and coffee's brewing. I'll be right back."

He disappeared into the bathroom, and a few seconds later Hannah heard the shower running. She turned to the counter where a bottle of scotch sat next to two highball glasses. The first sip burned her throat pleasantly.

She poked around his kitchen a little, curious to know more about him since her assumptions about his house had proven wrong. A bowl of fresh fruit sat on the counter, and the cabinets were filled with low-sodium canned goods, brown rice, and various spices.

The refrigerator mostly contained healthy foods—green leafy vegetables, eggs, chicken, yogurt—but the evidence of Evan's sweet tooth was obvious in the quart container of ice cream, the half-eaten slice of apple pie, and the canister of whipped cream.

Smiling to herself, Hannah closed the fridge and picked up her scotch again. He was like a boy sneaking cookies from the cookie jar, and she found his penchant for dessert rather ridiculously endearing.

By the time the coffee was finished brewing, Evan emerged from the bathroom. Clean and dry, dressed in a green T-shirt and a pair of black cotton pants, he looked both warm and deliciously edible.

"Coffee?" He nodded toward the pot.

"No, the scotch is doing a better job than coffee would." Hannah took another sip. "It's really good."

"Twenty-five-year-old Macallan, a gift from my father last Christmas. He knows his scotch." Evan gestured toward the living room. "Come and sit down."

As she walked into the living room, Hannah's breasts swayed beneath the overlarge T-shirt. Her blood warmed. Wearing Evan's clothes with nothing else on was damned sexy. Not to mention his tall, broad-shouldered presence filled her with warm, cozy pleasure like the scent of hot cinnamon.

She sat on the sofa, drawing her knees up to her chest as she looked around at the living room—the worn plaid sofa and big-screen TV, the cluttered computer desk. A bowl of Sugar Rush candy sat on the coffee table. The walls were bare, with only particle-board shelves filled with books giving any indication of Evan's personal interests.

"I didn't expect that you'd live in a place like this," she remarked.

"What kind of place did you expect?"

"A mansion like Luke's. Polly said it's some big monstrosity overlooking the ocean."

"Yeah." Evan took a swallow of scotch. "I don't know that he likes it much. He bought it when Sugar Rush hit the highest net worth in company history. It was a big deal to him. To all of us."

"What made you choose this house instead?"

"It came with the beach."

"The *beach* belongs to you?"

"Technically it belongs to the house, but I guess you could say that. It's a private stretch of beach between the two rock ledges."

Okay, so she hadn't been entirely wrong. Not many people in the world could afford to own part of the California coastline. Luke's mansion was a custom-made Nordic castle on a cliff; Evan's mansion was the sand and the sea.

She much preferred Evan's mansion.

She rose and wandered over to the bookshelf, running her fingers across the spines as if she could somehow absorb everything in his mind. History books, Shakespeare, thriller novels, linguistics textbooks, guides about marine life and conservation. The desk contained more books and papers, along with a few sticks of wood and a paring knife.

"What's this for?" Hannah held up a smooth stick whose bark had been carved off.

"I'm whittling a flute."

She laughed. He didn't.

Hannah blinked. "Seriously? You *whittle*? You're whittling a flute?"

"Yeah." Amusement rose to his eyes over her astonishment. "I was a Boy Scout when I was a kid and learned how to whittle. When I was recovering after my surgeries, I spent a lot of time perfecting the technique."

"Oh." A combination of admiration and sorrow washed over Hannah. "That's rather remarkable."

"Not really. It's just a hobby. Plenty of people do it."

"You're the first person I've met who whittles. Do you have any other sculptures?"

"There's some in the top drawer. I usually just give them to the children's hospital."

Hannah opened the drawer to find an array of intricately carved wood pieces—a bird, a rough-hewn bear, a sailboat. She stroked her fingers over the smooth edges of a driftwood elephant.

How many other things did she have to discover about Evan Stone? He was like an entire country, mapped with secret landscapes and hidden rivers that she wanted to navigate and explore until she found the very center of him. And there she wanted to curl up and rest.

"Can I keep this?" she asked, holding up the elephant.

"Sure."

Hannah set the elephant on the coffee table so she wouldn't forget to take it with her. Evan's giving away of his creations reminded her of her father and his paper airplanes. She had the sudden, strange wish that her father could have met Evan. They'd have liked each other.

She returned to the sofa and sat with her back against one of the arms.

"So you live here alone?" she asked.

"No, I live here with my girlfriend," Evan replied dryly.

She poked him with her foot. "I meant, do you live here with one of your brothers?"

"No, we all have our own places. Adam rents his out, so sometimes he stays at Luke's house or with our father."

Hannah set her glass on the coffee table and riffled through the glass bowl of Sugar Rush candy, selecting a package of fruit-flavored Puffles.

"Ah." Evan watched as she opened the package and ate a few of the gummy candies. "I knew I'd convert you, *Sahnehäubchen*."

Content to let him believe that, Hannah stretched out and put her feet in his lap. "Thanks for rescuing me."

He shot her a frown. "I'm still mad that you were out there in the first place. You should never go out on the rocks without checking for weather alerts."

"I promise I'll never do it again." She wiggled her toes against his groin.

Evan muttered something under his breath. Hannah smiled and leaned back against the sofa cushion, her limbs warm and languid. He put his glass down and took hold of her bare feet, rubbing them between his strong hands.

Oh, bliss.

She closed her eyes, letting him massage the soreness right out of her feet. He stroked her soles, pressed his thumbs against her arches, and caressed the pads of her toes. Heat sparked at the point of contact and glided all the way up Hannah's legs. She sank lower into the cushion, aware that beneath her ankles, the bulge in his flannel pants was getting harder.

"How did you see me out there?" she mumbled.

"From the kitchen window." He stroked his fingers over her instep. "I thought *I'm going to get that woman off the damned rocks and spank her.*"

Hannah's heart jumped. "You did not think that."

"I did."

"How did you even know it was *me*?"

"Lockhart." Evan's voice warmed, his mouth turning up at the corners. "I always know when it's you."

The area around Hannah's heart softened. She gave him a slow smile. His hand slid up the top of her foot to her ankle and beneath the hem of the pajama pants.

"You look good in my clothes," he remarked.

"You look good in your clothes too," she said. "Deliciously good."

He curled his hand around her ankle, tugging her closer so

her feet crossed his lap and her rear pressed against the side of his hard thigh. He moved his hand farther up her leg to her knee.

Between the hot shower, the scotch, and Evan, Hannah was already lost. She stretched out on the sofa and closed her eyes, letting him continue to rub his hand up and down her leg. Even without the shower and scotch, his touch alone would have melted her from the inside out.

Because his pajama pants were so big on her, he was able to slide his hand beneath them all the way up to her thigh and back down again. She spread her legs a little in invitation as the slow, languid sweep of his hand warmed her very core.

She opened her eyes. He was watching her, his disheveled hair falling across his forehead. Astonishing how he could trap her with his blue gaze, a universe unto itself. Her nipples pebbled beneath the T-shirt. She reached for the hem, tugging it up over her breasts, but not wanting to take the soft material fully off just yet.

Evan exhaled a heavy breath at the sight of her naked breasts. He stroked his other hand up to squeeze and caress them, his big, tanned hand a striking contrast to her pale skin.

"C'mere," he muttered gruffly, tugging at the waistband of her pants while simultaneously drawing her closer.

Hannah lifted herself up and draped her arms around his neck. Their mouths met in a hot, wet kiss. She moaned, loving the scrape of his whisker-rough chin against hers, the way he clutched her hips and shifted her to straddle his lap.

She shoved her hands under his shirt, stroking her palms over the warm, rigid muscles of his chest. He tightened his hold on her hips and pushed her down farther.

The sensation of his erection pressed right up against her cleft, with only the thin barrier of their pants separating them, rocked her with a shudder. Her whole body tensed with both pleasure and the urge to move against him until she came. He tugged at her shirt.

"Get this off," he growled. "I want to see you."

Hannah yanked the shirt over her head and dropped it on the floor. Cooler air brushed her skin, stiffening her nipples further. Evan pulled her closer, latching his lips around one nipple as if staking his claim.

Not that he had to. He'd already claimed her. Maybe from the moment he'd first kissed her.

"Come on," he whispered, gripping her ass. "Work yourself on me."

Oh my God...

She held on to his shoulders and shifted her lower body, rubbing against the hard bulge barely contained by his drawstring pants. She bit her lip, holding back a moan as her hips swiveled with increasing frenzy.

"Evan, I want you inside me," she whispered, though she was unable to stop herself from writhing on him long enough to divest them completely of their clothes.

"Oh, I will be." He twisted her nipples between his long fingers. "After you come, I'm going to rip these pants off you and sink my dick into your sweet pussy so deep you scream. Then I'm going to fuck you nice and slow...at first. I want to watch you take my cock in over and over, and then when you start begging for more, I'll give you more. But you have to earn it...and do you know how you're going to earn it?"

Hannah groaned, resting her forehead against his as her urgency mounted higher and higher.

"I'm going to make myself come," she gasped.

"Exactly." Satisfaction fueled his smoldering gaze.

She grasped the back of the sofa behind him, whimpers streaming from her throat as she continued writhing against his erection. She dragged a hot breath into her lungs. Her legs strained from their splayed position. Her blood burned.

"Evan...Evan, I'm so close...right there...*now!*"

She cried out, thrusting her body down on his. He gripped her hips and held her in place. Pulses of heat burst through her. She shuddered, knowing he would catch her when she slid down the other side.

And he did. She collapsed against him, breathless and quivering. He wrapped his arms around her, his deep voice a soothing murmur in her ear.

The sensations ebbed, and Hannah came back to her senses. She wiggled back on his knees and worked the drawstring of his pants, tugging them down just far enough to release his long, thick cock. Her arousal flared all over again at the sight of him so hard and ready.

Seized with an urge to taste him, she started to slide off his lap and to her knees. Then she stopped, an idea hitting her. Maybe it came from a liquor buzz or excess adrenaline from the storm, but more likely it was this combustible heat she and Evan generated. She half expected to see sparks when their bodies rubbed together.

"Take off your clothes." She sat up. "And wait here."

Evan muttered a noise of protest but let her go. Hannah hurried into the kitchen and grabbed the canister of whipped cream from the fridge. She returned to the living room, where Evan was taking a condom packet out of his wallet. Her body surged anew at the sight of him sprawled naked on the sofa, both feet planted on the floor.

For a moment, she just stared at him—his strong thighs and muscular arms, the slopes of his pecs bisected by the scar that only enhanced his masculine beauty. She admired his washboard abs with that trail of hair leading straight to his erect cock.

She shivered. Evan's gaze went to the canister she held. His eyebrows rose.

She paused in front of him and shook the can. Heated expectation stretched between them. Lowering herself to her knees, she twisted the cap off the canister and edged between his thighs.

She upended the can and squeezed a line of whipped cream right down his abdomen.

He twitched, his breath escaping in a rush. Hannah shot him a grin and lowered her head. Like a cat, she lapped up the thick cream, swirling her tongue over the ridges of his abs and into his navel.

She drew a few more little patterns around his abdomen and up to his chest, deliberately avoiding touching his cock even though her naked breasts brushed against it with almost every movement. Evan's breath hissed outward, and he reached down to curl his fingers into her hair.

"Lockhart," he growled. "I'm about to grab you and jack myself off between those gorgeous tits if you don't stop teasing me."

Hannah's heart crashed against her ribs at the thought of him thrusting his cock back and forth in her cleavage. She was tempted to keep teasing him just to reach that end, but she wanted to finish her task.

She moved back and squeezed a line of whipped cream over his shaft, then lowered her head to take him full into her mouth. He groaned, tightening his hand in her hair. The taste of him combined with the sweet cream fired Hannah with lust.

With a muffled moan, she worked her head back and forth, taking him in as deep as she could, sucking and licking. She moved away only long enough to apply more whipped cream before sliding him past her lips again.

"Ah, fuck, that's good, baby." Evan watched her, his hand in her hair and his eyes burning.

He thrust upward, swiftly but not fast enough to be startling. Hannah squeezed his shaft and sucked, feeling his tension break the instant before he came. After swallowing as much as she could, she pulled back, panting and rather astonished to see that he was still hard.

"Get up here," he ordered, fumbling to rip open the condom packet.

She couldn't move fast enough. In seconds, he'd sheathed his cock and hauled her up onto the sofa. She was spreading her legs for him before she was halfway to her back. He plunged into her with thrust that jolted a cry from her throat.

They moved together—hard, deep, delicious. Their lips met, clung, separated. The sound of their heartbeats filled the thick, heavy air. She dug her fingernails into his back. He buried his face in her neck. She tightened around him in the way she knew he liked as he drove into her, hitting the sweet spot that made her come almost violently. When she was still quaking with pleasure, he sank into her and stilled, his rough shout of release hot against her skin.

They collapsed on the sofa that wasn't big enough for both of them, but somehow Evan shifted them around so she was splayed over his long body. She pressed a line of kisses over the scar bisecting his chest, making her way up over his neck and chin until she reached his mouth.

"You did it," she whispered, brushing her lips against his.

"Did what?" His voice was a sleepy murmur.

"You found my sweet tooth."

He grinned lazily. She tucked her head beneath his chin and closed her eyes. He threaded his fingers through her hair. *Cafuné*.

As Hannah drifted to sleep, an unguarded realization made its way to the front of her mind.

With all her travel experience, she knew how to both arrive and depart a town or a city. She knew when to leave, what to pack, and sometimes where she was going next.

But now, for the first time, she had no idea *how* she was going to leave.

CHAPTER 18

$\mathcal{E}$van rolled over in bed and opened his eyes. Dawn light slanted through the blinds in his bedroom. Hannah sat on the chair by the window with a cup of coffee, her hair long and messy around her shoulders.

Wearing the striped knee socks she'd had on yesterday and his navy T-shirt, she looked both adorably tousled and so damned sexy that heat sparked through Evan's veins. He didn't think he could ever get enough of her. She was like an endless chili-chocolate cake, a mixture of sweet and spicy wrapped into one delicious, creamy package.

He could still taste her on his lips. His cock twitched. He wanted to walk over to her, spread her long legs, and bury his face in her pussy until she gripped his hair and begged him to make her come.

Hannah glanced up. Evan realized he'd groaned aloud.

"Morning." She held up her mug. "There's coffee, if you want some."

"C'mere," he ordered gruffly.

Her eyebrows lifted, but she set her mug aside and obediently padded back over to the bed. He liked it when she obeyed. He also liked it when she took control. Hell, he liked her any way he could get her.

He pushed the sheet aside and shifted onto his back. Hannah's lips parted on an O of surprise as she saw the hardening bulge in his boxer briefs. Her gaze flew to his.

"Really?" she breathed.

"Last night was just a warm-up." He stuck his hand into his boxers and grabbed his shaft. "This time, you're going to do the work."

A visible shudder ran through her, even as a flash of teasing defiance lit in her eyes.

"What if I don't want to?" she countered.

"Then I'll make good on my promise to spank you."

She folded her arms and pursed her lips, which made him want to kiss her. "I'm not in the mood for spanking," she announced.

"Are you in the mood for a fucking?"

"Maybe…" She glanced at his erection again.

Evan groaned and squeezed his shaft. "Come on, honey. Ride me."

"God," Hannah whispered, rubbing the back of her neck. "And here I thought you were such a nice guy."

"I'm a nice guy who wants to see his nice girl bouncing up and down on his cock until she comes like a rocket."

She shivered again, a flush rising to her cheeks. Locking her gaze to his, she grabbed the hem of her shirt and tugged it off, revealing her pale, burnished body. Evan's cock jerked to full hardness at the sight of her, all curves and soft skin, her nipples budding up into tight points that begged for his touch.

He shoved his boxers off. Hannah stared at his cock and licked her lips. He almost grabbed her and hauled her to him, but he wanted her to make the first…okay, the *second* move. And he really wanted to see her riding him.

Hannah took a condom from the nightstand and moved to

straddle him. She settled back on his thighs and rolled the condom slowly over his shaft.

Evan tensed. Pressure collected at his groin. Maintaining self-control around Hannah was not easy. Especially not with her delectable ass pressing against his thighs, and her hair falling around her naked body…and Christ, she'd left her knee socks on, which was almost disturbingly sexy.

He gripped her hips, urging her upward. "Do it."

She lifted her body and braced her hands on his chest. "Put it inside me."

Evan grabbed his dick and positioned it right at her slit. He knew without needing to touch her that she was already slick and ready. She curled her fingers against his chest and sank down on him, a slow, easy movement that had him gritting his teeth with pleasure.

Fuck fuck fuck. She was heaven. Her hot, honeyed warmth encased him like a glove, squeezing and rippling around him. She lifted her body and brought it down again. Heat flooded him. He tightened his hold on her hips.

With a moan, Hannah tossed her head back and rode him in earnest, her movements increasing in pace. Her body jostled with every descent, her ass slamming against his thighs and her breasts swaying.

Evan wouldn't last long, not with the combined onslaught of Hannah gripping him and the sight of her gorgeous body bouncing up and down. Her knee socks rasped against his sides as she worked herself on him, her skin flushed pink and her eyes half-closed.

"Oh my God, Evan, I feel you so deep." She gasped, spreading a hand over her belly. "All the way up here…"

She slid her hand down to her clit. Evan clenched his teeth, using every ounce of self-control to hold back while he watched her bring herself to orgasm. He knew the instant she started to come, tiny ripples coursing through her body before building into a wave that wrenched a cry from her throat.

He clutched her waist, driving up into her as deep as he could go. He came with a groan, shooting inside her with an explosive force that arched him off the bed at the same time that Hannah sank down, enclosing him in her body.

"Oh, you are so bad for me," she whispered, falling across his chest in a soft, damp bundle of sweetness. "I'd intended to get home and wrestle with my book proposal before my shift."

"I'll make a superhuman effort to leave you alone tonight so you can work." He stroked his hands down her back and squeezed her ass, then plucked at the elastic of her knee sock. "You got any more of these?"

"Yes."

"You're going to have to wear them more often."

Hannah's laugh was muffled against his shoulder. "All-righty then. Only for you."

"Good."

He pressed his lips to her temple. He'd never felt so right with a woman before. He'd known the moment he first saw her that his pull toward her was inordinately powerful. Kissing her at the auction had only intensified his need, but he'd ignored his own warnings to keep his distance.

After all, when it came to relationships, he controlled his heart. This fling with Hannah would be no different. Not even if he wanted it to be.

Evan slid scrambled eggs onto two plates and brought them over to the Formica table. Hannah, still wearing nothing but his T-shirt and knee socks, sat at one of the chairs, her gaze on the windows overlooking the ocean, whipped with whitecaps, and the gray morning sky.

"You wake up to this every morning," she said. "Must be nice."

"It's why I bought the house. I like being right next to the sea."

He opened the prescription bottle of his daily medication, dispensing two tablets into his palm. He swallowed them with a gulp of water. Only when he glanced up did he notice Hannah watching him.

She averted her gaze. A pained look flashed in her eyes. He put the bottle in the cupboard and slammed the door too hard. Tension threaded his shoulders.

"I think about views a lot when I'm in a place I love." Hannah pushed a tumble of hair away from her face and picked up her fork. "Waking up in Kenya, or Ireland. Brazil. If I have an amazing view, I always think how incredible it would be to wake up and see that every morning. It would fill you up."

Evan sat down and passed her the plate of toast. "What about when you wake up in a place that's not so picturesque?"

"Then I think how lucky I am to be there anyway. Not many people have had the opportunity to travel as much as I have. To have seen the things I've seen."

He took a bite of toast and considered his next words carefully. "You ever going to stop?"

"One day. Maybe." Hannah picked at the eggs with her fork. "I don't know. I make a living with my blog, so I don't know what else I'd do for money."

"What about your book?"

Her mouth twisted. "I still don't have any inspiring ideas. Even if I did, it would just be one book. I'd still have to keep up my blog for income."

She reached for her coffee, slanting her gaze to the window again. A swath of hair fell across her cheek. Even in the gray dawn light, her eyes were a striking aquamarine, the colors of the tropics.

Pride flared inside him, alongside a fierce sense of protectiveness. He hated that she'd been deemed the irresponsible one, the flight risk, the sister whose promises were suspect. More, he hated that she would even slightly believe those things about herself.

"It's amazing," he said. "What you've done with your life. Your writing, your photography. A lot of people dream of taking off to see the world, making a living, traveling wherever they want. You're one of the unique few who have actually done it."

"Thank you." She looked down at her plate. "Unfortunately, I've also been selfish. I didn't come back to visit my mother nearly enough. Or Polly."

"Don't make yourself feel guilty. You're here now."

"Maybe I agreed to help Polly out of penance." She shrugged. "I should have come back more. I think I knew it at the time, especially when my mother got sick. I felt like such a coward every time I left again. I just hated seeing her so sick, wasting away. She'd always been like Polly, vibrant and full of life. Sociable, likable. Then I'd come back from Malaysia or wherever, and she was so thin, almost skeletal. She lost all her hair and sometimes she was so weak she couldn't get out of bed. And Polly..."

Her breath hitched, and she shook her head. "Polly was so good. She'd have done anything for our mother. She did do everything she could. Even dropped out of college to come back to Rainsville and take care of her. Meanwhile, I had a hard time staying for more than a couple of weeks."

"Hannah. You're here now."

She lifted her head to look at him. A nascent glow burned in her eyes. He could almost see her thoughts shifting and working in her sharp mind.

"My mother always told me how much she loved my blog," she said. "That my posts made her happy."

"I'm sure they did. It sounds as if you make a lot of people happy."

There it was—the full-fledged smile that lit up her whole face and flooded Evan with warmth.

"Well, you make me happy, Heartbreaker," she said.

His heart flared with an emotion he didn't know what to do with. It was a combination of pleasure and sorrow—because of course Hannah made him happy too, but it would be a fleeting happiness, like eating a Sparkle Pop that he knew he'd be done with soon.

The front door slammed shut suddenly, and Adam's voice boomed in from the foyer. "Hey, man, you ready to go?"

Shit. Adam walked into the kitchen, clad in track pants and a T-shirt. He stopped in the doorway, his eyebrows lifting in surprise at the sight of them.

"Sorry." Adam stepped back. "Didn't know you had company."

"It's okay. Adam, you remember Hannah. Hannah, my younger brother Adam."

"Sure. Hi." She rose and extended her hand.

Adam's gaze flickered to her bare legs before he moved forward to shake her hand. "Good to see you again." He glanced at Evan. "Guess you forgot we were going to shoot hoops at the gym."

"Yeah. Sorry."

Adam rolled his eyes at the insincere apology.

"Have a seat." Hannah waved Adam to an empty seat at the table. "There's plenty of eggs and stuff."

Adam hesitated for about half a second, then pulled out the chair.

"Don't mind if I do." He sat, poured himself a cup of coffee, and filled a plate with eggs. "Looks like the auction worked out for you two, huh?"

Evan and Hannah exchanged glances. He didn't even want to think about what would have happened if she hadn't spontaneously bid on him.

"What about your date?" Hannah asked Adam.

"Nice girl." Adam shoveled a forkful of eggs into his mouth. "We had fun."

"Are you going to see her again?"

"Not sure. Maybe. I'm heading to Indonesia next week, so I guess it's up to her if she's going to wait for me to get back. I'm guessing not."

"What are you doing in Indonesia?" Hannah asked.

"Sugar Rush business."

"The Fair Trade Foundation crap I told you about," Evan explained. "It's turning into a crisis of corporate responsibility."

"Why?"

"Evan is all about strengthening Sugar Rush's social responsibility," Adam told Hannah, reaching for the plate of bacon. "It's always been part of the culture, but he wants it to be a division of the company."

"Isn't that what the Fair Trade Foundation is?" Hannah asked.

"That's why I started it," Evan said. "It's supposed to not only ensure fair compensation for farmers but also find ways to keep cocoa bean crops sustainable. Eventually I want the foundation to invest in local communities with building projects and programs to train people in the best agricultural practices. Unfortunately, the man in charge of it is taking things in a different direction."

"The wrong direction," Adam added around a mouthful of toast.

"Can you fire him?" Hannah asked.

"Not without evidence of wrongdoing, which we don't have." Evan told Hannah more details about the deforestation issues with Singa, as well as the potential for a PR disaster.

Hannah listened carefully, her hands wrapped around her mug and her gaze on him.

"Remember that trip to Mongolia I told you about?" she asked when he paused to refill his coffee. "Has Sugar Rush done any special programs with global tourism?"

"We've funded scientific expeditions in Venezuela," Adam said. "They're not for tourists, though."

"My friend Dave, he's into eco-tourism," Hannah continued. "He did some volunteer work for the Java Works Coffee Company's environmental project in Costa Rica. They were working on a farmer's collective or something. He can tell you more about it, but I think it was a big success. And Java Works is known all over for its commitment to the environment."

"All of our cocoa beans are sourced from family farms in Venezuela and the Ivory Coast," Adam said. "We've never done a volunteer project though."

"Dave said there were about three hundred people from all over."

Evan was silent. His brain started working in a different direction. A better one. The palm oil issue was specific to Sugar Rush's chocolate line. And the Fair Trade Foundation hadn't yet gotten off the ground—that was supposed to be Sam's job, despite his shitty start. But since Sugar Rush already had a framework in place in both Venezuela and the Ivory Coast...

He looked at his brother. "What if we created a program like that to launch the Fair Trade Foundation? A research and educational project with volunteers, scientists, students, Sugar Rush employees. We could recruit international donors, get journalists involved. We could start with the research about soil quality and improving crop yield of cocoa beans."

"Great idea, but Sam wouldn't want you encroaching on his territory," Adam said.

"Fuck him. Luke's the only one who would have to sign off on it." Ideas pinged back and forth in Evan's mind. "We need to go on the offense rather than the defense. Yeah, we still have to prove we're not involved with Singa, but a hands-on project about sustainable production and farmer support will take some of the heat off. Then we launch the project with applications, recruitment, maybe even scholarships...all emphasizing the foundation's charter of principles and Sugar Rush's worldwide initiative for corporate social responsibility."

Adam shook his head and chuckled. "Ambitious."

"I need your help," Evan told his brother.

"I'm here," Adam said.

Evan looked at Hannah, who hadn't taken her eyes off him during his whole speech. He leaned across the table and planted a kiss on her forehead.

"Lockhart, you're a genius."

"I am?"

"You're my genius." He stood and grabbed Adam's half-eaten plate of food away from him.

"Hey, I'm not done, man."

"Let's get over to Sugar Rush. We have work to do."

CHAPTER 19

*T*he Wild Child Bakery van rattled noisily over the straight, I-5 highway bisecting the center of California like a ribbon. The Rolling Stones crackled from the old speakers, and dry wind from the endless stretches of farmland blew through the open windows. Hannah opened a bag of Chocolate Crunchies from the stash of Sugar Rush candy Evan had brought along.

She passed the bag to him in the driver's seat. He took a few and popped them into his mouth, his gaze on the highway in front of them.

"*Tingo*," he said.

"The sound made by striking a bell with a metal spoon."

"Nice." He shot her a look of approval. "But no. It's Pascuense for stealing a person's belongings gradually by borrowing but not returning them. *Pochemuchka*."

"A cute little woodland creature."

"Russian for 'a person who asks too many questions.'"

"Really?" Hannah asked. "Russia has a word for that? Why? Where did it come from?"

He grinned. "*Gattara*."

"A special guitar made in a tiny Italian coastal town."

"A woman who devotes herself to stray cats. Basically a crazy cat lady."

"I have one," Hannah said. "*Fika.*"

"Swedish for a coffee break."

"*Sahnehäubchen.*"

He slanted her a sideways glance. "Look it up."

"Huh." Disgruntled that he still wouldn't just tell her, she reached for a bottle of water from the cooler. "Okay, what about great English words? I've always liked the word *kerfuffle*. It sounds like what it is, and it's fun to say."

"Like *hullaballoo.*"

"Exactly. *Gobbledygook.*"

"*Brouhaha,*" Evan said.

"*Gibberish.*"

"*Lollygag.*"

"*Serendipity.*"

"*Epiphany.*" Evan unwrapped a Sparkle Pop and nodded toward the bag of candy. "Try one. You'll have an *epiphany* about sugar."

"When you lived in Copenhagen, did you try and convert all the Danes into sugar addicts?" Hannah took a Chocolate Crunchie and popped it into her mouth.

"Actually they converted me." He stuck the lollipop in his mouth, rolling it across his tongue. "I became a huge fan of *ebelskiver*. Ever had them?"

"Those little round pancakes, right?"

"Fried and topped with jam and sugar. Couldn't get enough of them with a cup of coffee, some fruit and cheese." He made a deep noise of appreciation that settled in Hannah's core.

"Did you live with a family while you were there?"

"No, I was in the dorm at the University of Copenhagen, but I spend a lot of weekends and holidays with friends' families. You ever been there?"

"Once, but many years ago, and I didn't stay for very long. I don't remember much about it, actually."

"You should go. It's a phenomenal city. Still my favorite."

Hannah looked out the side window at the acres of field and low hills in the distance. A thought pushed its way upward from the seed that had planted during their trip to Napa Valley.

What would it be like to travel the world with Evan rather than alone? She'd taken short trips with other men before, but they'd always parted ways sooner rather than later, and she'd never longed for their company again.

But Evan...she could picture standing with him in the quiet stillness of the Roman Pantheon, walking along the Santiago de Compostela in Spain, eating ginger-lanced *siu mai* from a Hong Kong street vendor. She could hear him waxing rhapsodic about Viennese pastries and chocolate-dipped churros in Barcelona. She could imagine reaching out and finding his hand ready to close around hers, anywhere in the world.

"Are you planning to go back anytime soon?" she asked. "To Copenhagen."

"I don't know." He pulled the pop out of his mouth and set it back in the wrapper. "I'm going to Bern next year to work on the Alpine transition. I might stop in Copenhagen." He glanced at her, his eyes shaded behind his sunglasses. "Where are you going when you leave Rainsville?"

She wished she knew. For all her longing to leave, she hadn't yet made any specific plans—not that planning too much had ever been part of her repertoire. Her ability to uproot herself and move from place to place, buoyed by the wind like a dandelion puff, had always been one of her great sources of pride. And she didn't know what to make of her intense attraction toward a man whose family had roots that sank deep into the California soil.

"I'll probably go to the mountains," she said. "Since I'm now spending months near the sea, I'll go toward the sky next time. Maybe Italy. I've never been to the Apennine mountains."

The idea stirred inside her, though it lacked the quick-fire spark of excitement she'd always felt at the anticipation of a new trip.

Her phone buzzed. She glanced at the screen to find a message from Polly: *Are you seriously on a road trip with Evan?*

Hannah couldn't tell if her sister's tone was surprised or disapproving. She responded with: *Just for the weekend. Wild Child is fine in Ramona and Sophie's hands.*

I know. I'm asking about you and Evan!

Hannah chewed her bottom lip. She'd sensed Polly was hoping something would happen between her and Evan—Hannah had no idea why, since her sister knew she was leaving Rainsville soon.

Just so I can get material for new posts, she texted back. *No big deal.*

She turned off the phone before she could read Polly's response. Now that Polly was so happy with Luke, Hannah felt bad for having tried to dissuade her sister from *feeling* too much for the commanding CEO Stone. Polly wore her heart on her sleeve, and her genuine warmth and goodness had probably softened Luke's inflexible edges from their first encounter.

But Hannah wasn't Polly, and Evan wasn't Luke. They were having a fling, not a relationship.

Never mind how *good* she felt around him. Even the tedious drive south was turning out to be fun, only because she was sharing it with Evan and his inscrutable words, classic rock playlists, and Sparkle Pops.

She took over driving for a couple of hours so he could work on his tablet—brainstorming ideas for the cocoa bean research project he and Adam were devising. Not only was she immensely proud of his ambition and determination, she was happy he was convinced this was the way to pull the company out of the recent shadow that had fallen over it.

And she'd had a small role in giving him the idea. Not once

had she ever thought she'd one day influence the way a multi-million-dollar company conducted its business and social programs.

They neared LA. Hannah checked her travel guide and made a few calls to low-budget motels, finally locating one in East Hollywood that had a room available for the night. The urban sprawl of Los Angeles spread over the valley like a maze, divided by a tangled web of highways. High-rises shot toward the sky on either side of Wilshire Boulevard as Evan navigated the van through the clogged traffic of Westwood.

After registering at the neon-lit motel, they ate sloppy hamburgers at In-N-Out and wandered around Hollywood Boulevard. Though not nearly as high-end as Napa, there was a gritty, electric energy in the air that reminded Hannah the boundaries of the world didn't end in Rainsville. She took pictures of street performers, neon signs, graffiti.

They sat on the grass to listen to a free concert in the park, and Hannah realized her faint misgivings about this weekend road trip had disappeared. She'd known Evan was accustomed to expensive travel and dinners, and though the road trip had been her idea, she'd been anxious about how he'd handle it.

Clearly she needn't have worried. For all his wealth and family lineage, Evan was a man who would be comfortable anywhere—from a penthouse suite to the floor of a yurt. He knew how to eat caviar on blini, and he could appreciate a greasy burger from a roadside shack. He enjoyed both exclusive art galleries and tacky souvenir shops.

An ache nudged at Hannah's heart. Evan should be out in the world, a part of it, layered in all its joys and complexities.

"Did you ever want to travel more?" She held out a paper bag of nachos they'd purchased from a food truck.

"Yeah, but there are limits to what I can do and where I can go." He gestured to his chest. "High altitudes can be dangerous. And Luke wouldn't let me run the Fair Trade Foundation because it requires traveling to remote locations that don't have much medical care. I could do a lot of that, but knowing the worry it would cause my family..."

He shrugged. "Better to stay put."

That was the reason he'd stuck to the narrow path at Sugar Rush. After his mother's death, Evan hadn't wanted to be responsible for upsetting his family further. He still didn't.

A mixture of deep admiration and sadness rose in Hannah toward this warm-hearted man who'd spent years putting his family before his own ambitions. Only when his brother had taken away something Evan believed in had he stepped forward to make a change.

"Do you have any regrets?" she asked.

"None I could do anything about. I'll probably always wish for a whole heart, even though I came to terms with living with a defective one years ago."

She slipped her hand into his. His fingers closed warmly over hers. His heart was anything but defective. She'd never met a man with a stronger heart than his, one that had unlocked her own.

CHAPTER 20

"Take it in slowly," he murmured.

"It's awfully big." Hannah eyed the glossy knob doubtfully, even though part of her wanted to suck the whole hard length into her mouth, both out of curiosity and the desire to make Evan happy.

"Wet it with your tongue," he said.

She darted out her tongue and licked the red tip.

"See, it's not so bad." He brushed the hardness across her lower lip, his gaze darkening. "Now open wide and let it slide in."

Her heart thumped. Hannah parted her lips and waited. Evan gently pushed the cherry-flavored Sparkle Pop into her mouth. The overly sweet taste flooded her tongue along with a fizzy sensation like soda pop.

"Close your lips around it," he ordered.

She did. They were sitting cross-legged on the bed in a motel room, facing each other with their knees touching. Hannah took the lollipop stick from him. The fizziness in her mouth intensified.

"It sort of hurts," she complained.

"Hurts so good, baby." Evan unwrapped another cherry-flavored pop and put it in his mouth. "I'll do it with you."

They sucked on their respective pops. Bubbles popped in Hannah's mouth.

She wrinkled her nose. "When's it going to explode?"

"You never know." Evan watched the movement of her tongue as she slid the pop out of her mouth and back in again. "It's a pleasure explosion that happens without warning."

"I don't like explosions at all, warning or not."

"That's not the impression I got last night." He gave her a smug, very male look.

Hannah poked him in the chest with the sucker before sticking it back into her mouth.

The candy popped and fizzed. She didn't love the feeling, but Evan was looking at her with such hopeful expectation that she firmly told herself to see it through. Not to mention he was adorable sucking on the candy, his eyes almost glowing with unhidden pleasure.

Hannah sucked her pop harder.

Ah, the things we do for...

She quickly diverted that train of thought.

...the cute boys we like.

She squeezed her eyes shut, steeling herself for the "explosion" as the candy dissolved slowly in her mouth. She bit the outer shell. A burst of sweetness flooded her mouth, bubbles cracking and popping like little sparklers. She gasped, her surprise fading to both pleasure and amusement.

"You need to be the new face of Sparkle Pops," Evan remarked around a mouthful of candy. "You could swirl your tongue around the sucker and say things like *Come get your burst on.*"

"I suspect that would appeal to the wrong demographic." Hannah chuckled around the crunchy candy and tossed the empty stick into the trash. "This is the silliest thing I've ever eaten."

"But you look damned hot doing it."

Evan winked at her, biting the Sparkle Pop off his stick. He screwed up his eyes and braced himself as his candy exploded.

Hannah grabbed the front of his T-shirt and yanked him toward her. Their mouths collided in a hot, open kiss that popped with cherry fireworks.

The fizzing sensation combined with the feel of Evan's lips went straight to Hannah's blood, lighting her up with bursts of color. Their tongues tangled in a sudden frenzy, the candy still sparkling and melting until she no longer knew which lollipop was hers and which was his.

"Ah, hell, this is how candy should end." Evan brought his hands to the sides of her head and tilted her face so he could settle his mouth more securely over hers.

He shifted them both, pressing her back against the pillows and sweeping his tongue into her mouth. As the candy dissolved and disappeared, Hannah melted into his sticky-sweet kiss. She drove her fingers into his hair as her body surged with desire. Everything about him aroused her, from the feel of his chest pressing against her breasts to the way he tightened his grip in her hair with such possessiveness, as if he would never let her go.

She slipped her hands under his T-shirt and spread them over the warm, muscled planes of his chest.

"Take this off," she whispered, tugging at the hem.

Evan lifted himself off her only long enough to yank the shirt over his head and drop it to the floor. As he unbuttoned his shorts, Hannah wiggled out of her shirt and pants. Evan was already half hard beneath his boxer briefs, and her breath caught.

"Wow," she said, her blood warming. "Sparkle Pops turn you on, huh?"

"Sparkle Pops and you." He ran his hands over her body, rubbing his thumbs around her hard nipples.

Hannah shifted, her breath increasing. She rose slightly to unfasten her bra and release her breasts.

"Ah, fuck, you're so pretty." Evan lowered his head to capture one of her nipples between his lips, the warmth of his mouth sending a shock of arousal through her.

He slid his hand down her belly and between her legs, rubbing her panties into her cleft. His muffled groan rumbled over her skin.

"So ready," he murmured, his eyes smoldering. "Wet and hungry. You want my cock here already?" He slipped his finger beneath her panties and into her slick opening.

Hannah groaned, arching into his touch. "Yes."

"Then you need to come first." He lifted his head, a smile curving his mouth. "I want to feel it before I make you beg for my cock."

Flames shot through her. Hannah squirmed, still unable to reconcile the warm, gentle Evan Stone of everyday with the dirty talker who fired her arousal from zero to infinity in seconds.

He eased to the side, his hand still inside her panties, and the combined sight and feel of his fingers moving against her through the cotton drove Hannah's urgency higher. She curled her fingers around his wrist as he worked her with unbearably exquisite precision.

"Evan, harder," she gasped.

"Greedy." He chuckled, his breath hot against her ear. "Your body wants it now, but you're not getting it now. You're getting it nice and slow and you're going to work for it...ah, yeah, tighten your pussy around my finger...that's it..."

He circled his thumb slowly around her clit. Heat washed over her. The pressure broke with a hard snap. Crying out, she bucked up against him as vibrations shuddered through her.

She fell back against the pillows with a gasp, hearing Evan's low murmur as if it were coming from a far distance. His mouth covered hers again. He pinched one of her nipples and kissed a path over her neck, across her breasts and belly.

Hannah lifted her head, her heart thumping. She did not often allow men to go down on her. It was too intimate, too exposing. She never intended to be with them more than a few weeks at most. She had to give up too much control to let them put their lips and tongue on her most secret places.

"Evan…"

"Relax." He spread his hands over her breasts and moved his body between her thighs. "I want to taste you."

She shivered, tightening her fists on the bedcovers. "I really don't…"

He glanced up. His eyes burned with both lust and utter self-control. If she asked him not to do this, he wouldn't. If she asked him to stop, he would. That knowledge rose in Hannah like the first star of night.

"Trust me," he said.

She nodded.

He lowered his head, gently pushing her thighs apart with his hands. She gripped the bedcovers harder.

"Lift your knees," Evan said.

She did, trying to smother the feeling of intense vulnerability as he spread her open with his fingers. A tremble rocketed through her.

"Ah, fuck, you're so wet," he whispered. "So pretty."

She squeezed her eyes shut. He trailed his finger over her damp crevices, teasing and light. She bit back a moan. Her body surged and ached for his penetration. Then he touched his tongue to her swollen clit, and a low moan broke from deep inside her.

"Evan…oh, God…"

"Sweeter than sugar," he murmured, slipping his finger into her.

Hannah's body clenched around him, squeezing his finger as if it were a substitute for his cock. She opened her eyes, her heart hammering at the sight of her naked body splayed out on the bed and Evan's dark head moving between her spread legs.

Christ, it was fucking sexy. She shifted, spreading her legs wider. He murmured a noise of approval. He stroked his tongue over her as if he were licking a succulent candy, and then he took her clit between his lips and sucked.

"Evan." Hannah panted, her whole body quivering as her arousal intensified again.

"What do you want, sweet Hannah?"

A blush fired her from head to toe at the thought of voicing her desires. It was insane how he made her feel both shy and emboldened at the same time.

"I'm...I...oh..."

"Tell me," he insisted.

"I need you." She undulated her hips toward his face in a movement edged with desperation. "I want your cock inside me. I *need* you to fill me, fuck me deep...oh, please...Evan, make me come..."

"That's my girl."

He rose and mounted her again, bracing his hands on the bed as his mouth descended on hers. The flavor of cherry mixed with the taste of her own body fired her arousal to burning. With a moan, she opened her mouth and wrapped her legs around his hips.

Evan moved away from her only long enough to put on a condom and position himself at her sex. Fire burned in his eyes as he slipped partway inside her. Hannah arched upward.

"Do it," she gasped. "Hard."

He groaned, surging into her with one powerful thrust before stilling. For a second, they stared at each other, the air between them crackling with blue sparks. With his hair falling over his sweaty forehead, his eyes blazing, his features rigid with lust and control, Evan was nothing short of stunningly, heartrendingly beautiful.

Hannah gripped his biceps. "Fuck me now."

He pulled back, sliding out of her halfway before plunging

back in. She loosened her legs from his waist and spread them wider, giving him unhindered access to every part of her.

He lowered his head, burying his face against her hot neck, grunting with each deep thrust. His voice vibrated inside her, heating her blood. Harder, faster. Her body jostled against the mattress. She cupped her breasts, twisting her nipples. She was on fire inside and out, all thought subsumed beneath the intense pleasure of their union.

"Evan…"

"Again," he commanded, lifting his head to kiss her. "I want to feel your pussy clenching around my cock when you come."

She would never survive this. The pleasure would consume her. She slid her hand between their sweat-slick bodies to find her aching clit.

Evan clamped his hand around her wrist, pinning it to the bed. "No. You're going to come from my cock."

She shifted, emitting a soft groan as his shaft sank into her again. "I don't think I can…"

"Yeah, you can." His voice was low and gritty. "You will."

Hannah bit her lip, sudden uncertainty snaking through her. She flexed her hand in his grip. He seized her other hand, effectively immobilizing her. She was letting him do things she'd never allowed another man to do.

She stared at him. His eyes had darkened to navy, the color of the sky before a storm, the last hour of night.

"Come on, baby," he whispered, stroking his tongue over the arch of her collarbone. "Let me feel it."

Yes. The tension tightened, coiling around her with delicious pressure. Her hands curled into fists. Then she convulsed, clamping around his thick shaft as an orgasm tore through her.

She shrieked, bucking her hips up against him. The sensations swelled and crashed. Evan's muscles went rigid, his hands moving to spread her sweaty thighs wider as he increased his pace.

"I won't last," he grated through clenched teeth.

"I don't want you to." Panting, she raked her hand down his chest. "Come inside me."

He surged once, twice, and then gave a rough shout. His body arched. His muscles flexed beneath his taut skin. Hannah quivered anew, her pleasure spiking with the evidence of his release.

Evan collapsed on top of her, his breath harsh against her ear.

"Christ in heaven, you're incredible," he muttered, rolling over and tugging her against his side. "I want to fuck you in every way imaginable. And in ways that haven't been invented yet."

She chuckled. "If they haven't been invented, I'm sure you'll invent them."

"Mmm." He ran his fingers through her hair. "Next time you're getting on your hands and knees. I want to see your pretty ass bouncing against me while I fuck you."

Hannah shivered, astonished as a new wave of arousal rolled through her. She ran her hand over Evan's chest, letting her fingers linger on his scar.

"Clearly your heart hasn't affected your…ah, physicality," she said.

He didn't respond. Hannah waited a minute before she lifted herself on her elbow to look at him. His eyes were closed, his chest still rising and falling with his breath.

"Did I say something wrong?" she asked.

He shook his head, not opening his eyes. "When I was a kid, I tried not to let my heart affect what I could do physically. Sometimes I succeeded. Sometimes I failed."

She stroked his scar again. "How?"

"I grew up with five strong, athletic brothers," he said. "I had to keep up with them, or at least I tried. I couldn't beat them in team sports…not unless they let me win, but that didn't stop me from trying. I had a better shot with individual sports, so I did karate, track and field, strength training."

Hannah traced his pectoral muscle with her finger. "That

explains why you're so well-built, but it doesn't necessarily explain your sexual prowess."

He choked out a laugh. "Is that what I have? Prowess?"

"In truckloads." She stretched out beside him again, resting her head on his shoulder. "Surely you know that. Isn't that why the girls started calling you Heartbreaker?"

"I guess. I figured out pretty early that girls liked me, though at first I thought it was because they felt sorry for me. I learned differently in high school. Some people with CHD have issues with sex, but my experience was the opposite. Sex was the one area where I was in control. When I fucked, neither the girl nor I was thinking about my heart defect. That was all the more reason I wanted to do it."

"It was an escape," Hannah said.

No one understood the need for *escape* better than she did.

Evan opened his eyes. Something indefinable flickered across his face.

"Is that what we are?" he asked. "An escape?"

"I don't know exactly what we are." Hannah ran her hand over his chest. "It doesn't feel like an escape, though. It feels like a return."

CHAPTER 21

*E*van rubbed his chest, his gaze on the road in front of them. The late-afternoon sun shone in the pale, hazy sky, and a thin ribbon of clouds spread across the horizon. Desert towns stretched out on either side of the interstate, the faint smell of soil and vegetation drifting into the van. Cars and eighteen-wheelers rumbled along the road like a modern-day caravan.

"Your biggest pet peeve?" Hannah asked.

"Tardiness."

She slanted him a glance. "Really?"

"Yeah. If people say they're going to be somewhere at a certain time or do something by a specific deadline, they should be there and do it. Extenuating circumstances excepted, of course. What about you?"

"People who talk on their cell phones loudly in public. No one wants to hear their conversation. Your turn."

"If you were sent to live on a space station for three months and only allowed to bring three personal items with you, what would they be?"

"Camera, computer, and my packed suitcase."

"Cheating."

"That's how I travel. I take those three things everywhere."

"Ever had something stolen?"

"My wallet and camera, but that was years ago. I know how to be more careful now. So what would you take to a space station?"

"A loaded e-book reader and a girlfriend."

Hannah laughed. "Three months with a girlfriend in space, and you think you'd even open an e-reader?"

"Not if the girlfriend is the insatiable Lockhart." He shot her a grin.

"If I'm insatiable, it's because of you."

"I know. I get you going."

"I *mean* you're kind of dirty."

"Kind of? *Sahnehäubchen*, you wound me."

"In case you hadn't noticed, 'kind of dirty' gets me going. So does your sexy use of untranslatable words."

"I've noticed." He gave her a knowing glance. "*Komorebi. Mokita. Sillage.*"

"Oh, baby, don't stop," Hannah murmured.

They exchanged smiles. He liked her sitting beside him, her hair loose around her shoulders, her bare arm resting on the console as they headed off on the road together. It was good. A moment of *hygge*.

"I have to stop now or we'll be stranded." Evan eyed the fuel gauge before he pulled off the highway on to a narrow two-lane road leading to a gas station.

As he refilled the tank, Hannah went into the convenience store to stock up on water and snacks.

Evan caught a whiff of grilled burgers. His stomach rumbled. He glanced at a ramshackle bar on the other side of the street.

Their trip into the desert had taken longer than expected since Hannah had wanted to stop and see a bunny museum, giant dinosaur sculptures, and the Sriracha Hot Sauce factory. He'd have gladly taken her to a thousand other roadside attractions, except that he was getting hungry. He replaced the gas pump and took out his phone to check the map.

"Let's get dinner there." He nodded toward the bar when Hannah returned. "The motel doesn't have a restaurant, and it looks like it's in the middle of nowhere. We might have a hard time finding a place to eat."

"Okay. I told the motel guy we'd be there by eight, so that will give us plenty of time."

Evan paid for the gas and drove across the street to the bar. Music pounded against the walls, and neon beer signs flashed in the windows. People crowded around the bar at one side of the room. A dance floor was at the other side, a few pool tables arranged near the wall.

He took Hannah's hand and shouldered his way to an empty high-top table with paper menus stuck in the napkin holder. They sat on the stools, their knees bumping beneath the table. The waitress came by to take their drink orders.

As they waited, Evan admired Hannah because he could.

In a blue tank top that revealed her smooth, tanned arms and a hint of tempting cleavage, just the sight of her made him hot. Especially since he was so well acquainted with the taste of her skin—cinnamon and honey—and the spicy scent of her. He knew all the curves and hollows of her body too, from the soft undersides of her breasts to the flare of her hips.

She was different out here on the road. Freer. No tension lined her slender frame the way it did in Rainsville.

She caught him looking at her and smiled. She swayed a little to the music, shifting her gorgeous body. Her hair hung in a loose curtain straight down her back, framing the elegant arch of her neck and shoulders.

Mine.

She's mine.

He'd never felt this way about a woman before, never been

willing to let his heart control him to this extent. He no longer gave a damn about the dictates of their affair.

She was going to leave one day? He'd find a way to go with her. Or he'd convince her to stay. Either way, he'd keep her with him.

The woman he loved had bid fifty thousand dollars for a date with him. He sure as hell wouldn't let her go. Ever.

He grabbed his beer, ignoring the stab of unease in his chest.

He loved her. He loved Hannah Lockhart with her restlessness, her ambition, her talent, her uninhibited nature that fueled his lust like nothing else ever had. She hadn't treated him any differently after learning about his heart defect, and she didn't have a caretaker complex like some other women he'd been with. In fact, she liked it when he took care of her. He intended to keep doing just that.

She was saying something, her voice rising above the din of conversation and music. He leaned closer. Her breath brushed his ear.

"Dance a little after dinner?" she asked.

"Sure." He couldn't remember the last time he'd danced. Hadn't expected to until Luke and Polly's wedding.

Luke had fallen for a girl who was the complete opposite of "his type." That eased the discomfort in Evan's chest. Not only had they made it work, they were blissfully in love and happy together. Yeah, Luke had had to unbend, to loosen his rigid hold on Sugar Rush, but he'd done it because he'd wanted to be with his girl. He'd figured it the hell out.

Evan wouldn't let his older brother one-up him again.

His phone buzzed with a call from Adam. Under other circumstances he would have ignored the call, but this was likely related to the proposal he'd sent his brother.

"I'm sorry, I've gotta take this," he said to Hannah. "It's Adam."

"Go ahead." She waved him away, still bopping to the rhythm of a pop song streaming from the jukebox.

Evan stepped outside so he could hear the call.

"Good news, man," Adam said. "Dad said we can offer scholarships to encourage students to apply to the program. In addition to the scientific research, we can let volunteers know their contribution can be as simple as planting trees and helping farmers."

"Great. I have a call in to Alejandro about channeling all this through the Fair Trade Foundation."

"Have you talked to Luke yet?"

"No. I want all the details in place before I do. He's the one who has to deal with Sam."

"You want me to call a meeting for tomorrow morning?"

"Make it afternoon, around two. I'll be back in the morning. Talk to Kate. She'll set it up."

They spoke for a few more minutes before Evan stuck his phone in his pocket and went back into the bar. He started toward Hannah, then stopped.

A burly guy was standing next to her—too fucking close. Hannah's expression was tight, her hand up between them in a clear *back off* gesture. One the asshole was ignoring.

Evan didn't think. He didn't have to. He strode forward and grabbed Hannah's arm, shoving his body between her and the guy.

"Is there a problem?" he snapped.

The guy held up his hands and stepped back. "No problem, man."

"Good. Stay away from her."

The man's eyes shifted to Hannah. "Good luck with that. She's a cold fish."

"Walk away now," Evan growled.

Hannah tugged on his arm.

"Let's get out of here," she said. "Don't waste your time."

Evan allowed her to lead him a short distance away. He didn't like the hostility radiating from the other guy, as if he wanted revenge for her rejection. He took another step back, keeping himself in front of Hannah.

"Hey, you going to pay your bill before leaving?" the waitress called.

Evan dug into his wallet for a few bills, dropping them onto the table. Behind him, he sensed Hannah move to the side to grab her purse from the back of the chair.

It happened in a blur. The asshole drew his head back and spit in Hannah's direction. The glob splattered on her tank top. Her eyes widened in shocked horror.

Evan saw red. He launched himself forward like a torpedo, tackling the guy and bringing him down. They smashed into a table before hitting the ground with a thud. Screams and gasps filled the air from the crowd.

Fury scorched Evan's chest. He let his fists fly, slamming them into the fucker's face, his neck, anywhere he could reach. Hannah shouted, her voice sounding faraway, and pulled on his shoulder. He slammed his fists down again and again. Bone cracked. Blood smeared his knuckles.

A right hook caught his jaw, snapping his neck back. Pain radiated over his skull. He landed on his back. His opponent landed a fist to his solar plexus. All the air escaped Evan's lungs.

After a second of grappling, he regained the upper hand and brought his fist down on the guy's jaw. A knee to the groin had the man grunting in pain.

"Get the fuck off him."

Two sets of hands grabbed Evan's biceps and dragged him away. The other guy lay writhing on the ground, clutching his groin. Grim satisfaction filled Evan at the sight of the man's bloody face and split lip.

Evan let the two men yank him to his feet. Hannah was beside him, her voice in his ear, but he couldn't make out what she was saying.

He wiped the sweat off his face with his forearm. His breath burned his chest. His heart jackhammered.

He turned, folding one arm around Hannah. He focused on her face, her wide, scared eyes and flushed skin. His vision cleared.

"We don't put up with that shit in here," a bearded man snapped, waving his arm toward the scattered tables and chairs, and the bastard still writhing on the ground. "Either get the fuck out or I'm calling the police."

Evan took a few more bills from his wallet and tossed them on a table. He grabbed Hannah's hand and stalked toward the door. She stumbled after him, her fingers tightening around his. They stepped out into the warm night air.

"Are you all right?" Hannah pulled him to a stop beneath a streetlight, bringing her hands up to the sides of his face. "You're bleeding."

"I'm fine." He wiped his nose with his sleeve. "Are you okay?"

"Yes." She ran her hands over his neck and shoulders, across his chest, as if she needed to make sure he wasn't hurt. "You're sure you don't need to see a doctor?"

Evan leaned down to press a kiss between her eyes.

"Believe it or not, I've been in worse fights with my brothers. That asshole was an easy mark in comparison."

"Let's at least find a bathroom and clean up." She threaded her hands into his hair, brushing it away from his sweaty forehead. "Thank you. No one's ever defended me like that before."

A pain shot through Evan's chest. No one had defended her because she'd always been alone. Until now. He'd defend her for the rest of their lives.

They returned to the gas station and washed in the bathroom. Hannah changed into a clean T-shirt from her suitcase in the van, tossing the soiled tank top into the trash.

"Let me drive." She held out her hand for the keys.

Evan shook his head and opened the passenger side door for her. "I've got it."

She hesitated for the briefest instant, as if she wanted to argue, but then she climbed into the passenger seat. Grateful that she hadn't questioned his abilities after the fight, Evan got behind the wheel.

"We never got to eat." She peeled a granola bar open for him.

"Maybe we can find a takeout pizza joint."

He guided the van back onto the two-lane road leading away from the city. His jaw ached, but he didn't care. The sun sank into the horizon behind them, fields sweeping past in swaths of reddish gold.

Fewer cars appeared on the roads the farther they drove into the desert, turning on to a road that wound through the hills. Then they were alone, just the two of them, an old bakery van, and countless cacti and Joshua trees.

"I think it's about twenty miles." Hannah squinted at her phone. "I don't know, my GPS is acting a little wonky. Can I use your phone?"

He handed her his phone, but she had no better luck.

"Well, this is definitely the right road." She looked out the side window at the darkening desert hills. "I think."

Evan chuckled. Hannah shot him a grin. She reached across the seats and put her hand on his thigh. He felt the warmth of her palm through the denim of his jeans. His breath shortened.

He cleared his throat. "Lockhart."

"Hmm?"

"I—"

The van lurched. A sudden bang exploded from the engine. Evan swore, slamming his foot on the brake. Hannah gasped and grabbed the dashboard.

The tires squealed. The van skidded, spinning to the side before sliding to a hard stop on the shoulder of the road.

"Oh my God." Hannah pressed a hand to her chest. "What happened?"

"Not a tire."

Evan shoved open the door. A rush of dry, smoky air filled his lungs. He unlatched the hood and opened it. Smoke billowed out from the engine in a thick fog.

"Shit." He pulled a breath into his tight chest.

"I have a toolkit in the back," Hannah said, pausing at his side. "In case of emergency."

"I'd say this qualifies." He peered closer at the engine. "You call for help. I'll see if I can figure out what's wrong."

She hurried to get the toolkit. She took out her phone and swiped the screen as Evan checked the van's fluid levels.

"Bad timing, huh?" Hannah asked. "That's how it is with cars sometimes. I guess we'll just have to wait and see what happens next."

He glanced at her. "Well, as someone very wisely once said, 'That's how it is with cars sometimes.'"

Hannah lifted her eyebrows. "I just said that."

"Oh."

She laughed. "Are you kidding me? You like *The Love Bug*?"

"One of the best movies ever made." Evan grinned. "But I thought I was the only one who'd memorized the dialogue."

"I only know some of it." Hannah's eyes still twinkled. "First saw it at the old Vitaphone movie theater in downtown Rainsville. I thought it was silly and juvenile at the time, but it grew on me. Soon it became one of my favorites."

"Mine too. I had a thing for those old racing movies when I was a kid. *Around the World in Eighty Days, Cannonball Run, Gumball Rally.* I liked to think I'd go on a race like that one day."

She smiled, but it was tinged with sadness—as if she were picturing him as a little boy in a hospital room, dreaming grandiose dreams.

Once upon a time, he had been. But now the biggest dream of

all, the one he'd never imagined believing in, was standing right in front of him.

He chucked her beneath the chin. "I like you a lot, Lockhart."

"*Du bist mein Weltwunder*, Heartbreaker." Hannah turned to climb into the van, then glanced back over her shoulder at him. "Look it up."

Evan knew enough German to understand that phrase. *You are my wonder of the world.*

His heart skipped a hundred beats.

CHAPTER 22

*H*annah shaded her eyes against the glare of the setting sun, glad for the hundredth time that they'd brought plenty of water. The empty road stretched out to either side, not a single car passing.

"Maybe we should walk back to that gas station," she suggested. "It can't be far."

"At least ten miles, if not more." Evan squinted at the grimy innards of the van engine. "Any cell service yet?"

Hannah checked her phone and shook her head. To preserve what little battery power she had left, she turned it off and tossed it back onto the passenger seat.

"Someone will be by soon," she said, though two hours had passed without a single vehicle. This wasn't exactly a well-traveled road.

She climbed into the back of the van and grabbed another bottle of water. She took a drink and brought it out to Evan.

Everything inside her froze. He was slouched against the side of the van, one arm around the rearview mirror, and his left hand on his chest.

"Evan?" Hannah hurried forward.

He jerked at the sound of her voice and pulled himself upright. "Nothing. Just a twinge."

A *twinge*? In his heart?

Her hands shook as she opened the water bottle. "Here. You'd better get back inside and sit down. Nothing we can do about the engine anyway."

The fact that he didn't protest told her more than she needed to know. Evan hauled himself back into the driver's seat and took a drink of water. The color had drained from his skin, leaving him pale beneath his tan.

Hannah clenched her jaw against a surge of pure fear. She grabbed a T-shirt from her travel bag and wet it with precious water before climbing back into the passenger seat. She handed the damp shirt to Evan. He ran it over his face, his gaze on the bleak road in front of them.

"Y-you need to get to a hospital," Hannah stammered.

He gave a short shake of his head. "I'll be okay."

She looked out the side window, blinking back tears of rising anger.

What the fuck had they been thinking, venturing out into the desert when Evan had issues with his heart? How could he have put himself at risk like that? How could she have let him?

Evan's hand clamped around her wrist suddenly, the grip manacle-tight despite his weakness. She faced him, startling at the frustration rising hot in his blue eyes, the lines of tension bracketing his mouth.

"Don't," he gritted out, his breathing fast. "Don't you even *think* we shouldn't have done this. I've lived with this condition for thirty-three fucking years of my life. I know what I can and can't do. I know my limitations, though God knows I've fought against them every day. And I hate that Luke was right about it not being safe for me to travel to remote parts of the world. But there is *nothing* dangerous about driving east of LA to visit the damned desert. This is an accident, a case of bad fucking timing.

It is not a stupid thing to have done. In fact, this trip has been the best thing I've done in years. I'd do it again in a heartbeat."

Hannah managed a faint smile, even though a tear slipped down her cheek. She tugged her wrist from his grip and took his hand in hers, lacing their fingers together.

"I'll go," she said. "I'll head back to the gas station, and if someone comes by or if I get there first, at least we'll both be able to find the other person."

Evan shook his head. "You're not walking all the way alone. We're waiting. Someone will come by."

"But it will double our chances of getting help."

"No. It'll be dark soon."

Hannah smothered her protest, torn between wanting to stay with him and needing to get help. But the last thing Evan needed was for them to get into an argument. She released his hand and climbed into the back of the van, pulling their sleeping bags out and spreading them on the floor.

"Come back here," she said.

He followed her, lowering himself to sit. Hannah grabbed her phone and checked it again, as if somehow a signal would miraculously appear. Nothing.

Evan rested against the side of the van, his hand still on his chest. Leaving the back doors open for air, Hannah moved to sit beside him. She nudged the water bottle toward him, and he drank.

"Was it because of the fight?" Guilt rose thick and hot in her throat.

He shook his head. "It's…it's nothing new. Trust me."

"What do you need me to do?" Hannah asked.

He regarded her, the light in his eyes faded but still there. "Just be Hannah."

She tried to smile. "I can do that."

"That's all I need."

She settled beside him, resting her hand on his thigh. Her own heart beat too fast, the thumping sound echoing in her head. She wished she could somehow give part of it to Evan, to make his heart whole again.

The light began to fade. She tucked her body against his and looked into the gloaming.

The road remained deserted.

CHAPTER 23

*H*is breathing became labored, raspy. With every breath Evan took, Hannah's fear increased by increments, as if she were climbing the hill of a roller coaster that was about to plunge downward. She made him take sips of water and wiped his face with the T-shirt, but other than that there was nothing she could think of to do.

Her cell phone died after a few hours. The desert fell cold and silent around them. She didn't leave the van, not wanting to see the endless fields of stars, the moonlight that hadn't led anyone their way.

Finally they both lay down on the sleeping bags, Hannah pillowed against Evan's side as if the body contact would somehow help him. He folded one arm around her, guiding her head to his chest. His heartbeat thumped against her ear, the rhythmic sound reassuring despite his shallow breaths.

"Tell me more of the things you like." He stroked his hand slowly down her back.

"A little café in Stockholm called Sturekatten," Hannah said. "Mosaics. Grappa. Walking all the way up a mountainside cliff to a Tibetan temple. Local grocery stores. Postcards. Indian women's saris. Teapots. Spices. Welsh lovespoons."

"And when you leave here," Evan said, letting his fingers linger on her tattoo, "where are you going?"

Hannah closed her eyes, suddenly unsure if she could stand the idea of leaving any more than she could the idea of staying.

"I'd like to see the region of Umbria in Italy. Visit the San Francesco basilica in Assisi. Maybe I'll make my way there."

You could come with me.

The words hovered on the tip of her tongue, held back by the uncertainty of what the rest of the night would bring. But deep inside, Hannah knew the truth from which that wish had bloomed.

She wanted Evan to come with her. For all her solo traveling, for all her pride in being alone, she could now picture traveling the world with Evan. She could see herself taking him to her favorite places, exploring new ones, comparing notes about European cities. She could see them *together.*

"What else do you like?" she whispered.

"You. *Sahnehäubchen.*"

They fell silent. A low hum seemed to reverberate around them, emanating from the stars and the inky blackness of the desert. It took Hannah a second to realize that the hum was growing louder.

And it wasn't a hum…it was an increasing rumble…an engine.

"Evan!" Her heart jumped up into her throat as she hurried to yank on her shoes. "I think a car is coming."

He started to pull himself upright, but Hannah was already leaping out of the van and peering down the road. Sure enough, two bright headlights appeared through the dark.

"A truck!" Hannah called, excitement and relief flooding her like a tidal wave.

She ran along the side of the road, waving her arms as a small truck crested the hill and headed directly toward them.

Evan shouted behind her. She almost flung herself in front of the truck in the desperate attempt to get the driver to stop. Thankfully, she didn't need to risk life and limb, as the headlights caught her in their beam and the driver pulled off the road.

Hannah sprinted toward the truck. The door opened, and a middle-aged man wearing a baseball cap descended, his face shadowed and wary.

"You got some trouble, miss?" he asked.

"Yes." Hannah gasped. "I'm...our van broke down, and my... my boyfriend is sick. We couldn't get any cell service. Can you drive us somewhere or call an ambulance?"

"Take a while for an ambulance to get to you out here," he said, clambering back into the truck and reaching for the CB radio. "But I'll call for one to meet us back at the gas station. Can your boyfriend get into my truck?"

Hannah raced back to the van. The driver introduced himself as Charlie and helped transfer their belongings to the back of his truck. Once they'd gotten everything they needed, they sat in the front seat beside Charlie.

Hannah's insides churned with a combination of fear and relief. They returned to the gas station. Another short wait for the ambulance ensued, and she took the opportunity to start recharging their cell phones.

Evan barely spoke at all now—he sat in a chair by the counter, his skin tinged with gray and his blue eyes so dull it looked as if a light switch inside him had been turned off.

The wailing of the siren was the sweetest sound Hannah had ever heard. Tears of relief spilled down her face when the medics hurried out to tend to Evan.

Within seconds, they were checking his blood pressure, shining a penlight into his eyes, asking him questions, giving him oxygen. They got him into the ambulance and offered Hannah the front passenger seat for the trip to the hospital.

The lights of civilization appeared in the distance. The ambulance drove up to the emergency room entrance of a modest, one-story hospital on the outskirts of a town.

As they rushed to get Evan inside, he reached out and grabbed Hannah's hand. Her insides went cold at the sight of him—so pale his skin was white, his eyes shot through with blood.

"Don't tell my father," he said hoarsely.

Hannah stared at him. "You can't be serious."

"Don't tell him." His grip tightened on her wrist. "Not yet."

Not knowing what else to do, but needing him to get inside where medical care waited, Hannah nodded.

Evan released her. The medics wheeled him into the hospital.

"Miss, you can fill out the paperwork over there," one of them called over his shoulder, pointing to the reception desk.

Hannah stood outside, gulping in a rush of night air. A tremble rocketed through her, and then she started shaking so hard her teeth rattled. She pulled in a few deep breaths and walked to the desk, where a weary-looking receptionist pushed a clipboard toward her.

"Are you the next of kin?" she asked.

Hannah shook her head mutely.

"Fill those out, please. We'll verify the info with the patient."

Hannah sank into a hard plastic chair and stared at the paperwork through blurred vision. Name—Evan Stone. Middle name —no idea. Address—no idea. On a beach in Indigo Bay. Date of birth—no idea. Insurance—no idea.

She rested the clipboard on her knees and dragged her hands over her face.

He likes the color navy blue.

When he smiles, his eyes crinkle at the corners.

His stubble feels like fine-grained sandpaper against my skin.

He knows the history of cream puffs.

Cherry-flavored Sparkle Pops are his favorite.

Why was it the most important things you could know about a person were irrelevant in a situation like this? A sudden yearning rose in Hannah, so acute her chest ached. She pulled out her cell phone and dialed Polly's number.

"Hannah?" Her sister's voice sounded thick with sleep.

"I'm sorry. I woke you up."

"It's okay. Hold on." There was a shuffling noise in the background. "What's going on?"

"I...I'm at the hospital."

"What? Are you all right?"

Hannah wasn't certain she was, but she said, "Yes. I'm fine. It's...it's Evan."

"Evan? Oh my God. What happened?"

The shock in Polly's voice brought a fresh sting of tears to Hannah's eyes. "We're east of Los Angeles. We ended up heading into the desert. He started having chest pains, and we had to call an ambulance to take him to the hospital. They just took him into the emergency room."

"Is he all right? What did they say?"

"I don't know yet. I'm in the waiting area." Hannah stood and paced to the doors through which Evan had disappeared. "I don't even know how much they'll tell me since I'm not next of kin. Is Luke there?"

"No, he went out for a run. Did you call their father?"

"Evan asked me not to," Hannah said.

"Why on earth would he ask such a thing?"

"I don't know. I don't have his father's contact information anyway."

"Well, I'll call him then."

"No!" The word flew out of Hannah before she could stop it. "Can you just give me his father's phone number? I'll take care of it."

"Hold on." There was a pause before Polly recited the number.

Hannah scribbled it on the edge of the registration form, even though she knew she couldn't break her promise to Evan. He hadn't, however, said anything about not telling Luke.

"Will you tell Luke?" she asked her sister.

"I'm texting him right now, telling him to call me," Polly said. "But how are *you*? Are you all right?"

For a second, Hannah couldn't respond. It was just like Polly to ask about her. Not for the first time, she wished she had Polly's all-encompassing thoughtfulness about people.

"I'm okay," she finally said. "Scared. I had to tell someone."

"I'm glad you called me. I'll call you right back after I talk to Luke."

"No, I'll be all right. I'll let you know when I hear something."

"Okay. I have my cell right with me."

Hannah ended the call and set the clipboard aside. She waited for what seemed like hours—leafing through magazines, checking her phone, pacing back and forth from the emergency room doors. Finally they opened, and a gray-haired man with glasses and stooped shoulders emerged to scan the waiting room.

"You're with Evan Stone?" he asked.

Hannah nodded, her nerves jumping to alert. "Is he all right?"

"He's stable," the doctor said. "But his heart arrhythmia is pretty severe. I have a call in to his cardiologist."

Heart arrhythmia. Hannah had no idea what that was, and she wasn't at all certain she wanted to know.

"Can I see him, please?" she asked.

The doctor nodded, gesturing for her to follow him down a narrow corridor. They stopped at a small room where a curtain was half pulled around a bed.

Hannah fought an urge to flee, hating the sight of her beautiful, strong Evan lying in a sterile hospital bed. An oxygen cannula crossed his face, and he was hooked up to a heart monitor that beeped at regular intervals. A nurse stood on the other side of the bed, reading the sheet of paper feeding from the machine.

His eyelashes fluttered. Though still dull, his blue eyes fixed on her with the precision of a laser. Her heart bumped, her veins filling with a strength that anchored her to his side.

Of course she wouldn't *flee*. She would never leave him.

She stepped closer and rested her hand over his, giving him a tentative smile. "Anything for attention, huh?"

A responding smile tugged at his mouth. "Sorry."

"No. I'm just glad we got you here."

"When we hear from your cardiologist, we can make arrangements to get you back to the Bay Area," the doctor said. "I suspect he'll want to do the surgery as soon as possible."

Renewed fear clawed up Hannah's chest. She tightened her fingers on Evan's hand.

"Surgery?" she repeated.

Evan closed his eyes, fatigue washing over him like a shadow.

"He should rest now," the nurse said.

"Can I please stay with him?"

"Just for a few minutes."

After the doctor and nurse had left, Hannah dragged a chair up to Evan's side. She leaned in to brush her lips across his rough cheek.

"I tried to fill out the registration form, but I realized I didn't know any of the answers. Like your middle name."

"Matthew."

"And your address."

"1500 Turtle Drive."

"And your birthday."

"May twelfth."

Hannah swallowed. "And what surgery is the doctor talking about?"

"I'm having a mole removed."

"Evan."

He opened his eyes, resignation reflecting in their blue depths. "They need to replace a valve that pumps blood to my heart."

A chill raced over Hannah's skin. "The doctor can already tell you need surgery?"

"No. I knew a few weeks ago."

Hannah blinked. The chill turned into outright cold. She released Evan's hand and sat back.

"A few weeks?" she said. "You knew a few weeks ago that you need valve replacement surgery?"

"No." He held up a hand, as if he were trying to stop her from jumping to conclusions. "I mean, yes. I knew, but I didn't know I'd need it so soon."

"What are you talking about?" Confusion washed over her. "You agreed to go on this trip with me knowing you needed surgery. Didn't you think something might go wrong?"

His mouth tightened. "If I spent my life not going places because I was worried something would go wrong, I'd never leave the fucking house."

"But you thought it was okay not to tell me about it?" All her worry and terror tumbled out in a rush of hurt. "You thought it was okay to go on a trip that you knew wasn't safe for you because you need *heart surgery*? How could you put either of us in that kind of position?"

"How could I not?" Evan pushed himself up on the bed, his eyes flashing with blue fire.

The heart monitor beeped louder. Hannah put her hand out to stop him from flying out of the bed.

"Evan—"

"I thought I was done, okay?" he snapped. "I thought I was fucking done with surgeries, that maybe I could live a normal adult life without thinking about my pathetic heart. And though I've tried my damnedest not to let it stop me from doing what I want, the fact is there's always been stuff I just can't fucking do. And when *you* showed up with all your stories of travel and adventure, and telling me you're leaving as soon as you can, I knew it was my chance."

"Your chance for what?"

"To have an adventure of my own before I'd have to be the sick one again," Evan said. "An adventure with you."

Tears flooded Hannah's eyes, but she couldn't bring herself to move closer to him.

"You still should have told me."

"Would you have come with me, if I had?"

Hannah didn't respond.

Evan gave a grim nod. "That's why I didn't."

"And because you knew I'd leave again, right?" Hannah wiped her eyes with the corner of her T-shirt, trying to push down the bubble of pain rising and expanding in her chest. "We could hit the road together, have some fun, and then when you got back to your real life with its real problems, you wouldn't have to share any of that with me. Because I'd just leave anyway."

His mouth compressed. "You never gave me a reason to think you'd do anything else."

Hannah averted her gaze. She'd never given herself a reason to think that either. After all, leaving was what she did best.

Evan's phone buzzed on the nightstand. He picked it up. A pulse throbbed in his temple.

"You called my father," he said.

A pit opened up inside Hannah, dark and hollow. "I called Polly. I was scared and upset, and I needed to talk to someone. Don't you dare get mad at me for that."

"I'm not mad. But she must have told Luke."

"Of course she did. I asked her to, but she would have even if I hadn't. You're his brother. I'd be surprised if he didn't catch the next flight out here."

"He will." Rather than seem relieved that his brother was on the way, a cloud of defeat descended over Evan. He put the phone to his ear. "Dad. Yeah, I'm fine. I'll explain later, okay? No, you don't have to…Dad, it's not…I don't want a—"

He cursed under his breath and tossed the phone back on the nightstand. Tension bunched his shoulder muscles.

"Did Luke tell your father?" Hannah asked.

"The phone tree has been activated."

She should be relieved. She was no longer alone in trying to figure out what to do next. His family, the people who loved him, cared about him, and knew how to fill out a hospital registration form with all of his correct information, had been notified. They would galvanize into action, using their money and resources to help him in any way they could. They would take over and handle it all.

And she would step aside. Away from him.

"You're lucky they're all there for you." She swallowed past the lump in her throat. "One phone call, and half a dozen people flock to your side."

Evan shook his head, his expression unreadable. "That's exactly the problem."

"Why is it a problem?"

"I'm just tired of being the sick one."

"But they still need to know you're in the hospital. What if… what if something really bad happened and they weren't here for you when they would *want* to be?"

Evan dragged a hand through his hair, his face creasing with frustration. "It's not that simple. There's nothing they can do, and I know they want to."

"They can be here for you, Evan. So you're not—"

Alone.

Tears slipped down Hannah's cheeks. Pain, the cracking kind that felt as if it were breaking her in two, split through her chest.

"They want to be here for you," she continued, wiping her eyes again. "The way I *wasn't* for my mother and sister."

"Hannah…"

Evan pushed the covers aside as if he wanted to get to her. The heart monitor started beeping in a rapid-fire rhythm. Hannah's breath stuck in her chest.

"Fuck," Evan muttered.

The door flew open. A nurse came in, her gaze going accus-
ingly to Hannah. "Everything all right in here?"

"Fine." Hannah backed toward the door. "Everything's fine."

"You need to be lying down, Evan." The nurse bustled forward
to check the monitor, indicating sharply for him to get back into
bed. "You are not to become overwrought."

"I'm not, goddammit." He started to get to his feet.

The nurse flashed Hannah another glare.

She turned and fled.

CHAPTER 24

*A*fter hearing from Polly that Evan's family had arrived at the hospital, and that Polly and Luke were on their way back to Indigo Bay, Hannah set herself to the task of dealing with the broken-down Wild Child van.

She researched several local mechanics and made arrangements for one of them to pick her up at a motel the following morning and take her out to the van. It would cost a fortune, but hopefully Polly's insurance would cover some of the cost.

The mechanic towed the van back to the shop, where they took care of the repairs swiftly and expensively. She put the charges on her emergency credit card and returned to the hospital. She'd have to drive the van back to the Bay Area, but she couldn't leave without seeing Evan.

Unfamiliar male voices drifted from his room. Hannah knocked on the half-open door and pushed it open to peer inside. His brother Adam and a tall, handsome man with steel-colored hair stood near the window. The bed was empty.

Hannah's heart stuttered. She took a step back just as both men looked at her.

"Hannah." Adam strode toward her, his forehead creasing.

"Where's...where's Evan?"

"He's with the doctor. They're doing some last-minute testing before the flight."

"What flight?"

"There's a medical plane waiting for him at the airport." The older man approached and extended his hand. "I'm Warren Stone, Evan's father. We're hoping to have him back in Indigo Bay within a couple of hours. I'm grateful for all you did for him."

Hannah swallowed past the tightness in her throat. "I didn't do anything. Is he going to be okay?"

Adam and Warren exchanged glances.

"We'll know more when his cardiologist sees him," Adam said. "You're welcome to come on the flight with us."

"I...I have to take care of my sister's van."

"We can help you with that." Warren pulled out his phone. "Where is it?"

Hannah shook her head, not wanting Evan's family to worry about her when Evan's situation was so urgent.

"I'm taking care of it." She moved back toward the door. "Can you please tell Evan I'll call him soon? I should be back in Rainsville by mid-afternoon."

Before either man could respond, she turned and hurried back down the corridor to the parking lot exit. She got back into the van and ruthlessly pushed all thoughts of Evan out of her mind as she started driving. His family could do so much more for him than she ever could.

She merged onto Interstate 5 and tried to keep her mind off Evan by thinking of her blog—though not a single love tradition in the world could make any of this better. She drove straight through, snacking on granola bars and bottled water, stopping only to refuel the van.

She exchanged several texts with Evan, who told her he was back in Indigo Bay and going into a meeting with his cardiologist. The texts stopped after the first few hours. New messages came in from Polly that she and Luke had arrived in San Fran-cisco—the speed of their return evidence of Luke's take-control efficiency.

Hannah drove into Rainsville close to three in the afternoon. The sun was a golden glow washing over the low rolling hills of the valley. She left her belongings in Polly's apartment before heading down to Wild Child.

The instant she stepped into the bakery, she knew something had changed. The air was lighter, lit with a gentle energy like flowers blooming. Polly stood behind the counter, talking to Ramona.

For an instant, Hannah could only stare at her sister. Polly's hair was cut into a shoulder-length tumble of soft curls, she had a pale application of makeup that enhanced her features, and she wore a colorful, wraparound skirt and snug-fitting top that flat-tered her curvy figure. She looked both the same and somehow entirely different.

"Hannah!" Polly smiled, opening her arms as she crossed the room.

As her sister enclosed her in an embrace, Hannah's throat constricted.

"Hey, Polliwog. You look great."

"So do you." Polly pulled back and ran her gaze assessingly over her.

"How was your trip?"

"We were so anxious to get here that it seemed to take forev-er," Polly said. "But we managed to get a flight out shortly after I talked to you. I'm so glad we made it back before Evan goes in."

Hannah's vision darkened at the edges. "Goes in where?"

"For his heart surgery." A crease appeared between Polly's eyebrows the instant before shock registered in her expression. "You didn't know?"

"I...I knew he needed surgery but I didn't know it would happen so soon."

"Luke said Evan's cardiologist wanted to get it done right away, after the arrhythmia," Polly explained.

Hannah shook her head, as if to deny the truth. She didn't have to know much about medical procedures to understand that open heart surgery was both risky and frightening. Sometimes the surgeon even had to stop the patient's heart.

Hot tears stung her eyes. Her jaw tightened.

"It's scheduled for nine tomorrow morning." Polly reached under the counter to pick up her purse. "Have you seen him yet?"

"No."

"Come on." Polly peered into the kitchen and called to Ramona that they needed to leave for a couple of hours. "He's at the cardiac care center in Indigo Bay. Let's head over there now."

Grateful to her sister for taking charge, Hannah followed Polly out to a sleek, black Lexus. Rush-hour traffic hadn't started yet, and they made it into Indigo Bay in under forty minutes and parked in front of the cardiac care center. Polly guided Hannah toward the elevators and up to the twelfth floor.

Hannah's nerves tightened to the breaking point as they walked down the corridor to Evan's room. Voices drifted from the half-open door.

"You have to stay at your father's during recovery," Julia Bennett was saying. "Either that or I'm hiring a full-time nurse."

"Stay at my place," Luke Stone's deep voice carried into the corridor. "Polly and I will be there, but you know there's plenty of room."

"You and Polly need to go back to Paris," Evan said.

His voice flooded Hannah with light. She started into the room when Luke's next remark stopped her in her tracks.

"So you can keep an eye on Hannah for a few more weeks, huh?" he asked.

Cold trickled down Hannah's spine.

"I'm quite certain he was doing more than just babysitting her," Julia remarked, her voice dryly amused.

"Hope she thought he was worth fifty K," another man said.

"Did your date think you were worth almost half that?" The older man's comment prompted scattered laughter.

Polly frowned, taking hold of Hannah's arm before rapping sharply on the door and stepping inside. Hannah followed, taking in the people in the room—Warren, Luke, Adam, and Tyler Stone, and the matriarch Julia Bennett. She couldn't bring herself to look at Evan.

"Hannah." Luke strode across the room to stop in front of her.

With his sharp, corporate-power demeanor, Hannah had always found the eldest Stone brother to be more than a little intimidating. But he looked more approachable now in a wrinkled T-shirt and jeans, with lines of concern etching his handsome features.

"Thanks for calling Polly and letting her know," he said, his voice low. "We appreciate it."

She nodded. If she spoke, her voice would break. After everyone else greeted her and gave her thanks that she didn't deserve, Hannah gathered her courage and turned to Evan. Her whole body tightened in defense against the sight of him in the hospital bed, the knowledge of his upcoming surgery hanging like a pall in the air.

She approached him warily, forcing herself not to start shaking as she let her gaze roam over him. His skin had more color than it had yesterday, but his face was drawn, his eyes lined with dark circles. He looked weaker, diminished, as if his defective heart had gotten the better of him.

"Hey, Heartbreaker." She brushed her fingers against his arm, somewhat comforted by the feel of his strong, hair-roughened forearm. "How do you feel?"

"All right." He glanced at his brother Adam, and a wordless communication passed between them.

"Hey, let's leave them alone for a while." Adam gestured everyone else toward the door. "We can get a coffee at the café."

There was a rustle and murmur of conversation, but the others filed out of the room. Polly paused beside Hannah and rested a hand on her arm. Hannah gave her sister a nod of assurance that she was okay. Polly squeezed her arm and left, closing the door.

Silence fell. Hannah kept her hand over Evan's. His skin was as warm as it had always been.

"I hear they decided you need the surgery right away," she said.

He nodded. "Should take a few hours."

"Were you going to call and tell me?"

He stared at the opposite wall. A muscle ticked in his jaw. "I didn't want you to worry."

"Well, maybe I *want* to worry," Hannah said. "Maybe I want to be here for you. I know we agreed we were just having fun, but that doesn't mean I don't care about you...a lot. Even if we weren't involved, you're almost Polly's brother-in-law. That makes you..."

Family.

Longing flooded her veins. Was it possible that after a decade of escaping family and home out of fear of getting hurt, she could now actually find comfort in the idea?

Evan shook his head. "You didn't sign up for this."

"It's not a damned contract, Evan. I *want* to be here."

Silence descended between them. Hannah slipped her hand away from his arm. A chill shivered over her skin.

"Or maybe there was a contract between you and Luke." She swallowed, hurt rising into her chest. "Because you were just babysitting me, right?"

His mouth tightened. "That's not what Julia meant."

"That's what it sounded like." She held up a hand when he opened his mouth to protest. "Never mind. I get it. I was a flight risk."

I still am.

"He was going to come back, that was all." Evan dragged a hand down his face. "I couldn't let him. So I told him I'd make sure you stayed in town. That was part of the reason I asked you to Napa and offered to help with your blog content. I told you that. But *you* were the main reason."

"You didn't tell me you'd promised Luke you'd keep an eye on me."

"Hannah." Evan sighed, his expression flashing with frustration. "I'd had my damned *eye on you* since the day I met you at Wild Child. So when my big brother told me he thought you were about to bail because of whatever you told Polly, it was my golden opportunity. How could I not offer to keep you in town, especially since it gave me an excuse to be near you?"

Hannah's hurt softened a little, but not by much. She'd put herself in the position of being *babysat* because she'd been chomping at the bit to get out of Rainsville and she'd hinted to Polly that she wanted to leave *right now*.

Considering the number of times she'd bailed over the years, it was no wonder Polly had gotten nervous. Then she'd told Luke, and Luke had flown into action because that was what the CEO did—

Hannah stepped away from the bed and stared out the window at the rooftops of Indigo Bay. No one had believed her capable of staying. Not even her.

"Hey."

She turned. Evan was watching her, his eyes as blue as ever, the light in them undimmed by any weakness of his body.

"Come here, Lockhart."

She approached him again. He shifted to the side, making a place for her. Even as she hesitated, she was unable to resist the invitation. She lay beside him, closing her eyes as his arm went around her, pulling her closer.

The antiseptic smell of the hospital didn't dilute the delicious, musky male scent of him. Cedar and sage. She rested her hand on his chest. His heart thumped against her palm, still beating with a heavy, solid rhythm that belied all talk of defects and valve replacements.

Was this love? This wild, complex yearning for another person? The sharp fear of losing him mixed with the over-whelming joy of being with him right now, his body warm and solid against hers and his breath stirring her hair?

Was true love this tangle of emotions, this breathtaking need, the feeling that she would give anything to be with Evan rather than alone? Was it knowing in some deep-seated part of her being that she belonged to him, and only him?

Yes, whispered a little voice in Hannah's heart.

Every experience in her life—getting lost in the narrow streets of Trastevere, navigating a crowded Calcutta market, squeezed into an overcrowded bus on the hills of Argentina—all of her walking, hiking, train trips, flights, *everything* had been leading her back to Rainsville so she could stay long enough to find Evan.

But she had no idea what would happen next. She knew how to travel without a plan. She didn't know how to love without one.

"When are you leaving?" Evan asked.

Hannah spread her palm over his chest. What would she do if he asked her to stay?

"I…I promised Polly I'd stay until she comes back for good."

"She told me she's going to talk to Ramona about taking over for the next two months. Said you've done your time."

Hannah's spine tensed. She lifted her head to look at him. "I didn't think of it like that. At least, not after I met you. I've had an incredible time."

A smile tugged at his mouth. "So have I."

She shifted to press her face against the side of his warm neck. "I hate that you have to go through this."

"I'm in good hands. The surgeon, the cardiologist...I'm lucky to have them."

She slid her hand down his chest, letting her fingers trace the ridge of his scar. Though she was scared to know the details, she had discovered over the past few weeks that she wanted to know everything about Evan. She would not cringe from any part of him. She'd done that when her mother had fallen ill, and as much as she'd tried to justify her absence, the guilt would never go away.

"Do they have to stop your heart?" she asked.

"Yes." He threaded his hand through her hair. "Aw, Lockhart... don't do that."

She choked back a sob, even as tears fell in rivers down her cheeks.

"I got through it when I was eight," Evan said. "I'll get through it again."

Hannah wiped her face with the back of her hand. "I'll be waiting for you when it's over. Tell me more of the things you like."

"The smell of your hair." His deep voice rumbled through his chest. "Antique maps. Waterfalls. Jigsaw puzzles. Eating cereal for dinner. Your gorgeous ass. A new pen. When a little kid does a happy dance. Full moons. The way you scrunch up your nose when you're annoyed. Driftwood. A good stretch. Making love to you."

"Evan," Hannah whispered. "I love you."

His hand stilled on her hair. His heart beat faster.

"Have to check your vital stats, Mr. Stone." A nurse's cheerful voice broke through the tension-thick air.

Hannah pulled herself reluctantly away from him, the declaration having lifted a weight from her shoulders. She didn't expect to hear the words in return. She didn't even know if she wanted to, not with all the complications the tangle of their two confessions would bring.

But if nothing else, she would not let Evan go into surgery without knowing of her love for him.

The nurse approached the bed and attached the cuff to his arm. Voices filtered into her ears as Warren, Julia, Luke, and Adam came back into the room, followed by a tall, stern-looking man in a white coat who spoke with the authoritative voice of the doctor. Evan looked toward Hannah. Their gazes met with tangible force.

Raw tenderness passed between them. Everything inside her ached with the urge to grab him, haul him from the horrible hospital bed, and run away. She wanted him to see the majestic Incan ruins of Peru. She wanted to dance with him at Catalan festivals and walk with him in the wild, open landscape of the Serengeti. She wanted to curl up against him at his ramshackle beach house and watch TV.

She stepped toward the door. She tore her gaze from Evan, heard the doctor saying something about the surgery, risks, complications.

Fear slithered black and cold into the pit of her stomach. An image formed like a horror movie in her mind—Evan lying unconscious on an operating table with his chest split open. Attached to machines keeping him alive. A surgeon with bloody gloves cutting into him.

His heart—his beautiful, full, whole heart—stopping.

She wiped away her tears and forced herself to leave the room. She wanted to make him healthy again, to give him her heart.

But she already had.

CHAPTER 25

*T*he tests, doctor visits, paperwork, prepping—all of it was both foreign and vaguely familiar. He'd been through it all before, but so long ago that his memories had a fuzzy quality, as if it had happened in a dream.

His family was always near. Hovering around the room, asking questions, consulting with the doctors and nurses, answering a constant stream of calls and emails from friends and Sugar Rush employees.

"It wasn't because of the work," Evan told Luke, who was at his side all the time.

"I know." Creases lined Luke's forehead. "Once you're out of here, we'll talk about what you want to do at Sugar Rush. It's about time I got the hell out of your way."

"Are you going back to Paris soon?"

His brother shrugged. "I'll handle the Singa Corporation stuff first."

"What about Polly?"

"Once she gets things straightened out at the bakery, she'll go back to finish her courses. One of the chefs told her she could delay the internship, so she can go back next year for a few months, if she wants to. Gives her the chance to come back to Wild Child and implement everything she's learned."

Evan took his tablet from the bedside table and pulled up the documents he'd written about the Sugar Rush cocoa bean project. He handed the tablet to his brother.

Luke scanned the screen. "What is it?"

"An idea. Adam can tell you more. Read it soon."

"I will."

Evan pushed himself up on the pillows. It was getting harder to breathe. His lungs were tight. He hated his increasing weakness, his inability to do something to make himself whole.

"Look, if Hannah…" He glanced to where his father and Aunt Julia stood by the windows, speaking in hushed voices. He lowered his own voice as he turned back to Luke. "If she comes to the hospital after the surgery, don't let her in the room."

His brother frowned. "You don't want to see her?"

Evan almost laughed. Christ, yes, he wanted to see his girl. He could only imagine emerging from the deep fog of anesthesia— disoriented, in pain—and seeing *her*. If anything would make him not only realize he was still alive but revel in the glory of *being* alive, it was the sight of Hannah Lockhart.

But he knew the reality. In ICU he'd be on a ventilator with a breathing tube stuck down his throat. He'd be monitored for clots and infections. He'd have a new bloody incision right down his chest. Meds. Catheter. IV. Drain holes. Tests. Numbness. Pain.

"I don't want her to see me," he said. "Not like that."

Luke was silent before he squeezed Evan's shoulder. "Yeah, okay. She won't see you until you want her to."

Evan had already asked her not to come before the surgery —*way too much going on* had been his texted explanation, but in truth he was scared that seeing her would intensify his terror of all he could lose. That was just one of the reasons he hadn't been able to return her confession of love.

His phone buzzed the morning of his surgery. Her voice was a stream of light in his ear and straight to his heart.

"I love you," she said. "Know that."

"I do."

He thought of nothing else until the anesthesia dragged him under.

CHAPTER 26

"Wow." Polly spoke around a mouthful of cookie, her eyes wide. "These are really good."

Hannah took another bite of her chocolate-bacon cookie. As desserts went, it wasn't bad, though she suspected Evan's cardiologist wouldn't agree.

She put the plate of cookies by the cash register alongside the Free Sample sign. So far, she'd invented half-a-dozen pastries that were more spicy, savory, or salty than they were sweet, and all of them had been well-received by Wild Child's regulars.

Hannah would never be as happy at the bakery as Polly and their mother were, but she took pride in being able to finally, after so many years, make a small contribution to the family business.

Even better, Polly had genuinely liked the lemon-thyme cookies, the chili-chocolate truffles, and the rhubarb-lavender hand pies Hannah had made.

"They'll complement the sweeter stuff beautifully," she'd said.

Her sister's praise eased Hannah's despair over Evan, which she hadn't been able to talk to Polly about—although her sister clearly sensed it.

Instead of waiting through Evan's surgery with Luke and the rest of the Stones at the hospital, Polly had come to open Wild Child with Hannah. They'd spent the morning baking and setting out pastries, helping customers, serving coffee, and working with a compatibility that Hannah had never experienced before.

They both kept looking at the clock. Polly checked her phone every five minutes for messages from Luke, and then relayed the news to Hannah. *He's talking to the surgeon. He's getting prepped. They just took him in.*

Then there was nothing to do but wait, which they did in a flurry of cleaning, extra baking, and unnecessarily rearranging the baskets and the tables. Hannah counted the minutes, trying not to imagine Evan lying unconscious on the operating table. Instead she focused on *him*—the way the sunlight threaded his dark hair, the brilliant flash of his smile, the clear warmth of his blue eyes. How she loved everything about him.

Could she be happy and fulfilled living in Rainsville and working at the bakery with her sister? If she told Evan she was staying in Rainsville for herself, for Polly, for the bakery, for *them*, maybe they could make it work.

"Try not to worry, dear." Miss Purdy patted Hannah's hand as she brought a fresh plate of cookies to her and Mr. Becker's table. "My late husband had heart surgery, and he...well, obviously he's not quite fine now, but he was hale and *hearty* for several years afterward."

"And the techniques they use today are so much more advanced." Mr. Becker nodded sagely. "He'll be right as rain in no time."

"Not to mention he's fit as a fiddle," Mia remarked, lifting an eyebrow. "Heart issues aside, Evan is in amazing shape. Anyone that strong has to have a good prognosis. Right, Gavin?"

Gavin Knight barely glanced up from his laptop, but said, "Statistically, the mortality rate for surgery at the cardiac center is quite low."

"How do you know that?" Mia asked.

He slanted her a glance. "I know things."

"I'll bet you do," she murmured.

Gavin returned his attention to his laptop. Mia blew out her breath in a sigh, flipping her long blond hair over her shoulder.

Hannah exchanged amused looks with Polly as she went back behind the counter.

"You've really kept this place running smoothly," Polly said. "I appreciate it so much. It's just the way Mom wanted it, only better."

"I like it here, too." Only after she spoke did Hannah realize the truth of her words.

In all the weeks she'd been here, she hadn't even noticed that she'd started to *fit* at Wild Child. She knew all the regular customers and what they liked, she'd made friends, she understood the rhythms of the bakery. She cared about both the people and the pastries and cakes they offered. She even knew which dessert was the best.

It was almost as surprising a revelation as realizing she loved Evan.

Almost.

"I'm glad you've been enjoying Paris," she told her sister as they refilled cookie baskets. "You deserved to have an adventure."

"It's been amazing," Polly said. "And living in Paris with Luke has been a dream. But honestly, I'll be ready to come back when it's over. It's been such a whirlwind...meeting Luke, the success of the Declairs, starting the pastry-making course, all the excitement and learning...I'm looking forward to coming back home and just settling into a normal life, you know? Except it'll be a different normal life because I'll be with Luke."

"Any idea when you're going to get married?"

"Not yet. I'm just enjoying being engaged right now. I want to work on expanding the bakery and trying new things first, maybe opening a branch of Wild Child in Indigo Bay." She glanced at Hannah. "What about you?"

"I'll come back for your wedding," Hannah said. "And we both know I've gotten good at keeping promises."

Though Polly smiled, a flash of sadness appeared in her eyes. She tugged off her apron and nodded toward the door.

"Come on."

"Where?"

"Let's go for a walk. Get some fresh air. I'll ask Ramona to cover the front."

She disappeared into the kitchen. Hannah glanced at the clock. Three hours in. One or two to go. Hopefully.

Her chest was tight with anxiety. She took off her apron and grabbed her camera from upstairs before following Polly to the bakery van.

They drove to Rainsville Park and walked along the pathways winding through the grass, around the playground, and down to the Shingle Mill Creek.

"How could you stand it?" Hannah asked, as they stopped to sit on a bench beneath a tree. "Watching Mom suffer."

"Sometimes I couldn't," Polly admitted. "I hated it, but I also wasn't going to let her go through it alone. If there was anything I could do for her, it was be there. And honestly, we had some wonderful times together, even in the midst of her chemo and all her doctor's appointments. We went to the Codswallop music festival. We went to plays, dinners, art shows, concerts. And she had so many friends...people just rallied to help us and made sure we had a lot of light in the darkness."

Hannah's throat constricted. "I'm sorry I wasn't here more."

Polly squeezed her hand, and it felt like forgiveness. They stood and walked to the wooden bridge arching over the creek. Hannah paused to take a picture of the wildflowers and brush growing along the banks. She focused her lens on a leaf shaped like a heart.

Polly leaned her elbows on the bridge railing and gazed at the water rolling across the smooth rocks.

"I know you never intended to stay here, Hannah," she said. "And I...well, I admit I was trying to find a way to make you change your mind. I think I secretly hoped you'd fall in love with Wild Child and decide to stay. But I also know Rainsville and Wild Child never meant as much to you as they have to me. So you have my blessing if you want to leave. I don't want you to feel trapped here anymore."

Being given the freedom to leave didn't fill Hannah with pleasure and relief. Just the opposite, in fact. Her heart flooded with dismay.

"I don't feel trapped," she said. "Not anymore."

"Because of Evan?"

"Yes. And Wild Child. I understand why it was so important to you and Mom." Hannah stopped beside her sister and leaned on the bridge railing. "There are cafés and bakeries like that everywhere in the world. In every city and town I've been to. Warm, cozy places where people come for coffee, food, conversation. In Japan, they're called *kissaten*. *Pastane* in Turkey. *Kahvila* in Finland."

Polly smiled. "When you run out of love tradition ideas for your blog, you can write about café culture. Not that you'll run out of love traditions."

"I thought I would, until I met Evan. Turns out that showing me around was his way of making sure I didn't jump ship."

"From what Luke tells me, Evan was very quick to offer. And based on the photo of that kiss you two shared at the auction...I'd say you were destined to end up together."

Hannah thought the same thing. But she didn't know what happened after the "ending up together" part. Come to think of it, she didn't know what happened *after* all the love traditions and customs she'd written about over the years.

Curiosity flared in the back of her mind. Faces and names

appeared in her memory. The couple she'd met in Rome who threw a coin together into the Trevi Fountain. The heart-struck Welshman in Cardiff who'd spent hours carving a wooden spoon for his beloved.

The group of girls serenaded by hopeful suitors in China. The young Fijian man who'd presented his girlfriend's father with a polished whale's tooth, a *tabua*, as a request for her hand in marriage.

She remembered the Hindu couple who'd bucked their families' tradition of arranged marriages by falling in love. The parents had united and thrown them a marvelously elaborate wedding that Hannah had, to her delight, been invited to attend.

What had happened to all those people after the rituals had been carried out? Did they have children? Where did they live? Where did they work? Were they living happily ever after?

She took out her phone and pulled up the email address of an old travel acquaintance through whom she'd met the Indian couple, Rajiv and Amrita. She sent Melanie a quick message of greeting and asked for the couple's contact information. For some reason, she wanted to know how they were, what they were doing. She wanted to know their story.

Polly's phone buzzed. Hannah's nerves jumped into high alert.

Polly took out her phone and swiped the screen. The creases of worry on her brow eased.

"He's done." She smiled, lifting her phone to display the text from Luke.

All okay. In ICU. Will call you in five min.

Relief flooded Hannah, weakening her knees. Unexpected tears sprang to her eyes and spilled down her cheeks. Then she found herself wrapped in Polly's arms, her sister's embrace a circle of unending warmth.

CHAPTER 27

*H*annah was not allowed to see Evan in ICU, but he
texted her when he was moved to a regular hospital
room. She went to see him often, torn between relief that the
surgery had gone well and despair over what he still had to
endure.

He was quiet much of the time, reading, watching TV, or
listening to mostly one-sided conversations from his visitors.
When she visited, Hannah stayed near the periphery of the room,
uncertain how much she either should or could be part of his
close-knit family circle. She was never alone with Evan since
both his family and the nurses stayed close to his side.

She met the Stone twins, Carson and Spencer, both younger
versions of Luke with their strong, masculine features and dark
eyes, and their sister Hailey, a pretty girl with light brown hair
who closely resembled Aunt Julia with her fine features and high
cheekbones.

Their relationships seemed to be typical sibling—teasing and
good-natured arguing, though Hannah wondered how much of
that was to keep the atmosphere light for Evan's benefit.

Because she still didn't want to shy away from the reality of *him*, she educated herself on both his surgery and the recovery period—what to expect, possible complications, diet, and all the things he needed to do.

Every time she saw him lying against the stark white pillows, his skin so pale he looked bloodless, the chest bandage visible beneath his gown...she wanted to rail at the universe for forcing this on him.

But she had seen enough of the world to know that no one was immune from anything. And in many ways, Evan was lucky —he had a constant stream of visitors, his family members loved him deeply, his doctors and nurses were knowledgeable and attentive caregivers.

For the week of his hospital stay, Hannah divided her time between Wild Child and Evan. The deadline for her revised book proposal came and went. She sent an email to Elaine Miller of Franklin Publishing with an apology and the truthful explanation that she just couldn't think of anything else to tie all her posts together.

Polly had to return to Paris for her classes, but Luke stayed in Indigo Bay temporarily to both ensure Evan's recovery and take over Sugar Rush again. Though it was none of her business, Hannah hoped that Luke had at least recognized Evan's contributions to the company.

Evan resisted his aunt's efforts to have him live at Warren's house for the remainder of his recovery, and with Luke and Adam backing him up, he returned to his house after a week in the hospital. Knowing he was back in his shabby little cottage on the beach with his books and whittling tools eased Hannah's persistent tension and worry.

She was busy packing up a box of pastries to bring to his nurses at the hospital when the wind chimes over the Wild Child entrance jingled.

"Hey, girlfriend who lasted all of fifteen minutes."

Hannah turned at the sound of her friend Dave's familiar

voice, pleasure rising inside her. As shaggy and unkempt as ever, he was carrying his ratty backpack and a duffle bag.

"Where are you off to?" she asked.

"A friend made me an offer I couldn't refuse," he said, helping himself to a cookie from the Free Sample plate. "The Love International Festival in Croatia is next week, and he said I could crash in his apartment. Plenty of room for you too. Think of it, Banana. Three days of music, parties, sun, sand...not to mention the potential for *love.*"

Hannah rolled her eyes. "I'll bet."

"Hey, don't mock or I won't tell you what else I have for you."

"I'm not sure I want to know."

"Oh, you want to know." Dave pulled a wrinkled sheet of paper from his duffle and handed it to her. "Free registration for the Travel Bloggers' conference, which is being held in Venice this year, which is not all that far from Croatia, which is why you need to go with me on Tuesday, which is when flights are cheapest, which is how we'll make it in time for the first day of the festival."

Hannah scanned the letter with the free registration offer. "Where did you get this?"

"I got contacts, baby." He quailed a little under her skeptical look. "Okay, I entered a drawing on their website and won. But you gotta go, Banana. Tons of big travel companies go to the conference looking to sponsor bloggers. You could score some killer free trips and really get your name out there. That would totally help with the publisher and your book, right?"

Right. The book she'd just killed because she couldn't come up with any new ideas.

"Thank you, Dave." She pushed the registration form back across the counter to him. "But I can't go."

A look of bafflement crossed his features. "You're kidding, right?"

"No. I can't go. I need to stay here and run the bakery."

"Oh, man." He stuffed the form back into his duffle and shook his head. "I was afraid of this."

"Of what?"

"You've gone soft."

"Isn't that what your girlfriend said?"

"Ha ha." He frowned and stabbed his finger toward her. "When you told me you were staying in Rainsville for all this time, I thought you might lose your edge. Turns out I was right."

"Oh, please. People can change." *She* had changed. In ways she'd never have imagined.

"Fine, but the Hannah I used to know would never turn this down, for *Lock Heart* if nothing else." Dave hefted his duffle onto his shoulder and headed for the door. "You know how to reach me if you change your mind."

She wouldn't. She watched him go, ignoring the pang of sorrow over not knowing when she would see him again. Exactly what Polly and her mother must have felt every time she left Rainsville.

Well, Polly wouldn't have to feel that anymore. No one would.

She packed up a second box of Declairs and drove to the hospital to leave the pastries for the nurses. Then she headed to Indigo Bay with the Declairs and pulled up in front of 1500 Turtle Drive.

Only Evan's SUV and another car were parked at the front of the house. An older woman in a cartoon-patterned nurse's uniform opened the door at Hannah's knock.

"Is it all right to see him?" Hannah asked.

"Yes, he's out on the deck," the woman replied. "Would you like some coffee or tea?"

Hannah thanked her and declined. Her nerves tensed as she walked through the quiet house, remembering the evening she and Evan had come in after the storm and warmed up in such a hot, delicious way.

She opened the door to the deck. A rush of cool sea air

brushed against her face. Evan sat on one of the wooden chairs, bundled in a jacket with his hands shoved deep into his pockets. On the table beside him were a whittling knife and a stick of wood shaved clean of bark.

He turned at the sound of the door closing. His tense expression cleared.

"Hey, Lockhart." His voice was weakened, but still contained that same deep rumble that curled Hannah's toes delightfully.

"Hey, Heartbreaker."

He was thinner, pale, his jaw unshaven and his hair messy, but his eyes were as blue as ever. She paused to rest her hand on the back of his neck. Her breath hitched at the feel of his cold skin— he was so warm and strong that she'd never felt *coldness* radiating from him before.

She pressed a kiss to the top of his head, inhaling his familiar scent of cedar and sage. She set the box of Declairs on the table. "I'm not sure if you're allowed to eat these yet, but I figured I'd bring them anyway."

"Thanks." He didn't reach for one, turning his gaze back to the ocean.

Hannah sat beside him. Faint awkwardness crackled in the air. Now that they were finally alone, she wasn't quite sure what to say.

"So how do you feel?" she finally asked, then winced. "Not that you don't get asked that question multiple times a day."

He smiled faintly. "Coming from you, I don't mind it so much. I'm good. Well, I will be. Hard to do a lot right now."

"How much pain are you in?"

"Depends on the time of day, how I'm sitting." He gestured to his sternum. "It's all here. Meds help, but I don't like taking them too much."

She rested her hand on his arm. Knowing him as she did, she suspected the physical recovery would be almost easy compared to the complexity of his emotions. The reminder of his mortality had always been the scar on his chest, which would now be starker than ever. And with his five big, healthy brothers never far from him...

"How's the book proposal going?" Evan asked.

"I missed the deadline." She tucked her hands into the pockets of her running jacket and followed his gaze to the horizon line where the ocean met the sky.

"You missed it? Why?"

"I couldn't think of anything beyond love traditions to incorporate into a book, so..." She shrugged. "Something else will come along."

"Hannah." Frustration edged his voice. "You can't lose this chance."

"It doesn't matter."

"It does matter," he argued. "Do you know how many people would kill for a chance like this? Don't throw it away. You'll find an idea, either here or somewhere else."

"But the deadline has passed."

"So ask for more time." Evan turned to face her, his eyes glinting. "Tell the editor where you're going next, so she'll know you have plans. That you're not just sitting here stagnating."

"But I...I'm not going anywhere," Hannah said. "I'm still working at the bakery."

"You know as well as I do, and as Polly does, that you don't need to stay at Wild Child. Polly always knew that. She was just hoping you would want to stay."

"I do want to stay."

His mouth twisted, but his eyes softened as he looked at her. "No, you don't."

Irritation scraped Hannah's insides.

"Don't tell me what I do or don't want," she said. "I've gotten used to Rainsville and the bakery."

"Getting used to something is not the same as loving it."

"I love it then," she retorted peevishly.

"What about *Lock Heart*?"

"Like I said..." Hannah tried to give a nonchalant shrug. "Something else will come along."

He was silent. She stroked her gaze over the line of his strong jaw, the way his hair curled over his ear, the column of his throat.

Her mind flashed with all the things she'd experienced in the short time they'd been together—the pleasure of his perfect kisses, the warmth he evoked just by looking at her, the bliss of waking up curled against his side. The possessive way he put his hand on her lower back and touched her hair. The knowledge that she belonged to him, and him alone.

A sudden rush of hope rose in her, desperate and raw.

"Evan, I want to stay." The words spilled out of her. "I mean that. I'll work at the bakery, and I can help during the rest of your recovery. I know you have your family and all, but I can..."

She could do what? Cook him dinner when he probably had a special chef making his meals? Drive him to the doctor's office? Help him with physical therapy? Sneak him forbidden desserts?

He had his family and a whole medical team on his side. At most she could go for walks with him and read books to him, but everyone else had been handling Evan's heart condition since he was born.

They knew exactly what to do. And though she'd done her research, she, on the other hand, had very little idea.

"Lockhart." Evan brushed his thumb across her bottom lip, then pulled his hand away almost sharply, as if touching her had been a mistake. "You can't stay in Rainsville."

"Don't tell me what I can or can't do either," Hannah said. "Look, I let Polly handle everything during my mother's illness. I knew even then that I could have done more, but I didn't. It was so much easier for me to stay away. Well, I won't do that this time. I'm staying to help you because I love you."

His mouth compressed. "I don't need your help. I don't want it."

Stung, Hannah drew away from him, repelled by a sudden sense of cold. "Why are you pushing me away so hard? You told me about your heart early on. You don't have to protect me from it. I knew what I was getting into."

Except that she hadn't, not really. She'd known his health carried a certain risk in terms of their relationship, but she hadn't known her love for him would deepen to the point that she *felt* him in the marrow of her bones.

She hadn't known she'd fall asleep at night with a half-finished thought of him that concluded the instant she woke. She hadn't known all the magnificent experiences of the world would pale in comparison to the idea of a lifetime with Evan.

"You didn't know." Evan voiced her thoughts as if he'd read her mind. "No one knows, not my doctors, not my family, not me."

"So that means I'm not allowed to love you?" she retorted. "Is that it?"

Evan looked at her, a faint smile tugging at his mouth. He reached out to put his hand against her cheek.

"Lockhart," he said. "You are bold, beautiful, and daring and you make me want to run off and travel the world with you. I want to climb mountains, cross deserts, and swim rivers with you. I want to wake up in Patagonia and find you sleeping beside me. I want to sit with you in a hillside temple in Nepal and drag you around Vienna in search of the perfect dessert. I want to go everywhere, do everything, *be* everything...all with you."

Hannah wiped her eyes with her sleeve, her heart flooding over with a riotous combination of both love and apprehension.

"Then I'll wait for you," she said, unable to dispel a sudden spark of excitement. "Your recovery isn't that long. I'll work at Wild Child until you're better again, and then we'll take off together. Evan, there's so much I haven't seen yet, so much I want to show you. A little mountain town called Iuygar in Argentina where there's a craft festival every day. A valley in Burma with the most incredible archeological complex of Buddhist temples. Of course, we'll take it easy at first, but the world is huge. There are plenty of cities and towns. We can do it together. Everything."

She tried to smother the pain rising inside her, mingling with the hope that danced like butterflies. Evan's hand still cupped her cheek, his thumb moving to brush away the tears still falling. Regret shone in his blue eyes. Hannah's throat closed over.

"Please," she said.

"I *can't* do everything. Even if I wanted to try...and God knows I do...I won't leave my family to worry themselves sick over me. I've always tried not to let my heart affect the way I live my life, but the fact is I'll never have a normal heart. I'll always be at risk for health problems. I won't let that affect you, too."

"It wouldn't!" Hannah sat up, the ache inside about to crack her chest open. "The only thing that affects me is the fact that I *love* you. I want to be with you. If you can't come with me, then I'll stay here. We can make this work."

"No, we can't." Lines of tension bracketed his mouth. His hand fell away from her. "You can't have a life with me. There's no telling what complications I could face in the future, and there's no reason you should have to deal with them too."

"I'm not dealing with you, for God's sake," Hannah snapped. "I love you. I *choose* to be with you. Why are you forcing me away?"

"Because you deserve more than to be stuck here with a man who could end up stifling you," he retorted. "After ten years of freedom, do you really think you'll be happy working at the bakery and being my caretaker?"

"Evan, you're going to recover! And I'll do anything for you, but I don't expect to spend my life being your nurse. You've already come so far."

"Yeah, but for how long?" Bitterness cut through his voice. He looked away. "Next time, it could be worse. And you wouldn't leave my side no matter how bad it might get."

"I wouldn't leave your side because I love you, not because I'd feel guilty. And what if something happens to me? What if I get sick? Don't you think the only person I'd want with me every step of the way is you? Why don't you think the same thing about me? Why don't you want me with you?"

"It's not a question of *want*," he said. "It's that I'd hate knowing I was the reason you were trapped."

Hannah wiped her wet face, feeling as if she were facing down an immovable brick wall.

"You'd never be the reason I'm trapped," she said. "You're the reason I'm free. The reason I'm finally not afraid anymore. Do you know why I love you?"

He shook his head, not looking at her.

"Because you're worth it. You've spent so much of your life trying to prove yourself, but you never had to prove anything to me, Evan. I've known the truth all along. You're worth everything, especially my heart."

His throat worked with a swallow. He stared at the ocean, his jaw rigid. Hannah pushed to her feet, sudden defeat washing over her.

"But until you believe that," she said, "until you *know* it, then I can't be with you. I won't let you devalue my heart or my feelings. You need to trust that I'll see anything through with you, that I won't leave, that I'll keep my promises. I'm all yours for the taking, but if you don't believe in us, then we'll never make it together."

She paused beside him, willing him with everything she had to give them a chance, to say something that would allow her to stay. He was silent. Her heart split right down the middle.

"Now I know why they call you *Heartbreaker*," she said.

She turned and left him, blinded by tears.

CHAPTER 28

*M*issing Hannah hurt a fuckload worse than open-heart surgery. At least the physical pain had eased up over the past few weeks. But the *missing Hannah* was a goddamned permanent hole in his chest.

One he'd drilled himself because…she'd wanted to stay. She'd wanted to make it work. As much as he'd hated letting her go, Evan still couldn't find any way around it. He'd rather spend his life alone than be the reason for trapping Hannah.

That's not how she sees it.

That's how it is.

According to you.

According to my fucking ruined heart.

That's not how she sees it.

That's how it is.

Since when do you let your heart control you?

Bitter irony that. He'd spent his life refusing to be constrained by his physical limitations, but he'd just let Hannah go because of his heart. And yet his other heart, the one that was bigger and more powerful than the weak organ inside his chest, was still full of crazy hopes that somehow, Hannah had been right. Somehow they could make it work.

Or not. Because...his heart.

And his head, which was ready to explode with all the wrangling he'd been doing trying to figure it all out.

He pushed away from his desk at the Sugar Rush corporate headquarters. At least he'd had work to distract him, though it didn't have the same appeal as it had before. Nothing did, not without Hannah.

He tossed a few folders into his briefcase beside a flat square package wrapped in brown paper. For the hundredth time, he picked it up and ran his fingers over the edges that were worn from his constant handling. The package had arrived in the mail two days after he'd heard from Polly that Hannah had left Rainsville.

His name and address were written on the front in Hannah's curly handwriting, with Wild Child listed as the return address. He'd been carrying the package around in his briefcase for the three weeks she'd been gone, both wanting to open it and dreading what might be inside.

It was his final connection to her, this goodbye gift. Once he opened it, he felt like he'd lose her forever.

Did that mean he still had hope?

No. Because he was the fucker who'd pushed her away when her whole being had glowed with love for him.

He put the package back in his briefcase and headed out of the office. The elevator doors at the end of the corridor opened. His father and Aunt Julia stepped out, their heads turned toward each other in conversation.

The sight of them—his big-shouldered, authoritative father and his beautiful, fashionable aunt—struck a chord in Evan. Though they sparred and argued, somehow over the years they'd become a team. As if Julia had known, even in the aftermath of losing her sister, that family had to stick together to stay intact. To heal.

"Evan." Julia caught sight of him, a flash of relief crossing her face. "Your father said your appointment with Dr. Kumar went well."

"Very well." This time, Evan didn't conceal the truth. "Really good, actually. My recovery has been faster than he expected."

"Best test results he's had in years," Warren added.

Evan gave Julia the details of Dr. Kumar's assessment as they walked to the boardroom. His concerns about ending up on the Sugar Rush sidelines after his surgery hadn't come to pass—Luke and his father had kept him apprised of business issues when he was recovering at home, and neither of them had protested when he'd said he wanted to return to the office.

"Do you want to get some lunch after the meeting?" Julia pushed back the cuff of her suit to glance at her slim gold watch. "I don't have to be back at work until two. We can stop at Wild Child."

Right. As if he could ever set foot in the bakery again, knowing Hannah wouldn't be there.

"I'm not going to Wild Child," he said.

"Somewhere else then." Julia waved a hand. "That's for the best, I suppose, considering the calorie count of those pastries. I need to talk to Polly about offering a salad menu."

Evan exchanged an amused look with his father.

"It's a bakery, Jules," Warren reminded her. "You want a salad, go to a farm."

She sniffed. "I don't like dirt."

"That's not what Hannah seemed to think," Evan remarked. "She said Polly told her you have some secret past involving astrology and hippie music festivals."

"I most certainly do not." Julia flipped a lock of her smooth blond hair away from her shoulder.

A thought occurred to Evan, much as he couldn't reconcile

the idea of his Chanel-wearing aunt having once been a beatnik teenager.

"Aunt Julia," he said. "Were you a *groupie?*"

Warren chuckled. Julia shot him a glare.

"Don't be a fool, Evan Stone," she scoffed. "I would never consort with the *hoi-polloi.*"

"You no longer have an issue with Polly," Evan pointed out. "And you had her pegged as all kinds of lowbrow."

"I admit I was wary of her at first," Julia allowed. "But she grew on me. Not to mention, she changed your brother for the better. I'm sorry Hannah didn't do the same for you."

Irritation prickled Evan's spine. "What does that mean?"

"Just what I said." Julia shrugged, stepping aside as Warren opened the boardroom door for her. "I know the surgery was a blow, but she was there through it all. As far as I could tell, she didn't flinch."

Of course she didn't. Because she was brave. Because she loved him.

To avoid getting into this conversation further, Evan followed his aunt into the boardroom. Luke and Adam were seated at the table, discussing the final details of the Alpine acquisition that had closed last week.

"It's done." Luke clamped his hand on Evan's shoulder. "Good job, man. Really good. Even with the Singa Corporation crap, the Alpine acquisition went through without a hitch. Now we have a new inroad into the European chocolate market."

"And more support for the cocoa bean research project," Adam said.

For the first time in the three weeks since Hannah had walked away from him—hell, since he'd gone under anesthesia—Evan experienced a rush of pride and satisfaction. At least he'd gotten one thing right.

"The project is already generating buzz." Luke sat beside Evan. "It's a great idea, especially now that we have Alpine. You were right that Sugar Rush needs to be a leader in the sustain-ability of cocoa bean crops. Funding a large-scale research and volunteer project intended to help local farmers and crop production is a slam-dunk way to start."

"What about the Fair Trade Foundation?" Warren asked.

Unease rippled through the room. It was a question Luke and Evan hadn't talked much about. Not that they'd had a chance. Luke cleared his throat.

"I told Sam I was removing him as director," he said. "I made a mistake giving it to him in the first place. Evan should always have been the one directing the program."

Silence fell. Though it was gratifying to hear his brother admit the truth, Luke had always been right about Evan's ability to direct the foundation to the level it required. There were things he couldn't do, no matter how desperately he wanted to.

Like be with Hannah.

He forced the thought of her aside, knowing it would never fully go away.

"We need to change its name," he said. "The Fair Trade Foun-dation is too generic. I didn't think of this at the time, but for branding alone the name needs to be specific to Sugar Rush and cocoa bean production."

"The Sugar Rush Cocoa Bean Team," Julia said.

Evan and Luke exchanged glances.

"It's truthful, but cute," she said. "If you're going public asking for students and volunteers, then you'd better believe you want something catchy."

"She's right," Warren put in. "And I try not to say that very often."

Julia tossed him a glower. He winked at her.

"Evan." Julia turned back to him with a roll of her eyes. "Who wouldn't want to be part of the Cocoa Bean Team?"

"Actually, that's not bad," Evan said slowly, his brain clicking into gear. "Since we want to get into the education sector, we could launch a Cocoa Bean Team program directed toward K through twelve students. Get marketing to design a fun logo, like Captain Cocoa or something, and put together activity packets and curriculum guides about fair trade and sustainability."

"Why didn't we think of that before?" Adam spread his arms out, his eyebrows lifting. "Of course we need to get this into the schools. That's fucking brilliant, man. We're a candy company. Kids love us, love our products. We need to start with them."

"And you have an avenue through your mother's foundation," Warren added. "The literacy and education programs are intended to help young people develop viable skills that they can put to use. You can start there."

They all looked toward Luke. Their older brother sat with his forehead creased and his mouth turned downward, as if he were thinking very hard.

"Dude," Adam said. "Don't tell me you don't like the idea."

"I don't like the idea," Luke said. "I love the idea."

For the first time in what felt like ages, a smile cracked Evan's face.

"Evan needs to direct the whole thing," Adam said.

Much as he wanted to be the one in charge, Evan shook his head.

"We'll figure something out," Luke told him. "Talk to your doctors and—"

"No," Evan interrupted. "Even before the research project launches, we'd still have to visit all the farms, staying to help establish infrastructures and make sure we can support the research. I can't do that. I was stupid to think I could."

He paused to take a breath, hearing his heart beating inside his head. Steady. Strong. His admission didn't make him feel weak, not anymore. There was strength in acknowledging one's limitations and finding a different way.

"I have another idea," he said.

"Which is?"

"Adam and I can run the program together," Evan said.

Luke and Adam looked at each other, then back at Evan.

"Together?" Adam echoed.

"I can't go to most of the remote farms or anywhere too far from a hospital," Evan said. "Especially now. But you can. You still wouldn't have to work full time, only as needed. I also want to talk to European chocolatiers about getting on board and starting an annual multi-national conference. Now that we have Alpine, that shouldn't be difficult to arrange. I'll run the Cocoa Bean Team from here with you as the international field director."

Silence fell. Evan's heart beat faster. Then Julia spoke.

"As Adam so eloquently stated," she remarked. "That's fucking brilliant."

"She's right," Warren said.

CHAPTER 29

Saudade. A longing for a loved one who is lost to you.

Damned if he didn't feel the meaning of that word down to his bones.

Waves crashed against the base of the rocks, a spray of salt water washing over the outcropping. The early morning November sun shone bright and clear, the sunlight dusting the crests of the white caps rippling across the water.

He walked close to the edge, squinting at the horizon as if he could imagine Hannah on the other side of the sea. Maybe he could. That was where she belonged. But much as he knew she needed to be out in the world, he hated the thought of living his life without her.

He turned, shifting his gaze to the tidepools perforating the rocks. He crouched beside one and poked gently at a sea anemone, which closed its tentacles in self-protection. Barnacles clung to the edge of the pool like little volcanoes. Kelp, sea stars, crabs, sea urchins. Rocks in which he could find heart-shaped formations.

Evan stood. Miniature universes in and of themselves, sustainable ecosystems. There were a lot of worlds in the world.

But none of them had such an endless capacity for both happiness and pain as the human heart.

He rubbed his chest. Almost four weeks after his surgery, his sternum hurt only occasionally now, and he'd regained a lot of strength. It would be several more months before he was "fully" recovered, but at least he felt more like himself.

Working on the details of the Cocoa Bean Team had been an enormous help as a new project he believed in, one that was already strengthening Sugar Rush's culture and influence. If all went as planned, next year the first team would head to Venezuela to start working with a farmers' collective on research and education.

He walked back to the beach, passing the spot where he'd grabbed Hannah when a wave had crashed into her. The fear that had gripped him was still a sharp, vivid memory, the unimaginable notion of *losing her* like a black, endless pit.

And though he'd lost her in another way, at least he knew she was living the life she was meant to live.

That's not how she sees it.

That's how it is.

He walked back to his bungalow, passing the kitchen table that was scattered with pieces of wood and whittling tools. He spent every evening whittling. He thought of his father, who used model airplanes and boats to escape his pain. Evan didn't want to live the same way, but he couldn't see any way out.

He showered, and changed into a suit and tie before driving to Sugar Rush. He parked next to Luke's Porsche—his brother planned to stay in Indigo Bay for another few days—and went up to his seventh floor office. A sharp knock on the door signaled his executive assistant's entrance.

"Mr. Stone, I compiled binders of all the Alpine documentation for the transition meeting." Kate approached with an armload of thick, three-ring binders. "They're color-coded according to subject, and each one includes a flash drive containing the digital files."

"Impressive." Evan stood to take the heavy binders from her.

Kate opened one and showed him the Table of Contents and organization of the files. Evan had hoped Luke wouldn't want Kate back as an assistant, but his brother had already sent him several reminders that Kate was only working for him "temporarily" and that she'd return to the duties of her position as "executive assistant to CEO Luke Stone" as soon as he returned from Paris.

Maybe Evan could wrangle his brother to let her work on the Cocoa Bean Team. She'd whip that program right into shape with her spreadsheets and interactive calendaring. Not to mention her uncanny ability to anticipate the needs of executives before they did.

The office door banged open. Kate and Evan both turned. Luke stalked into the room, his expression tense and his phone clutched in his hand. Julia was at his heels, looking worried.

"Where did Hannah go?" Luke asked.

"Hannah?" Evan's heart started beating too fast. He swung his gaze from his brother to his aunt. "What do you mean?"

"Where did she go?" Luke repeated, urgency edging his voice. "Polly can't reach her. During their last phone call, Hannah told her she was going to Italy."

"Yeah." Evan tried to suppress a rising apprehension. "She'd mentioned going to the Apennine mountains, maybe Assisi. I don't know if she did. I haven't been in touch with her. Polly can't reach her?"

"Not since the earthquake."

The fear broke through, seeping into his veins like ice. "Earthquake?"

"Six point three." Julia strode to the computer and brought up a news website. "Centered in Perugia. Reports of extensive damage."

Curses blistered Evan's brain. The screen flashed with a video of horrific images—piles of rubble from destroyed buildings, flashing lights of rescue vehicles, downed power lines, people out in the streets, shell-shocked and scared.

She wasn't there. She couldn't be there.

He grabbed his phone and called her number. Voicemail picked up.

"She's not answering." Luke's brow furrowed. "She hasn't called Polly or anyone else we can think of. No sign of her on social media."

Evan's heart hammered. "How long has it been?"

"We heard about it an hour ago. The quake was three hours ago."

Heavy silence descended. Evan stared at the news. A gut-wrenching helplessness gripped him.

"Try texting her rather than calling." Kate hurried to the door. "Texts are more likely to go through. I'll contact the Red Cross and the Department of State to find out what other measures we can take."

After she left, Evan and Luke both returned to their phones.

"Is Polly okay?" Evan asked his brother.

"She's scared." Luke frowned at his phone. "She spent so many years not even knowing where Hannah was, but since Hannah left Rainsville they've called or texted a few times a day. It's not like Hannah not to respond right away."

Evan sank into a chair, hating the fear clawing through him, the knife-blade uncertainty of not knowing if the woman he loved was all right.

The woman he loved. His jaw tightened. He'd pushed her away because of the uncertainty she'd have to live with by loving *him.* He'd suppressed the knowledge that anything could happen to her too.

He felt Julia sit beside him. She settled her hand on his knee.

"There's not much chance that she's there," she said.

"'Not much' doesn't mean *no chance*." Evan scrolled through his phone again, his shoulders tense. "People get hurt all the time. Everywhere."

"Yes, they do. But that doesn't stop us from living."

Her voice carried an echo of grief. Evan knew she was thinking about his mother and the aftermath of the accident. They'd all dealt with it in such different ways—Julia and Luke went into action, Adam left town, Warren turned toward Hailey, Spencer focused on work, Tyler got into trouble. Evan retreated to the sidelines.

He'd wanted to prove himself at Sugar Rush, but not until Hannah had he known that he also wanted to prove himself at *life*.

By not giving him and Hannah a chance, had he failed?

He stared at the text screen on his phone, willing her name to appear.

Luke's voice rumbled through the room as he spoke to Polly again. When he ended the call, he looked at Evan and shook his head.

Evan shoved to his feet and went to his desk, needing to do something. Luke had the same idea because he pulled a chair up beside Evan and reached for the desk phone.

"Dad alerted the Sugar Rush disaster relief team, and they're getting supplies and medical kits over there. They're going to see what they can find out from the ground."

Evan scoured disaster relief websites, social media, traveler message boards and forums. He had no other contact info for Hannah—no friends or fellow travelers. He didn't even know how to reach her friend Dave. He checked her blog, which had last been updated a week ago with a post about Prague.

"Can we track her cell?" he asked.

"No signal."

If she was okay, she'd call Polly.

He texted again. *R U OK?*

No response.

The next two hours passed in a blur—futile attempts to get through to government agencies and disaster relief organizations, endless attempts to call and text, all while the aftermath of the earthquake and rescue efforts played across the computer screen.

Evan's phone buzzed. So did Luke's and Julia's phones. His heart stuttered. The three of them swiped the screens. A forwarded text message from Hannah came from Polly's number.

Polliwog, if you heard about the quake, don't worry about me. I'm fine. Back in Florence from Assisi, where I couldn't get a signal. Then left my bag w/phone on a train, was gone when I went back. Using a borrowed phone, no intl connection. Will call you as soon as I can. Heading out of Italy. Love you.

An overwhelming relief swamped Evan in a wave, weakening his knees. She was *fine.*

"Thank God," Julia breathed.

Evan scrubbed his hands over his face. He suddenly felt everything—the beating of his heart, the rush of breath through his lungs, the blood flowing through his veins. He was awake. Alive.

Luke's hand settled on his shoulder.

"Okay?" he asked.

Evan nodded. "Thanks."

His brother moved away from him, and after a short discussion about sending disaster relief aid from Sugar Rush, he and Julia left him alone.

Evan looked at the screen on his phone. He typed in the original number of Hannah's text and slowly wrote the words *Come back.*

His finger hovered over the send button. Then he deleted the message and typed *Stay safe.*

He sent the text, even though he didn't know if she'd get it on the borrowed phone. He turned to toss several folders into his briefcase. The brown-paper wrapped package was still there, unopened.

Evan picked it up. After carrying it around for almost a month, a sudden urgency flooded him. He tore off the paper wrapping in a haste. Inside was a square, handmade scrapbook with a drawn picture of a heart on the front.

He opened it to a photo of cotton candy. Only after staring at it for a second did he realize it was the photo Hannah had taken of him at the boardwalk, after he'd pointed out the cotton candy had formed the shape of a heart.

He looked through the rest of the photos. The book was filled with images Hannah had taken of heart-shaped objects. A knot in a piece of weathered wood. A wine stain on a glass. A leaf, a rock, a sugar cookie. A fried egg, a padlock on a bridge, a piece of Sugar Rush candy. The last picture was a self-portrait of her— smiling into the camera with her hands and fingers creating a heart.

Evan closed the book. For thirty-three years, he'd believed his heart wasn't whole enough to give away, that he couldn't trust it. And then from the moment their hands touched, Hannah had proven him wrong. He just hadn't wanted to admit it.

She had made him complete, healed him, enforced his urge to *live* with every fiber of his being. He had always belonged to her, just as she belonged to him.

He had to tell her that. He had to hope she still wanted both him and his whole heart.

CHAPTER 30

*F*ernwah. The feeling of missing a place she'd never
been.

Was there a word for missing a person she'd never met? If so,
that was what Hannah had felt all those years before she met
Evan.

All her escaping and running away had concealed the void
inside her, the one into which Evan fit so perfectly. All the loneliness and fear she'd denied, the search for belonging…everything
had led her back to a town she hadn't liked. A place where she'd
felt acute loss.

And there Evan was. The answer to her unasked question.

Stay safe.

For him, she would. Because even now, she couldn't rid
herself of the hope that she would one day find her way back to
him. How else could she explain why every single circumstance
and choice she'd made had brought their two lives together? As if
her locked heart had been seeking his damaged heart all along.

After leaving Rainsville, she'd boarded a plane to Tokyo,
where the neon-lit skyscrapers and jam-packed marketplaces

failed to enthrall her as they always had before. In fact, nothing about travel held the same appeal.

Now, the best part of being away were the calls, texts, and emails she exchanged several times a day with Polly—sometimes quick sentences about what they were doing, sometimes longer discussions about the holidays or Polly's plan to meet Hannah somewhere during a break from her courses. The new connection to her sister was a bright, shining thread through Hannah's days.

Until she saw Polly again, she continued to travel alone. She went to Italy, though the earthquake happened before she made it to Assisi. From there, she boarded a train to Munich and then Vienna, where she stayed for several days.

She visited various cafés and sampled a decadent cake, warm apple strudel, chocolate hazelnut pudding, and vanilla cookies. Evan would definitely choose the *Sachertorte*, a chocolate sponge cake layered with apricot jam and topped with dark chocolate ganache, as his "perfect" Viennese dessert.

As the weeks passed, she heard from Polly that Evan's recovery continued to be smooth and uneventful—exactly what they had all hoped for and what the doctors had anticipated given Evan's youth and overall excellent health. He was busy with cardiac rehabilitation and a new position at Sugar Rush.

Hannah was happy to hear all of that. She only wished she could be there with him. She'd always been a solo traveler, intrepid and fearless. But for the first time, she felt as if the world was too big for her. As if she needed another hand to hold.

After Vienna, a series of emails led her back to India at the invitation of Rajiv and Amrita, the young couple whose wedding she had attended five years ago.

Her *Lock Heart* blog post about the wedding remained one of her favorites, as she'd been genuinely delighted to join the festivities. She'd loved everything about the Hindu wedding, from the jewel-toned saris to the intricate henna *mehndi*, the sacred rituals, and the reception laden with food and joyful *bhangra* music.

The warmth extended to her by the families continued during her visit, where she found the couple living close to both their parents with Rajiv working at a network services company near Delhi. They had two young children, a boy and a girl who kept Amrita and her mother-in-law busy.

Hannah took pictures of the gorgeous, black-eyed children, of their teatime and family meals around the dinner table. She went with them to a cricket match, accompanied Amrita during her daily shopping, and played with the children. She gave the girl, Leena, the wooden elephant Evan had whittled.

Love wound through everything the family did, even if it was expressed in subtle ways. Amrita buying a packet of Chiclets for her daughter and pouring her husband's tea. Rajiv asking for his wife's opinion and bringing her a jasmine flower to wear in her hair. The grandmothers' endless stream of advice about the children and housekeeping. Amrita's mother-in-law giving her a new type of coconut oil.

With their consent, Hannah wrote a follow-up post called *After the Wedding*, in which she wrote about the daily lives of this family who had been formed by a traditional ritual.

This is what happens next. They live, love, grow, and change together.

She emailed Elaine Miller of Franklin Publishing, asking if she'd still accept a revised manuscript.

Yes, definitely, Elaine replied. *Just let me know when to expect it.*

Hannah went to Copenhagen next and immersed herself in the city Evan loved. She found a cheap apartment, rented a bicycle, squeezed into crowded basement bars with crackling fires, visited museums, shopped at flea markets, and took photos of the winding canals and elegant townhouses.

Between her explorations, she wrote a new proposal for a

book about the real-life stories beyond the world's love traditions.

She wanted a new avenue for her blog as well. She would no longer *report* about love. She would write about the people who both celebrated joy and weathered storms together.

She wrote a blog post detailing her new direction.

I have spent ten years writing about the ways people around the world commemorate love. Only now do I realize that I've neglected the single most important part of all those customs.

I haven't written about love itself—its complexities, meaning, shadows, and importance. I haven't talked about what brings two people together and why they fall in love. I haven't written about how love makes you feel because I had never experienced it for myself.

But now, for the first time in my life, I know how thrilling, frightening, and exhilarating it is to fall in love. I know what it feels like to sit in contented silence with a man. I know a desire that breaks open thunderclouds. I know butterflies and breathless laughter. I know the song a heart in love sings.

How did I know I was falling in love with him?

When telling him my secrets was like being caught in free-fall by the universe. When he put his hand on the back of my neck, and I knew I was not alone. When he kissed me, and I felt as if I had come home. When my heart started beating in time with his. When I wanted nothing more than to stay with him forever. When he became my world.

How did you know you were falling in love? What did it feel like? How did you meet and where are you now? Why do you love your partner?

It's your turn, my dear readers. Tell me your love stories.

After publishing the post on *Lock Heart*, she refocused on her book proposal, and when she logged on to her blog two days later, dozens of reader responses filled the comments section.

Hannah scrolled through them, both astonished and delighted by not only the stories, but the fact that they came from all over the world—Australia, Mexico, France, England.

There were stories from couples who were childhood friends, who'd met at school, on blind dates, at work, by sheer chance. A reporter and a cop. A musician and a bartender. A rekindled old flame. An arranged marriage that turned into love. A World War II nurse and an army officer. A foreign exchange student and a taxi driver.

Hannah posted a message of thanks, adding that she would read and respond to all of the stories soon. With the new incentive, she quickly finished her revised proposal for Franklin Publishing.

TO: Elaine Miller (e.miller@franklinpublishing.com)
FR: Hannah Lockhart (hannah@lockheart.com)

Elaine, thank you for allowing me more time to complete my proposal, which I have attached.

With a new angle on true life love stories, I suggest the title be Locked Hearts.

All the best,
Hannah Lockhart

She hit the send button and walked to the nearest café for a coffee and a cherry-chocolate kringle.

CHAPTER 31

Comment posted by: Anonymous
Dec. 2, 8:56pm

My love story starts with a broken heart.

A heart that never formed correctly, one that will always be damaged and defective. A heart that has to be watched and sometimes feared.

But it's my heart, the only one I'll ever have. Maybe I've always guarded it too closely, like a wounded animal, scared that allowing it to feel too much would cause greater damage.

Then I met her. She has an incredible, perfect heart. One filled with wonder, loyalty, and a wild sense of adventure.

I wanted her badly. I thought I could have her for a short time, that it would be fun and casual, and that my heart wouldn't get involved.

Yeah.

When did I start falling in love with her?
When my heart started doing all sorts of good things it had never
done before.
When she told me her secrets.
When I told her mine, and she didn't flinch.
When I kissed her.
When she brought me a Declair from her secret stash.
When I couldn't wait to see her again.
When she baked a cake.
When she put her hand on my chest.
When she laughed.

How does she make me feel?
Like my heart is whole.

Why do I love her?
Because she's bold and brave.
Because she cares right down to her soul.
Because she has eyes the color of a turquoise sea.
Because she tried a Sparkle Pop for me.
Because she doesn't give up.
Because she's as sweet and delicious as a *Sahnehäubchen*.
Because she makes me believe in happy endings.
All the sexy things I'll never tell anyone but her.
Because when I'm with her, I see hearts everywhere.

Treasure hunt clues:

Latitude: N 35 31 55.899
Longitude: W 120 42 20.617
Die Brücke

2:00am GMT, xxvii, studeni
ILY

CHAPTER 32

*H*annah's plane landed at SJC shortly after noon. A month had passed since she'd left Rainsville, but it felt as if it had been much longer. She rented a car and drove the hour and a half to Indigo Bay. An electric, nervous excitement simmered through her.

As she navigated the Pacific Coast Highway, the ocean stretched out beyond the sand dunes like a bucket of spilled blue paint. Sunlight glittered on the water, and people walked along the beaches clad in windbreakers and jeans.

She had always thought of the world as *big*. It was filled with widespread seas, golden deserts, mountains stretching toward the sky. There were always new places to go, countries to visit, things to see. She could travel her whole life and not see it all. She'd gotten lost in the world countless times.

But not until Evan Stone loved her had Hannah ever been found.

Close to Indigo Bay, she turned east toward Rainsville. The landscape changed to stretches of farmland and low rolling hills, the charm of the seaside fading into the background.

Wild Child had closed for the day, and Hannah parked in the

alley behind the bakery. She let herself into Polly's old apartment, where she showered and changed into the blue dress she'd worn on her and Evan's boardwalk date.

At five minutes to six, she drove downtown and parked on Main Street. Her nerves jumped and danced. She looped her satchel over her shoulder and walked to Rainsville Park. A few children played on the playground, their parents standing watch nearby. An older man walked his dog on the path.

Everything was the same as Hannah remembered it, but brighter, clearer, as if she were viewing it all through a prism that enhanced all the good.

The Shingle Mill Bridge arched over the narrow creek, the wood worn and cracked from the sun. She crossed the bridge and stopped in the middle. Water splashed over smooth rocks below, wandering south to join the watershed.

A glint of silver caught her eye. A padlock was attached to the railing of the bridge. Her heart did a crazy kind of twirl she'd first felt two months ago—the moment when Evan's lips had first touched hers.

She took the padlock in her hand. It was smooth silver, engraved with a heart and the initials H and E. A key was still inserted into the lock. She twisted it, securing the lock to the bridge.

"You still owe me $8.56, Lockhart."

Hannah turned at the sound of Evan's voice. Her soul filled with more colors and light than existed in the world. He approached from the other side of the bridge, still thinner but no less beautiful in jeans and a navy blue, button-down shirt that made his eyes look like the ocean.

"I'll write you a check," she said.

"Or you could kiss me."

Hannah smiled, her hand tightening on the railing as she restrained herself from running to meet him. She wanted to look at him, reacquainting herself with the lines of his body, the strong planes of his face, his well-shaped mouth and thick eyelashes.

"You figured it out." He stopped a few feet from her.

"Your use of the Julian calendar threw me off for a while," she admitted. "But the rest of it was easy."

"It was supposed to be. I don't..." He paused and cleared his throat. "I don't want this to be difficult. Other things are difficult. We need to be easy."

"Oh, you're easy, Heartbreaker," Hannah murmured.

A smile tugged at his mouth. She took a wooden object out of her satchel and held it out to him.

He ran his fingers over the coarse wooden spoon, engraved with a rough design of a heart, a lock, and an anchor.

"You carved this?" he asked.

"*Carved* is a rather subjective term, I suspect," Hannah said. "But yes. Welsh sailors used to carve lovespoons during their long journeys, which is why anchors were often part of the design. And since being away from you was a very long journey..."

He slipped the spoon into his breast pocket, right next to his heart, and extended both his arms. Tears stung Hannah's eyes as she moved forward.

And then his arms closed around her in a strong, secure circle. She had come home. She breathed in the cedar scent of him and pressed her face to his shirtfront, hearing and feeling the beat of his everlasting heart.

"It's lonely in the world without you," she said, her voice muffled against his shirt. "I don't want to be lonely anymore. I don't want to be without you anymore either."

"I love you." He pressed his lips to the top of her head, tightening his hold on her. "And I don't want you to give up the things you love because of me."

"You are the thing I love."

A chuckle rumbled through his chest. "I mean travel, writing, and photography. Your need for adventure and experiences."

"None of that matters anymore, Evan. I just want you."

"I want you too. But it all matters to me because it's part of what makes you who you are." He pulled away to look at her, his warm gaze tracking over her face. "And I'm crazy about every part of who you are."

Hannah wiped her eyes. "So what are we going to do? I don't want to go, but you won't let me stay…"

"I'm hoping we can do both." Uncertainty flickered in his expression as he held both her hands. "We'll go and we'll stay."

"How?"

"I need to live in Indigo Bay," Evan said. "My family is here, and I worked out an arrangement with Luke and Adam to do exactly what I want to at Sugar Rush. I have a ton of ideas I want to implement, and I know it's going to take the company in a new direction. But I also have my doctor's okay to travel occasionally, with certain conditions. I can't do everything you can, and I can't spend weeks away from home, but we can start with Europe and see where it leads us. If you'll come back here with me."

"Evan, I'll go anywhere with you." Hannah tightened her hands on his. "I'll stay anywhere with you."

"You know it's…" His throat worked with a swallow. "It's a risk being with me. I'll do everything in my power to live a long, healthy life, but there are no guarantees."

"There are no guarantees with anyone or anything."

"If you need to travel for your blog or any other reason, and I can't go with you, then I still want you to go. For a week or two, however long you need to. And when you come home, I'll be here waiting for you. I don't want you to miss any adventures."

"Evan." Hannah untangled her fingers from his and put her hand on his cheek. "*You* are my adventure."

The faint tension in his shoulders eased. He turned his head to press his lips against the center of her palm.

"I love you, Lockhart."

"I love you, Heartbreaker." She brushed her thumb across his jaw, thrilling in the knowledge that she now had the right to touch him as much as she wanted. "Though I'm really glad I bid fifty thousand dollars on you, you're worth so much more. You're my gold at the end of the treasure hunt."

Evan smiled, his eyes crinkling at the corners. "This treasure hunt doesn't end with gold."

"What does it end with?"

"I told you there's always a kiss at the end."

And so there was. A perfect kiss.

ABOUT THE AUTHOR

New York Times & USA Today bestselling author Nina Lane writes hot, sexy romances about professors, bad boys, candy makers, and protective alpha males who find themselves consumed with love for one woman alone. Originally from California, Nina holds a PhD in Art History and an MA in Library and Information Studies, which means she loves both research and organization. She also enjoys traveling and thinks St. Petersburg, Russia is a city everyone should visit at least once. Although Nina would go back to college for another degree because she's that much of a bookworm and a perpetual student, she now lives the happy life of a full-time writer.

www.ninalane.com

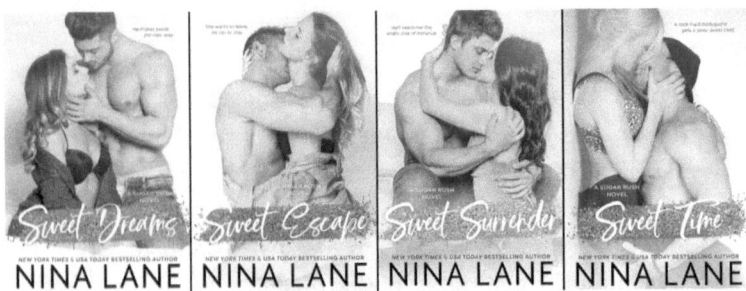

THE SUGAR RUSH SERIES
Sweet is the new sexy.

From the Stone family patriarch down to the youngest
bad boy, follow the lives and loves of the Sugar Rush men and the
women who bring them to their knees.

THE SPIRAL OF BLISS SERIES

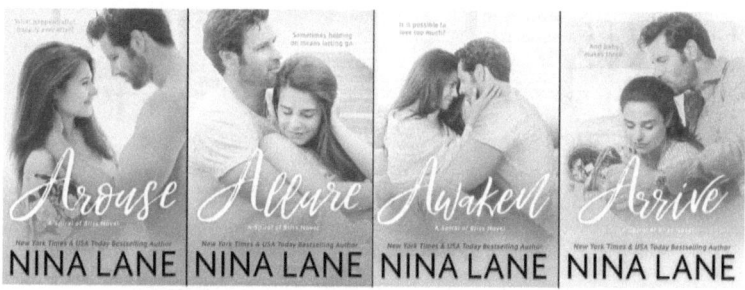

"Give me a kiss, beauty."

From an exhilarating crush to the intensities of marriage, Liv and Dean West embark on a passionate lifelong journey together. As the medieval history professor and his beloved wife face both personal challenges and painful battles, they never lose sight of the hope, humor, and devotion that belong only to them.

Liv and Dean's everlasting romance will melt your heart, turn you on, and enchant you with the power of a love to end all loves.

First we fell in love. Then we fell apart.

Shattered by tragedy a decade ago, two lovers fight the secrets that could destroy them.

"This book is a work of art."

A woman fleeing scandal. A town's mysterious recluse.

Lust and secrets collide in this provocative romance.